POVÍDKY

Other titles in the series

Afsaneh: Short Stories by Iranian Women

Galpa: Short Stories by Bangladeshi Women

Hikayat: Short Stories by Lebanese Women

Kahani: Short Stories by Pakistani Women

Qissat: Short Stories by Palestinian Women

Scéalta: Short Stories by Irish Women

POVÍDKY

SHORT STORIES BY CZECH WOMEN

Edited by
Nancy Hawker

TELEGRAM
London   San Francisco

British Library Cataloguing-in-Publication Data
A catalogue record for this book is available from the British Library

ISBN 10: 1-84659-007-8
ISBN 13: 978-1-84659-007-8

copyright © Nancy Hawker, 2006
Copyright for individual stories rests with the authors

This edition published 2006 by Telegram Books

All rights reserved. No part of this book may be reproduced or transmitted in any form or by any means, electronic or mechanical, including photocopying, recording or by any information storage and retrieval system, without permission in writing from the publisher.

This book is sold subject to the condition that it shall not, by way of trade or otherwise, be lent, re-sold, hired out, or otherwise circulated without the publisher's prior consent in any form of binding or cover other than that in which it is published and without a similar condition including this condition being imposed on the subsequent purchaser.

Manufactured in Lebanon

TELEGRAM
26 Westbourne Grove, London W2 5RH
825 Page Street, Suite 203, Berkeley, California 94710
www.telegrambooks.com

Contents

Acknowledgements

'Mininovel' is from *Knížka s červeným obalem* ('Little Book with a Red Cover', Práce: 1986 and Petrov: 2003); 'The Path of Medium Sinfulness' was first published in *Proglas* magazine (1993); 'One Pistachio Ice Cream' is from *Červené botičky* ('Little Red Shoes', Petrov: 2001); 'Owlet' is from *Želary* (Paseka: 2001); 'Every Civilisation Has Its Heyday' is from *Sůl, ovce a kamení* ('Salt, Sheep and Stone', One Woman Press: 2003); 'How I Went to School' is from *Sar me phiravas andre škola – Jak jsem chodila do školy* (ÚDO České Budějovice: 1992); 'All the Colours of the Sun and the Night' is abridged from *Alle Farben der Sonne und der Nacht* (Aufbau Verlag: 2003); 'The Forest' is from *Noci, noci* ('Nights, Nights', Torst: 2004); 'A Day in the Half-life of Class 4D' is abridged from *Jeden den ve IV.D* (Torst: 2005); 'Elegy' is from *Bůh z reklamy* ('The God from the Advertisement', Československý Spisovatel: 1964); 'Don't Tell Mum' is based on a motif from the author's *Nordickou blondýnu jsem nikdy nelízala* ('I Have Never Licked a Nordic Blonde', Concordia: 2005); 'A Child' is from *Nechci se vrátit mezi mrtvé* ('I Do Not Want to Return Among the Dead', Triáda: 2004); 'Spades' is from *Ikariana* (print cancelled in 1969, Samizdat 1984, Práce: 1991).

Introduction

What springs to mind when people think of the Czech Republic? Prague, beer, perhaps Václav Havel or *The Good Soldier Schweik* (*Švejk* in Czech). Classical music aficionados might know Martinů or Dvořák; ice hockey fans will know the Czech team. At Christmas time some might briefly think of Czech history while singing 'Good King Wenceslas Looked Out on the Feast of Stephen'. Well, there won't be much of all that in this collection, except for some views of Prague, two or three beers, and the fleeting appearance of Saint Wenceslas himself.

Recently, the biggest signpost in the development of Czech writing has obviously been the lifting of censorship following the collapse of the totalitarian communist regime in late 1989. Czechoslovakia had shared the fate of other countries in the Soviet orbit for forty-one years, during which censorship was alleviated only briefly, in the run-up to the 1968 Prague Spring. During this time literature was required to conform to the demands of building a socialist society, or more cynically, of supporting the ruling power. Those who did not conform suffered in various ways. Some authors wrote and published in exile: we have in this collection a work by Viola Fischerová, whose short story was written in 1975 in Basel, Switzerland. Others kept their manuscripts in their desk drawers, like Květa Legátová who could finally bring *Želary* out to great acclaim in 2001. Some used 1968's window of opportunity to publish, but saw complete stocks of their books shredded soon after the Warsaw Pact brought Czechoslovakia into line by the positioning of Soviet troops around the capital in the late summer of that year. Such was the fate of the first editions of Věra Stiborová and Lenka Reinerová's volumes. Others managed to circulate their manuscripts in typescript via dissident channels, the 'samizdat' method, beyond the reach of official censors; this is where Svatava Antošová marked her debut.

Not surprisingly, there emerged among the intellectuals of political dissent a feeling that they were persecuted because they were the 'conscience of the nation'. Paradoxically, it seemed that both the regime and the dissidents placed a high value on the political and social power of ideas, therefore for the one side ideas had to be destroyed, for the other they had to be promoted at all cost. After the changes in 1989, an appraisal of this struggle took place. Some accused the dissidents of arrogance in claiming the moral high ground, while publishers rushed to publish previously forbidden literature in print runs of 100,000. After the euphoria of finally having a free press had died down, it became clear that not absolutely everything the dissidents had written during the dark years was of high literary quality, and not absolutely everything sanctioned by the regime had to be sent to the rubbish heap. In fact, it was one of the luxuries of freedom not to have to view things in such black-and-white terms. Even Lenka Reinerová, the most ideologically categorical in our group, changed her title for the re-edition from the original *The Colour of the Sun and of the Night* to *All the Colours of the Sun and the Night* to denote that opinions exist on a sliding scale between 'yes' and 'no'. Two of the authors in this collection were published under the Communists, but at a time of relative political thaw – Alena Vostrá in 1964 and Alexandra Berková in 1986; these writers pushed the boundaries of what could be published when the censors were not so vigilant. Their political critique is explicit in places, and at the time their two slim books came as a breath of fresh air amidst the putrid recycling of socialist-realist themes. In this collection, the rotten atmosphere of the eighties is wittily described in Kateřina Sidonová's story; she herself is the daughter of a dissident and therefore has her own angle on the issue.

During the nineties, there was a growing feeling of disenchantment with all political ideologues, be they apologists for the authorities or dissenting. Some critics lamented 'the end of history', 'of politics', of '*intellectuels engagés*.' This misses the point that it is very political to say that ideologies are irrelevant or wrong. Luckily, the year 1989 was not the end for literature, and intellectuals today still seem to find issues to debate. Whether they are considered politically significant is another matter; certainly their prestige is not guaranteed, any more than their books' publication: their work must compete on an open market against pulp fiction. One of the intellectual debates of the nineties was over feminism: a war seemingly broke out between the feminists and the anti-feminists. The latter probably won in terms of public opinion, as feminism became synonymous with radicalism. Some commentators have expressed surprise, even dismay, at this turn of events. The Czech women's rights movement had started out so promisingly a century ago, and today we find in the opinion columns views on women more backward than ever. Although indignation is justified, I think there is little ground for imagining that women's liberation makes a linear progress until it reaches emancipation. Rather, it would seem that the 'woman's question' crops up in public debate whenever communities are in a state of transition and social functions are being redefined in general; why precisely women are the object of the fiercest arguments, while the question of men's roles is only implicit, is perhaps beyond rationality. In our anthology, Alexandra Berková is perhaps the most significant avowed feminist, although nearly all authors touch on gender roles.

In another way women might have gained, at least in the publishing field. The year 2000 seemed to mark a turning point as far as publishing women writers is concerned. 'Women's literature' is no longer relegated to the category of 'Romance and Relationships', and the prevalence of male writers is not as automatic as it used to be. Perhaps this is because literary works are no longer circulated solely in the clubs of the (traditionally male?) intelligentsia, and it is certainly because the books have found their market. Moreover, women writers have put their fingers on issues that not many men have raised. In this collection, Anna Zonová mentions attitudes toward Roma, Sabrina Karasová the tricky legacy of the Sudetenland, Magdaléna Platzová deals with pornography, Kateřina Rudčenková with broken families, Svatava Antošová confronts sexual abuse of children and Erika Olahová rape. It makes for a cheery list, yet all of these pieces are also about how humans (and an animal or two) live, for better or worse, and about things that are beyond them. We are far from the wasteland of 'post-history', and we have plenty to read.

It will be noticed that two of the contributions were not written in Czech at all, making it difficult to classify them as Czech literature. Moreover, they happen to be memoirs, thus not easy to label as 'short stories'. I hope that the reader will be open-minded. Tera Fabiánová's story is translated from Romani, the language spoken by the older generations of Roma in the

Czech Republic and Slovakia, and in other dialects elsewhere. In terms of literary production, Romani used to recite poems and sing songs, and to recount tales that either preserved a certain cultural and ethnic history, or present a moral yardstick (Erika Olahová's piece can also be understood in this way). It has only been used as a written language since the 1960s, when a few Czech sociologists and anthropologists saw the transformation of Romani culture into a written one as a tool for raising the profile of Roma in Czechoslovakia. This occurred after decades of drastic resettlement and re-education since the Second World War, when most of the Czech Roma were exterminated, while the Slovak Roma saw the economic foundations of their lifestyle disappear. While an educated Roma class has emerged around the Romani rights movement, of which written Romani is a component, most Roma live today in poor ghettos near industrial centres, on the periphery of society.

Nowhere has this social fiasco been more evident than in the Sudetenland. Much property was left vacant after the expulsion of the Sudeten Germans, a large linguistic minority with nationalist and secessionist tendencies in pre-Second World War Czechoslovakia. The Sudetenland was incorporated into Czechoslovakia when the state was created in 1918, according to principles of national self-determination in Central Europe – even though there was a seeming contradiction in including such a large German group that had to be satisfied with minority rights rather than the self-determination awarded to the Czechs and Slovaks. After their expulsion on the grounds of collaboration with the Nazi Protectorate, the Sudeten borderland experienced an economic decline that communist-planned industrialisation was supposed to reverse, and the resettlement of labour force, including Slovak Romas and Ruthenians (Ukrainians), was meant to counteract the depopulation. Anna Zonová and Sabrina Karasová, who have experienced life in the Sudetenland, have dealt with these issues.

Lenka Reinerová's story is translated from German. The oldest author in this collection, she is a testimony to the Czech Republic's multilingual and multiethnic past. Her Prague Jewish community, most of which was traditionally German-speaking, did not share any of the political preferences of the Sudeten Germans. After their community had been virtually exterminated in the Holocaust, the Jews who did return, among them many Communists, found their existence threatened in other ways. The Stalinist purges staged by the Czechoslovak government in 1952 fabricated accusations that implicated Jews in a Zionist conspiracy and in contacts with the Western imperialist powers. Reinerová and Fabiánová's stories are so extraordinary that one might wish they were fiction and not reality, in order that one might have read them as surreal short stories. The Foucauldians among the readers might appreciate the prominence in these accounts of two institutions for 'disciplining and punishing', the school and the prison. Their experiences might also give the reader an idea that the Czech sense of nationhood evolved in a context where clear-cut nationalities were not self-evident.

I must apologise to all those who aimed to map new Czech literature, who wished to draw some conclusion about the fate of women in Eastern Europe, or who wanted to grasp the essential Czech literary style. To some extent, I have shied away from answers, and I disagree with the premise of some of the questions. My aims are modest: to offer a collection of stories that have never been published in English to an interested readership that wishes to be entertained and edified. This introduction perhaps betrays the fact that I am a sociologist at heart, but the above is definitely not meant to imply that a sociological reading of the texts is necessary or important; rather, it is meant to give the context of the literary creation by considering points of interest without striving for academic precision. It is something to add to the list under Švejk, Martinů and Good King Wenceslas ...

I would like to thank the many people who have helped me in my endeavours: Kathleen Hayes, Robert Pynsent, David Short, Jana Nahodilová, Tim Beasley-Murray, Marie Chřibková, Rajendra Chitnis, Bernie Higgins, the late Milena Hübschmannová; I thank my friends Magdaléna Herová, Magdaléna Hodková and Catherine Eden for their assistance, my meticulous parents Mary and Nigel Hawker for their comments and my husband Alaa Owaineh for his support. The team at Telegram Books provided unfailing backing. Above all, I thank all the authors and translators – it was a pleasure to work with them.

Nancy Hawker

Pronunciation Guide

'á': long 'a', as in bl<u>ah</u>-bl<u>ah</u>

'c': 'ts' as in hi<u>ts</u>

'č': 'ch' as in <u>ch</u>eck

'ch': 'kh' as in <u>Kh</u>rushchev

'ě': as in 'wh<u>e</u>re oh wh<u>e</u>re ...'

'í': long 'ee' as in sw<u>ee</u>p cl<u>ea</u>n

'j': 'y' as in <u>y</u>awn

'ó': as in d<u>oo</u>r

'ou': 'o' as in bl<u>ow</u>

'ř': as in bou<u>r</u>geois (approximately, it's a consonant that only 95 per cent of Czechs can pronounce, apparently Václav Havel cannot, so you are in good company)

'š': as in <u>sh</u>eep

'ú' and 'ů': long 'oo' as in b<u>oo</u>

'ž': as in plea<u>s</u>ure

ALEXANDRA BERKOVÁ

Mininovel

When Mum and Dad ran into each other they said, it's been ages, what have you been up to all this time. And Mum said, I guess I'll have to get married. And Dad said, why have to and why guess, and Mum said, have to because I don't want to, and guess because I guess I'll do it. And Dad said, marriage is an outdated institution, let's go to the cinema. And Mum said, thanks but I don't have time. So they went.

And a week later Mum said, come on quick, let's go for a glass of wine, I'm a terrible coward and I'm hiding from Karel and I can't stand being alone because I'm such a coward.

And a week later she passed her final exams and she said, I'm so relieved not to be going out with anyone, and Dad said, there must be some mistake, you're going out with me.

And a month later Mum said, where were you, I was looking for you, and Dad said nothing and then he said, I was at the cottage with that young one of mine. Mum fell silent and then she said, I wanted to show you this, and she pulled out a calendar. And Dad stared at it and said, we'll have to do something about that.

And Mum said, you do what you want pal, and she stood up. Dad said, I've already broken up with her, and Mum said, you needn't have bothered, and she left.

Then she dialled a number and said, hi Jarda, let's go for a glass of wine, and he said, for you, my long-lost love, anything, and they went. He said something and he looked at Mum and Mum smiled and he said, girl, you're in a bad way, let's buy a bottle and go back to my place. And Mum said, I'm an idiot, I'm sorry I dragged you out, I'm a stupid idiot. And he said, think it over, and Mum said, I feel bad inside and out, don't be mad. And she went outside to cry.

Then she went home and Dad was standing in front of the door and he sneezed and said, you shouldn't wander about like this at night or our daughter will catch cold. And Mum said, mind your own business, and Dad said, don't be mad any more, after all we're both adults. And Mum said, you've got a long way to go before you reach adulthood and you can relax, I was only testing you. And Dad said, you're very silly, too bad I didn't notice before, and he left. Mum stood in front of the house and it started to rain. Then she went to make a phone call and she said, hi Zdena, can you please lend me some of little Honza's things, I'm going to be a single mother. And Zdena said, you're crazy, I'm coming over, and she came and said, why did you insult him like that, and Mum said, because he doesn't know what he's doing and it's easier to take care of one child than two. Zdena talked for a long time and Mum said, don't feel sorry for me, I can manage, and Zdena said, I don't feel sorry for you, I feel sorry for that child, in one room with a toilet on the corridor, you've got an inflated opinion of yourself. And Mum said, thanks a lot for the great advice, and Zdena said, you're more selfish than crazy and she left. It was still raining and Mum couldn't fall asleep for a long time and the next morning she was late for work.

A week later a twenty-year-old girl came and said, Petr loves me. And Mum said, congratulations, even though I couldn't care less. And she said, Petr claims that you're going to get married but I know that it's not true, I know him, we've been going out for half a year. And Mum said, I understand that that seems incredibly long to you, but I still couldn't care less. And she said, you're jealous because you're almost thirty, but you won't steal Petr away from me. And Mum said, no, I won't because I'm not trying, and say hello to him for me, and she opened the door.

Then she lit a cigarette and someone knocked and Dad entered and said, don't smoke or our daughter will suffocate in there. And Mum said, don't be so hard on your teeny-bopper, you can still catch her on the stairs. And Dad said, my mother sent her here, I announced that we were getting married. And Mum said, to think that's the first I've heard of it, Dad said, I was just coming to tell you, Mum drew a deep breath and Dad said, you're lucky, you're so dumb you might have spoiled everything. Mum said, that's my concern and I don't want anything from you. And Dad said, more proof you're crazy, and all the more reason I have to stay close to my daughter. And Mum said, you don't have to do anything and it will be a boy. Then they talked for a long time and Mum said, what will happen now and Dad said, from now on everything will be fine, and Mum said, I don't have any clothes.

Then she travelled home and she said, I'm going to get married, and grandma said, you already were married. Mum said, I'm going to have a baby, grandma said, whatever you say, grandpa said, god help you, and he left. And Mum said, well, take care, we're getting married in July, I'll send you the notice, and she left.

A week later Dad lay on the ground and drew and said, we'll have to install gas and water and put in a shower, we've got a lot to do by December. And Mum said, do you think we'll fit in here, and Dad said, yeah, if the girl isn't too big. And Mum said, we hardly know each other, it's strange that I'm not afraid. And Dad said, there's nothing strange about it because I don't bite and we've got tons of time to get acquainted. Mum kissed him and said, I love you, I'm lucky I met you.

A week later someone knocked and Karel entered and sat down and said, I hope I'm not interrupting, you look fabulous and he offered Mum a cigarette. And Mum said, thanks, I don't smoke, what do you want. He said, I just want to see you, Mum was silent and he said, I heard you were going out with someone, I hope it's nothing serious, Mum was silent and he said, watch out for yourself, a person of your calibre shouldn't be chained to the stove, and Mum said, it's not serious, it's fun, I'm going to have a baby and I'm going to get married. He said, you're naive, even rabbits can procreate, but there aren't many specialists in your field. Then he said, I'll find a doctor for you and we can get back together, and Mum said, thank you but I don't want to. And he said, I know that I'm not always charming but you've got to understand that a man like me has a lot of worries, I don't have time for lovey-doveying. Mum was silent and he said, I'm a nervous wreck because I have to take care of everything on my own and I can't always be charming, you simply have to understand that, that's why I have you. Mum said, you don't, and he said, don't be silly, you won't have it so good with anyone else as you do with me and don't be coy, I don't like that, you know all too well that I don't like that. Mum said, I know, and he said, there you go, I want to have clean shirts and I'm not willing to eat out of tin cans because the wife is writing a novel. And Mum said, you said something about the stove, and he said, don't nit-pick, you're always nit-picking and that winds me up, so don't wind me up and you can keep that fling to yourself, I'm even willing to get rid of that unpleasantness. See, another worry, and he lit a cigarette. Mum said, how did I put up with you for almost two years and he said, I was the one who put up with you and I'm willing to put up with you even longer because I need you, I admit it, I need you. But don't be coy, you're not exactly first prize and I can easily get a replacement, even though that will involve more expenditure and more time. Mum said, yuck. He said, don't get precious, I won't fall for it, I just call a spade a spade and I'm willing to take care of you, call that love if you like. And Mum said, I wouldn't dream of it, go away. And he said, whatever you want, but in that case don't forget that I was the one who paid for Yugoslavia and you owe me four thousand. And mum said, I truly have more luck than sense, you'll get your money, get lost. And he said, you're an ordinary twit, I'm amazed that I ever loved you, after a fashion, nonetheless I hope it's an easy labour, and he left.

And Mum bawled and laughed and called Dad and Dad said, what a bastard, he promised that he wouldn't go to see you, he was here the day before yesterday. And Mum said, darling today let's go out for dinner instead of cleaning, our son has a craving for a steak. And Dad said, anything for our daughter, but while we're on the subject, my mother may drop by to see you too. And Mum said, ah. Dad said, be nice to her, she always wanted to find me a bride and we sort of side-stepped her. And Mum said, ah. And Dad said, maybe she won't come, I told her to leave you alone. And Mum said, ah, hm.

And three days later, a fifty-year-old lady came and said, I came to see who's taking away my only son. And Mum said, please sit down, and she said, my son is still a child, you have no right to take him from me. Mum drew a deep breath and the lady said, you're taking away my only son, you're devious, three years older than him and divorced, if I'm not mistaken, but I'm willing to reach an agreement with you, and she took out her wallet. And Mum blushed and said, we won't reach an agreement that way, please, sit down. And she remained standing and said, no need to be ashamed, obviously you've found out what sort of family little Petr comes from, otherwise you wouldn't have picked him, and if you knew who his father was you wouldn't have dared. And Mum said, won't you take a seat, and the lady said, little Petr has only just finished his studies, he has to build a career, I must protect my child. And Mum said, don't you care about Petr's child? And she said, is it really his? And Mum went red in the face and said, I don't know about you, madam, but I – and the lady said, I won't be insulted by some – and Mum said, I apologise for wasting your precious time, and she stood up. And the lady said, I know that little Petr is not sure either. And Mum said, goodbye and she opened the door. Then she sat with her head in her hands and then she called Karel but he wasn't in.

After work she dragged her feet, she bought a cinema ticket but threw it away, then she wandered through the streets and looked at shop displays and at people and she went into a shop. She said, I want a dress, something to boost my self-confidence. And the salesman said, but young lady, how could you lack self-confidence – Mum tried on two dresses, she said, I look like a blob of ice cream, and she left. She called up Karel and he said, I knew princess would change her mind, and Mum said, only partly, I need that doctor. And he said, there you go, you've come to your senses, I'll pick you up tomorrow, Mum said yes and she hung up.

In the evening she came home, Dad was waiting there and he said, don't say a thing, I talked with mother. Mum said, she's right, you don't know what you're doing, I've changed my mind. And Dad said, nonsense, you're both nuts, the guy for the gas is supposed to come the day after tomorrow and I'm going to stay here and he inflated a mattress. And Mum drew a deep breath and Dad said, it bothers me that any little thing can put you into a state but I'll save my reproaches until after the birth, until then I'll cook and he unwrapped six little sandwiches. And Mum whispered, you're crazy, and Dad said, that's not true, I'm the only normal one here. And Mum said, what about your mother, and Dad said, my mum has a heart of gold, but she's snooty and a little slow on the uptake, before the week is out we'll be invited for lunch. And Mum said, I've already arranged for a doctor, and Dad said, if I hear such rubbish again I'll do something rash. And Mum said, I love you, Dad said, it hardly looks like it, Mum said, I'm happy, and Dad said, so try not to screw it up, for the moment everything's fine except you, now let's get our daughter some air, I read that you have to take walks. And Mum said, it'll be a boy, and they went for a walk and then the repairman came and then they went to the Prague grandma's for lunch and then they painted and installed gas and water and then they went to the town hall, but Dad forgot his identity card so they went another time, but they arrived an hour late and then Mum said, let's leave it until later, I don't want to get married in a tent dress, and Dad said, you're right, it doesn't matter anyway.

And then Mum lay in a room with green tiles and she sweated and a doctor arrived and he said, I'm only an orthopaedist, but I've brought you a visitor, and Dad came in a white coat and he said, hold on girls, I have to leave now so that they don't catch me here with Honza, and he squeezed Mum's hand.

And two hours later another doctor said a little more – that's it – well done – you have a daughter.

They washed me, checked and measured and weighed me and showed me to Mum. And Mum said, oh, she's beautiful, can I touch her? My name is Dita.

Translated by Kathleen Hayes

VIOLA FISCHEROVÁ

The Path of Medium Sinfulness

Were Jakub to turn right out of the school gates and then walk further down the road, Father Nosek would ride past him on his bicycle still in the tree-lined avenue. Were he to cut across the castle grounds, the priest would only catch up with him in the steep street leading to the church. The third option was to hide behind the petrol station. For that he had to wait until the black silhouette appeared in the gateway and then set out on the right-hand pavement towards the main square. The third tactic was the most inconspicuous but also the most risky: in the flow of traffic and cyclists, Father Nosek could easily overlook him and Jakub would then have to wait until Sunday Mass. Nevertheless, he was convinced that only by alternating all three methods would their encounters seem coincidental, a matter to which, for some reason, Jakub attached great importance.

Yet today – of this Jakub was certain – Father Nosek was anticipating their meeting just as he was. This too weighed on his mind during the two hours of lessons that were left until he could go home, and although it wasn't *the main issue* – although Jakub's sense of expectation was for completely different reasons – he had to think about it anyway. Now, standing on the pavement, choosing which path to take, he was ashamed. He checked that Father Nosek's bicycle was standing in the rack and ran across the avenue to the park, to where the tall maple faced the school gates.

It was only the end of October, yet the trees were nearly bare. Four hollows filled to the brim with water from the incessant rain were all there was left of the bench that had stood here in summer. Uncle Johan had been under ground twenty days already, Saracen nine. Water probably didn't leak from the grave's walls into the heavy oak coffin, but Saracen's box was certainly full. He imagined Saracen, head on paws, staring with unblinking eyes into the watery darkness.

Were it summer, he would have buried Saracen as is, straight into the earth. When they were uprooting the dead apple tree in the orchard last spring, Father Nosek had said that there was only as much matter in the universe as God had created. It doesn't disappear, nor does it increase – it only changes. The black stump of the tree truly was no longer wood. The splinters Jakub collected in a pile were soft and fluffy and turned to dust under his touch.

In summer, in the warm soil, Saracen would have transformed faster. Jakub imagined the crumbly loam mixing with the shaggy fur, the hair close to the body white and coffee-coloured like rootlets and, closer to the surface, the hair greener, germinating until springtime when the dog would bask in the sun afresh, rather like a shadow in the grass: the green shadow of a dog.

Yet the box was sturdy, and in a sudden need to protect Saracen from the mud and the cold Jakub had decked it with an old blanket and nailed it shut. In the middle of the empty parkway he was overwhelmed by the feeling that he had walled Saracen up.

But was this all that was left of Saracen? When he had left for school that morning, Saracen had been lying stretched out in front of Uncle's bedroom door, his eyes closed, looking as if he were dead. But he still recognised Jakub, and what's more, *showed his recognition* by taking milk from Jakub's hand with his chapped tongue – just a couple of drops, the only food he had accepted since Uncle's death. By noon he had stopped moving. His eyes were open and his gaze fixed on the distance, somewhere beyond the wall.

Mother had been preparing him for this all week. The animal will die of longing for Johan, you must come to terms with it. He had come to terms with it. He even let himself be convinced that Saracen could not be buried in Uncle's grave, even though neither of them would have wished for anything else. With time he would have reconciled himself to that completely. In his mind, both had found their place in heaven, next to that tall man in a swimming costume at the seaside, laughing on Mother's night table, the man who was supposed to be his late father although he was so young.

When Jakub was little, he used to take the photograph out of its frame when his mother wasn't looking. He would hold lemon candy to the man's lips, half-believing that they could share the sharp taste through some mysterious connection. At least he thought such a thing wasn't completely out of the question. He observed with trepidation the expression in the laughing eyes, which he saw changing each time they rested on him. He felt such joy and supreme pride at those moments that he would usually burst into tears.

But that was before. Since he had been attending school these last three years, he did not think about his father in such concrete terms. Daddy was in heaven, where Jakub and mummy would join him one day. His plea for that day, which he addressed every night to the Almighty, started with the invocation:

Lord, let me ascend to my father in the heavens,
So that I may not remain without him
(sometimes he added, And without his love),
Who sees me,
And who does not forsake me.
Amen.

To this fixed part he would add extra verses composed on the spot in moments of particular piety. Lately the prayers had been for Uncle Johan and his loyal servant Saracen, who had loved him so much that he died of woe for him.

And yet, Saracen was not in heaven – that was as clear as it was certain that Uncle Johan was. Father Nosek had said so one afternoon in religious studies. Animals don't go to heaven because they don't have immortal souls. He tried to recall the kindly voice, pronouncing that sentence.

'That's not true!' he had cried out from the back of the classroom. Then, as if he had not heard anything Father Nosek had said about man's free will to choose God, he had whimpered, 'None at all? Not even old horses or dogs ... not even Saracen?'

'No horses, no dogs, not even Saracen!' he now answered himself out loud, stunned by the boldness of that statement. And yet it must be true. Father Nosek did not lie. He could not. Neither did he have any reason to. One could look into his face for hours and no shadow of danger or evil would cross it.

Jakub stared intently at the gates. Once in a while they would open, but only a few straggling pupils would slip out. Four had not struck, but the light was already on in the staffroom. None of the teachers came out. He pulled the sleeves of his sweater down over his fingers. It occurred to him that he could wait in the cloakroom by the stairs, but he rejected that option and immediately forgot it.

All right – he reflected – people have immortal souls and when that soul leaves the body the person dies. But animals too must have a soul, otherwise how would they live? What if they have just a tiny soul, a mortal one – do they die when that soul dies? In that case, when Saracen refused to eat after Uncle's death, he destroyed his soul by starvation. That was a ridiculous idea, that a sausage could keep Saracen's soul alive. Or even a string of sausages! Jakub laughed briefly. For an instant he caught a faint glimmer of hope that everything might be otherwise; but the flicker vanished and he tried in vain to bring it back.

Geese and chicken died when their necks were wrung, he had seen it with his own eyes. Blood came out of the cut and then life escaped from it too. What else could life be but the soul? The only difference is that the human soul knows where it should go: to God. But what do rabbits and lambs know? He imagined their little fluffy white souls wandering helplessly around the yard, chased from one corner to the other and eventually torn apart by the wind and blown away.

Saracen died because he *wanted* to die. Because he had to go after Uncle Johan. If he had refused to eat and drink, it was because his soul had ordered him to do so. His tiny soul had at last exterminated the big dog's body, so that it could escape and follow its master. Besides, Saracen's body was hungry and thirsty; one could tell by the way, at least for the first few days, he would look at his bowl. Also, Saracen cried. Silently, he always had two wet sticky trickles of tears under his eyes.

Is it possible for a soul like that to be dispersed like fluff, like nothing? Wasn't it much easier to imagine it setting sail, finding its wind and dashing off like a rocket, over hills and dales, to join its master?

And what about Uncle Johan? Did he not turn around to see what Saracen was doing without him? Had he not seen how he was lying in front of the door, how he was languishing in his absence, and how he would die? Would he not wait a little so that they could go together, as they had done all those long months when Uncle had spent all his time walking to and fro between the rooms, never deserted by his one and only Saracen? It just couldn't be so!

Uncle Johan never spoke to them about Saracen, to Mother and him, nor to Father Nosek. In the end he spoke very little in general and when he did it was only to Saracen. Jakub could hear them at night through the wall when he was falling asleep. What could they have been talking about, if not about *it*? No, Uncle Johan would never have abandoned Saracen!

But what if he had had to? Jakub breathed in deeply. What if he could wait no longer? Uncle's soul needed to get out and Saracen was dying too slowly, the soul had to leave, to go to heaven, to hell, or to purgatory. What happened then, when Uncle's soul couldn't breathe on earth any more? First it held its breath, trying to hold on to pillows and blankets until it went red in the face and had to let go and soar. The day after the funeral Father Nosek had said that Uncle Johan was in heaven rejoicing with the angels, because he saw God and Jesus Christ and was blessed.

Then what happened to Saracen, if dogs are banned from paradise? Did they just leave him outside, running back and forth, sniffing around in front of the gates? Did they leave him to languish and starve once again?

What does God have against dogs, when he loves all people, even the ingrate and the evil ones, since He sacrificed His son

Jesus Christ for them, whom they took and nailed to the cross? What grudge does He hold against dogs and colts and old horses who pulled their loads every day and could never gallop in the field because there are no fields in the city? Does it mean that the Lord doesn't like animals?

He stopped himself short. He was overcome by a sudden wave of shame and fear, as when Viktor talks on purpose about angels while he's peeing. Yet wasn't what he had just thought an even greater heresy? He blushed.

Nevertheless, here were these dumb creatures, God's creatures, *sacrificed* for no good reason, burnt offerings on the altar. And the lambs that God ordered to be slaughtered towards the evening of the fourteenth day. He imagined it: men kneeling on top of a cliff, laying down the bleating lambs, their legs tied, on the stone, and slashing their necks. In the whole town, in every house, they wrenched the youngest lamb from its mother. Once they had killed it, they wiped their bloodied fingers on the doorframe.

Even Christ had had a lamb slaughtered. And when his disciples had nothing to eat, he ordered Peter to cast his net into the sea, and Peter pulled out 153 fish, which they grilled on red-hot coals.

He had seen it on holiday by the sea. A man in a white apron picked out fish thrashing about in a bucket and threw them straight into a pan of boiling oil. He had cried out in horror and mummy had carried him away whispering in his ear that the fish was half dead anyway and couldn't feel anything. But he had seen all too well how the fish was struggling under the counter, floundering against the stones covered with blood.

He had never told Father Nosek about it. Only once on the dam he had asked him whether killing fish was a different kind of killing. It was a different killing, because killing for a useful purpose is not a sin. There, above the outfall, he had explained it to himself in terms of a sacrifice, insofar as God had provided the animals for humans to eat so that they may not suffer from hunger, and in recompense for their sacrifice, all the animals, even predators and snakes, would go to paradise.

'Paradise,' Father Nosek had said at the end of the lesson, 'is God.' Then, after the bell had rung, in the midst of the bedlam that was breaking out, just for Jakub: 'Only humans agonise in their desire for God. All their lives.'

It was possible that animals know nothing of God. But does that mean that they do not long for a green field, where they can gambol and graze, in reward for all the suffering, for their hunger and cold, for the whipping and the hunting and the killing? For sure, animals have an idea of paradise. And Saracen? Saracen had not cared so much for God as he had for Uncle Johan. Had Saracen not loved Uncle Johan with all his heart, with all his soul and mind, and had he not followed him wherever he had gone?

If God will not hear Saracen out, someone at least will hear his howl in front of the gates. Jesus will, or the angels.

'Someone must take care of him!' he screamed. 'You can't just leave him there like that!'

A tractor with an empty trailer clattered down the road. Two more windows shone into the dusk from the ground floor. Behind one of them the caretaker's wife was hanging up curtains. For a moment, when she was resting her arms, it looked as if she were looking straight at Jakub. But she was only observing her own reflection, and when she had rearranged her scarf and tucked in her blouse, she resumed her work easily and naturally, as if there were nothing outside the window, as if no one could see her.

Jakub detached himself from the trunk and started pacing

between the trees, around and across, treading an indiscernible web in the grass.

It was dark when Father Nosek appeared in the doorway. Teachers were now emerging in pairs and threes. Father Nosek came out last and alone. Below the steps he halted and lit a cigarette. Jakub didn't move. Only when the last cluster of teachers disappeared around the corner did he pick up his satchel, swing the straps over his elbow and step out into the light of the street. His knee hit the bag with every pace as he walked, his eyes fixed on his feet. His mind was blank. The happiness he had denied himself all afternoon, the wayward joy which he nevertheless suspected to be in every thing, even in the water that flooded Saracen, this happiness now surrounded him, light and effortless, and there was no reason to resist it. Jakub dragged his shoes through a long puddle and then skipped onto the pavement.

Father Nosek was not looking at him. He stood with his head turned away towards the street and when he faced Jakub his expression was different.

'I cannot make it easier for you, Jakub. I cannot tell you what you would like to hear. Even if it might seem incomprehensible to you,' Father Nosek sighed, 'there are no ... I have no evidence for the existence of souls in animals. Perhaps I would have ...'. Father Nosek spoke sharply with agitation, as if he were angry. In his first year at school, when Reiner had thrown Jakub's satchel out of the window, Father Nosek had taken him into his arms – in front of the whole class. On Sunday there would be a daytrip to the hills. It began to rain; it was late. Father Nosek put on a raincoat, straddled his bicycle and rode off. With his head against the corner of a wall, Jakub wept.

There is a place that God doesn't know about, that he doesn't think about, that he didn't even tell the prophets about. Behind the back wall of paradise there is a meadow full of mist. Animals who have no one to go to come to this meadow after they die. All of them are there, horses and dogs, mice and lambs. But no one knows about them and no one looks for them there. So they are all waiting there for nothing.

Until now Jakub had gone to great lengths in order to get into heaven. He did not take God's name in vain, he did not indulge in sinful thoughts and he almost never stole anything. Suddenly that seemed easy, or at least a lot easier than what was ahead of him. For from this day on he must live in sin. Not completely, not enough to descend to hell and eternal damnation, but enough not to deserve paradise. The soul grows through union with God, he recited quickly to himself to stifle his growing anxiety. Loss of faith brings damnation. Somewhere in between is medium sinfulness. He must pray, but God mustn't hear him. He must believe, but only in paradise. He must gain a tiny soul. And he must never tell anyone about it.

He shook with cold and distress. The face of the young man, smiling at him from the seaside, appeared before him for an instant, and he felt such an intense pain that he had to shut his eyes.

Someone has to be there with them, to stroke them and talk to them.

He started to run. When he opened the front door, it occurred to him that he would be but a poor consolation for Saracen, but, he told himself, better than nothing. Before he entered the bathroom, he took some glue and a brush out of the tool cupboard, and chose a sharp pencil from his case. Under the corner of the linoleum floor that had come unstuck he wrote in delicate lettering: *God is not the father*. After a pause for thought he added the signature: Jakub. Afterwards he glued the flooring back and locked the door. He prayed for a long time, carefully choosing the right words. In his new prayer the word father did not appear once.

When she came back, Mother found Jakub in the kitchen. While the soup was heating on the cooker, he was eating cakes. He spat the cherry stones across the table in long arches, straight into the coalscuttle.

Translated by Nancy Hawker

ANNA ZONOVÁ

One Pistachio Ice Cream

Renáta and I used to be contented. During the first years of our marriage. After all, that's how I'd been imagining it and planning it: having a healthy breakfast together. Usually muesli and half a pint of low-fat milk.

We have lunch on our own, I in my canteen, Renáta in a bistro. I suspect that she often just grabs something cold on the run and washes it down with coffee. Of course, coffee. Can't be without it. Despite several scientific studies proving the harmful effects of caffeine I brought home for her. But Renáta doesn't care. Lately, at least. She simply ignores all scientific proof. Which she shouldn't, considering she has a university degree.

The supper she prepares is always very light – just for me. Two slices of buttered bread with something on top. I could eat more, but have to watch my figure. Renáta always pours herself only a big glass of white wine. 'To lose weight,' she used to say.

Keeping her weight down is not at all desirable in her case. You can count her ribs, and her hip bones stick out, whether she's wearing a skirt or a pair of trousers. When I first tried to explain it to her, she accepted my explanations with understanding and from then on I refrained from commenting on her wine-drinking.

She also sometimes irritates me with her obsession with smells and her intolerance towards people in tracksuits. I can't understand it. I simply can't smell anything. Three months into our relationship we agreed that she was not going to bother me with this. Still, I often catch her walking around the flat with the tip of her nose visibly twitching. Like a rabbit's. 'Renáta!' I scold her. I'm sure she has discovered something she's not happy with.

'You haven't rinsed your mouth!' Or: 'How long have you been wearing that underwear?' She would embarrass me with such comments and that's why we finally came to an agreement: for our relationship to grow and to be a positive influence on our children, I too have to have sufficient self-esteem.

The Pelners moved into our block of flats five months ago. They are both around thirty. Mrs Pelner may be younger, I would say perhaps twenty-five but I'm not going to ask about her exact date of birth. 'What do you need to know that for?' she could very well retort. I'm not going to explain to her my sense of responsibility and accuracy. Miroslav Pelner works as a maintenance man for the City Council's housing department. I see him regularly leave the building at 5.55 AM. That's when I make tea. I warm up the milk later.

Renáta usually sleeps in.

She finds the Pelners happier than us. 'I have the impression that they live a full life,' she said last week just before we went to sleep.

'What do you mean, a full life?' I said. 'Can you define what you mean by that or describe it more precisely?'

'Mrs Pelnerová sells ice cream from a stall in front of the confectionery shop.'

'I didn't know that,' I replied.

'I'd love to be a twenty-four-year-old gypsy woman weighing eighty kilos,' she went on. 'I would sell ice cream at a stall. I would make slow, lazy movements, not ungainly, just unhurried, taking pleasure in every step, movement and bow. I would have eight different flavours of Algida ice cream on offer. Chocolate, hazelnut, lemon, strawberry, pistachio, banana, orange and blueberry (that's the one I love best). In the evenings I'd feed my five children and get properly laid by my fifth man, and again in the morning. I would feel happiness. I wouldn't worry about the pain and suffering of refugees from any country, the starving people of Africa, the uprootedness of American Indians or Sudeten Ruthenians. I wouldn't be brought down by unhappy relationships, by my friend's terminal illness, I wouldn't miss orgasm and my thoughts would not turn to promiscuity.'

Her declaration startled me.

'We can analyse this,' I said. 'Your wish to change profession is not normal. I hope you realise that the position of a City Council official is socially respected and well paid. I would, of course, welcome a certain weight gain on your part. I know we have already discussed this several times. If only you would eat a proper lunch and ...'

'You idiotic moron!' she screamed.

Then she grabbed her blanket and went to the living room. She had never used such swear words before. I couldn't decide what to do. She can't call me that, can she?

After all, she doesn't even realise the full meaning of the words she used. After a while I got up and found the dictionary, but the notebook I use to explain things to her was in the kitchen and I didn't want to walk past her. I didn't want to face her just after this critical clash. For that reason I used the home accounts notebook, where I wrote down: 'Idiot: from the Greek *idiotes*, a person of profound mental retardation having a mental age of a three-year-old and generally being unable to learn connected speech or guard against common dangers. Moron: A person with mild mental retardation with a mental age of between seven to twelve years and generally having communication and social skills enabling some degree of academic or vocational education. The term belongs to a psychological classification system no longer in use and is now considered offensive.'

I'll present her with the notebook at breakfast. I think we ought to have a proper talk.

I woke up half an hour earlier than usual. I thoroughly aired the room and sprayed the toilet with air-freshener. I was hoping that nothing would irritate Renáta first thing so that we could devote attention to our problem. I used the time I had gained by getting up early to draft an outline of what I was going to say to her. It was important for her to understand how senseless and degrading it is to bring vulgarity into our marriage.

I made neat little mounds of muesli on the plates. I warmed up some milk and brewed the tea.

'Good morning,' said Renáta as if nothing had happened the night before.

I remained silent. She must always be the first to ask forgiveness. I'll assess her apology and, depending on the nature of her lapse, I'll decide how to behave towards her.

She noticed the notebook lying open on the table. 'Ah yes, our little daily lesson,' she grimaced.

She has never behaved like this before. It seemed to me that she might have some kind of a female problem. Very well, we shall tackle it. But first things first. Renáta went back into the living room. She brought out a bottle of vodka from the bar and returned with it to the kitchen. She poured some vodka into a glass which we use exclusively to serve coffee to visitors. Scooping the muesli with a spoon, she washed it down with vodka.

'That's not exactly a healthy combination,' I remarked. I expected her to burst into tears, the way she does when she can't handle a situation. But she put down the spoon with a slow, deliberate movement, raised a clenched fist and shot out her index finger.

'You need to see a doctor,' I responded without delay.

'It's you who needs one,' she said, amused.

I phoned the City Council and excused Renáta from work for the day. During lunch-break, I'll think about what to do next, but before that I'll give her a ring around ten to see how far she got with her drinking.

In the end I decided to take half a day off from midday. My boss is never pleased about his employees taking time off, but this was only the second time I took a short leave in fifteen years.

The first time was when Renáta had refused, at the very last minute, to have an abortion. Although taking time off could have affected the smooth running of our office it was unavoidable. I had to discuss the whole situation with her several times. It would have been extremely irresponsible to bring a child into a half-furnished flat. On top of that, we had planned to buy a new computer and a leather sofa. We both needed a computer for our professional development, she was well aware of that. The same applied to the sofa. My manager had come for dinner at our place twice in the past two years and the sight of an ordinary old corner settee didn't make me feel at all proud.

First of all I would visit the library to prepare for my discussion with Renáta. I knew very little about the Romani people, but I was aware that my wife used the inappropriately pejorative expression 'gypsy'. That's what I'm going to start with, I thought. If you can't sort out your terminology, you'll never achieve anything. Renáta was going to nod in approval. So far, she had always followed my suggestions.

I couldn't concentrate very well and I randomly leafed through Nečas' history of the Roma in the library reading room. Signs forbidding Roma entry into cities, punishment for vagrancy by beheading, an MP's proposal that they be painlessly branded like cattle, imprisoning entire families for petty thieving, creation of Romani ghettoes. After fifty years of war.

Dear God, the world has gone mad!

And Renáta with it, by pointlessly making me feel so anxious. Until now, we've always been such a well-co-ordinated pair. What got into her?

I shut the book and returned it to the counter. I was at a loss. I simply didn't know what to do.

When we come home, we have our meetings, as Renáta calls them. Still in our work clothes. At the most, I would loosen my tie and unbutton my jacket, if it's too hot. Renáta remains dressed in her suit, even keeps on her high-heeled shoes. The heels leave marks on our Finnish lino, but luckily these disappear in two hours. She disapproves of slip-ons.

'I don't look good in them,' she says apologetically.

'As you like,' I reply. I can be patient. I know sooner or later she will accept my arguments.

We then evaluate everything that happened at work that day together. It is me who usually comments on her working methods. I have more experience.

Now Renáta was greeting me dressed in my old striped shirt, her thighs bare. I realised with relief that she had not gone to work.

She has never, I repeat never, behaved so casually. The sight of her excited me, I have to admit that. Despite being so thin, she has beautifully shaped limbs, like those of a doll.

She noticed my excitement and raised her chin. She probably expected a kiss.

'You smell of vodka,' I said.

'And you smell like an old goat,' she replied irrationally.

I didn't say anything.

There was coffee on the table as usual. But instead of the usual white cups with a blue stripe we used for afternoon coffee I stared in disbelief at two pint-sized mugs with a dreadful picture of a brontosaurus and the words Zum Glück. They must have been purchased by Renáta's mother who has a remarkably plebeian appetite for kitsch. I have pointed this out to Renáta several times. Especially one Christmas, seven years ago, when she gave us a ghastly table lamp made of a plastic kitchen bowl filled with water, with a couple of artificial flowers floating on the surface. The light bulb was fixed to a moulding attached to the bottom of the bowl.

'Old Polášek makes them,' she declared. 'I'll buy you another one, with tulips. When I get my pension payment.'

They both looked very satisfied. Renáta always greets every present, no matter how absurd, with almost childish joy.

I saved my comments concerning breach of electrical appliance regulations – if that dreadful object, regardless of its unattractive appearance, could be called an appliance – until after our festive dinner.

I didn't feel like coffee. I wasn't even hungry. That was unusual. I had made myself and my body accustomed to a regular regime.

'You are going to kill us with that discipline of yours,' Renáta would tell me. Lately more and more frequently.

Now she was sitting on the chair, legs slightly apart, bringing the mug to her lips. I stared at the brontosaurus with revulsion. Renáta smirked. I noticed that the umlaut over the letter u was missing in the word Glück. Renáta wasn't drinking. Instead, she plunged her nose into the mug and started making air bubbles.

'It's fun, don't you want some?' she asked without stopping blowing bubbles.

I was silent.

After a while, she got tired of it and removed her nose from the mug. It had a greyish-brown colour, like the bottom of her face. She let the coffee run down behind the collar of her shirt.

'I'll wipe you clean,' I moved close to her.

'Really?' she grinned again. But this time it was that vulnerable kind of sneer I was used to.

I wiped her face with the edge of the shirt. Underneath, she was wearing red lace panties. I can't remember her ever wearing coloured underwear. She pressed her face to my body, wiping the rest of the coffee on my light grey woollen jacket and leaving two visible smudges. I also noticed her hair was several shades darker than usual.

I couldn't stop wondering about those red panties.

We were not due for our regular intercourse until Thursday. Today was only Tuesday. I couldn't get my head around it.

We got up late at night. Tangled clothes were strewn around the kitchen table. I drank the cold coffee. Renáta finished a sandwich.

'I don't know what to do with this,' I told her. 'I don't feel well, what with our regular regime and all the rest.'

'I'm sure there's a way,' she smiled.

'I don't know how to deal with all this,' I wanted to shout.

She turned to me and wiped her face again with my shirt.

Translated by Alexandra Büchler

SABRINA KARASOVÁ

Barbed is the Wire in the Sudetenland

The sun is shining and the weather is so clement that out of love I'd go to the seaside. My father and I are fixing barbed wire to the fence around the garden. I put this inimical act down to his mental disorder.

'Dad, why are we doing this?'

'Against the children,' he says uncompromisingly, to make clear where he stands.

It is very clear to me where he stands.

Suddenly the wire starts coiling in my hand like a snake. Somebody is pulling on the other end. I glance down the line of wire: children! They are climbing over the fence in the corner, trampling down the barbed wire with their trainers.

Dad advances threateningly: 'What do you want?'

'You have cherries,' explains the eldest, continuing to trample on the wire.

Dad stands directly by the fence, so the boy cannot jump down, crosses his arms and shouts: 'You could have had some too, if you'd got your act together! Had Mummy and Daddy not wanted to kill the first daddy! Why did you expel him?'

'On account of the second daddy being better than the first,' explains the boy, sitting on the wire like a chicken. 'But then again now he's doing time. I'll come tomorrow,' he promises.

Translated by Nancy Hawker

Owlet

1

Šelda penetrated deeper and deeper into the forest, holding fast to the river, in the same way as one clings to a guiding hand. With the self-irony that rarely left him, he thought to himself: my prize – and punishment.

He was surrounded by colours that soothed him. Green, purple, blue, grey, white. A misty haze caressed the countryside so lightly that it didn't conceal the verdure.

When he reached the cliffs, he thought to glance upwards. He saw human legs. They were hanging above the abyss, white and immobile, legs without a body. Barefoot. He guessed they belonged to a child.

He reached the top of the cliff from the sloping ridge. The girl was sitting on the ground and her legs were hanging over the edge of the rock. Her head was drooping, as if she were falling asleep. She could not have chosen a more precarious spot for a quick nap.

As soon as she felt his presence, she sat up. She contemplated him with the same amazement as he contemplated her.

'What are you doing here?'

'Good morning,' she answered. Perhaps she didn't even realise that she had automatically greeted him, because her eyes widened and her cheeks flushed with a hatred that he didn't understand.

She considers me an intruder. I'm guilty of interrupting her. Interrupting what?

He had to squint so that the sun would not blind him. He was standing at an unfavourable angle. He saw her lips curl in ridicule. For some reason, she despised him to death. It was quite strange, since they had just met for the first time in their lives.

She moved and slid down closer to the abyss. Provoking him.

He was the only person far and wide and he had the right to scold her. She was waiting for him to say something like: 'Don't flail about, you'll fall!'

He didn't say anything.

He came right up to the girl at the edge of the cliff. A wisp of wind snaked around his ankle, like an imperceptible, murderous noose.

He stepped back.

The wind tore at his hair and deafened him.

He sat down near the girl. They observed each other without shyness – their situation was unreal.

Dark chestnut hair, lively eyes, a delicate face filled with naïveté and spite, calmness, wisdom and courage.

Her gaze was childlike, and yet tantalizing.

They were so alien to each other that there was no need for pretence. He grasped a handful of her hair, expecting her to wince. Instead she drew her face closer to him in calm expectation. Even before he realised what it all meant, he felt her hands on his neck.

She hung onto him, and her eyes, very close to him, were no longer filled with calmness, but rather with sheer dread.

'What has happened to you?'

'Nothing. Except tomorrow they're marrying me off.'

God knows why those words stung him. He tried to shake it off – it's none of his business! His attempt failed.

She moved her lips to his face and touched him at the corner of his mouth. He drew back to arm's length. He had never seen a more expressive face. She closed her eyes and wilted. He held her in his arms like a big doll.

'Do you know what you want to do?'

'I know.'

'Why?'

'Because you're a stranger. Because we'll never meet again.'

How you're mistaken, poor thing, how you're mistaken! But it was too late to get up and leave. Again she clung to his neck and her gaze was triumphant and hard.

2

At first no one even thought to relate Šelda's presence in Látal's bar with Pavlína Cigošová, who scrubbed the spit-splattered floors there. Not that the local gossips lacked tongues to wag, but they were busy analysing a different facet of the engineer's privacy, the manifest disharmony in his marriage. This was also taken as an explanation for his drinking habits: he behaved in the way any man who has an exquisite, yet unhappy and fickle wife would.

There wasn't a man in Želary who didn't desire her. She was fragile, sweet-scented, carried herself like a fairy and could smile in such a way that each man who greeted her felt as though she had been waiting for him all her life. It was not surprising that their Adam's apples bobbed and their voices cracked. The excitement she stirred was palpable; it rose to one's head like spirits. It was only a matter of time before the engineer ended up in the ravine with a jackknife in his ribs.

He was saved from this universally expected fate by Kazda the factory-owner, who drove the charming Aduša off in his sparkling car to who knows where.

As if he had a premonition, the engineer sat in the tavern that day and didn't return until morning. He was greeted by plundered cupboards and a cradle filled with the crying of a child.

Her mother had forgotten twelve-month-old Lízinka.

It was then that Šelda invited Pavlína to be his housekeeper. It was a slap in the face of the chaste young women of Želary; it coloured their cheeks blood-red. Pavlína Jirešová, nicknamed Cigošová – 'from the gypsies' – married as Lipková, was a whore to be precise, about whom public opinion, very indulgent in these parts, couldn't find so much as a clean speck.

Not only had she had an affair before marriage – all the more insulting because no one knew with whom – but within a year she had trampled the sanctity of marriage and ran off with the first person at hand, that being her husband's friend, or actually his buddy, Štěpán Gryc. As for him, he's now sitting out a life-sentence in jail, for murder. He had had a fight with the tramp Floryšek and had the fortune or misfortune – it depends how you take it – that, unlike his rival, he got out of the encounter alive. Pavlína, convicted of a vaguely defined theft, spent a couple of weeks in prison and was then shoved back to her hometown. Every detail of her life with the tramps was public knowledge circulated by Floryšek's dear old dirty beggar of a wench, Sefka.

Jireš, nicknamed Cigoš, publicly disowned his daughter, an act he sealed in a tumultuous pub hullabaloo with his like-minded and like-inebriated mates.

The publican, her uncle, had mercy on her and allowed her to slog away from morning to night in return for food and a mouldy straw-mattress in the attic.

Pavlína's sins were not really that clear-cut. Everyone knew that Štěpán won her from Michal in a game of cards. Many considered this to be a significant point.

Mining engineer Šelda led Pavlína off to his villa, the spanking new luxurious villa from his wife's dowry, where even the garden was designed by an architect.

His behaviour, although understood as desperate, excluded him from the circle of people who thought better of themselves once in a while.

Quite clearly, he didn't care.

The only one who profited from the whole affair was little Lízinka. She scrambled into Pavlína's arms, without being the least bothered that she was a loose woman.

Pavlína loved her with slavish love. (Her master deemed her incapable of any other kind.) She let her eyes be poked, her hair tugged: she kept watch over her on nights when she was colicky and cried with such distress that it broke her nanny's heart. She would secretly go and ask Lucka for some herbs which would help instantly.

'I see that the young missus has enslaved you,' the engineer admonished.

'She's crying,' she feebly defended herself.

'Let her cry herself out. And don't look at me as though I were a werewolf.'

He knew he was just beating the air, and so he at least untied her apron strings, which she couldn't fix while holding the baby. Embarrassed, she became all flustered and flushed.

It occurred to him that he should marry her. His first marriage had ended in divorce. It would mean no real change for him, but for Pavlína it would change everything.

As soon as he mentioned marriage, she panicked. On the verge of breaking down, she refused, with simple-minded certainty that she would humiliate him. He didn't like to see her suffering, although he could seldom prevent it.

'You know who I am, sir,' she said.

'I know.'

Each of them meant something different by that, but only Šelda realised it. He had a special gift of knowing how to place people perfectly, without having to listen to prompters. Even more extraordinary was his ability to place himself equally precisely.

He gave up hope that Pavlína would understand him. He could either renounce her or forgive her. He chose the latter.

With time, he even allowed her her tears, which disgusted him above all else. The only thing he wouldn't have tolerated was empty words. But Pavlína spoke little and usually when he wished it.

After failed attempts at courtship, he realised that public contempt was a precondition for Pavlína's existence. In order to kill her, he only had to repeat that she was not a loose woman. He had enough sense not to engage in skirmishes with demons. Deep in his heart, he believed that Pavlína would come to see the light – it was one of the few small mistakes that he committed.

In his relationship with her he was honest. He cared for her with the affection she deserved and which would have been a source of suffering to her had she understood it.

'You're unbelievably good,' she said. She considered him a saint.

Usually he left it at that, without commenting. Only once did he dare argue.

'I'm not good. I love you.'

He said it without passion, as he would have uttered any other statement of fact.

She stood petrified.

'No!' she cried hoarsely. Beads of sweat pearled above her eyes. She ran off under some pretence, so that he would not see that she was trembling.

He wasn't one for emotions, but this time, he buried his head in his hands.

The image of Aduša with her proud smile on her beautiful face flashed before his eyes. That revived him. He imagined what would happen if Pavlína suddenly turned into the product of hairdressers, beauty parlours and perfumes. And how everything he valued would dissolve into boundless twaddle.

Aduša belonged to those people who passionately profess only one truth, their own. Then they remain misunderstood their entire life. They consider it their strong point.

They consider it the fault of others.

Aduša couldn't believe that Šelda could snub, in her words, 'such sensibilities'. And that along with that sensibility, he could even spurn money, social status, simply everything that might be termed valuable: it indicated the mentality of a madman.

Šelda was no madman.

'What else do you want?'

'Nothing.'

She considered it defiance. Monstrous pride.

He wasn't defiant and he didn't suffer from wounded vanity. He was not playing games with her.

Precisely because of that she couldn't believe him.

'You don't love me!' she cried out, an accusation she believed preposterous. She expected repentance.

'Why are you not saying anything?' She forced a fake sob from her throat.

He stood silent, thinking, 'My dear, we don't tell women that we don't love them. It suffices that we don't tell them that we do love them: then they should know where they stand. To love you means to be your vassal, and I am not created to be that. You are driving me into a circle in which I would be lost. Luckily I see the limit.'

When she left him, he sighed in relief. Arguments exhausted him.

He began to play the piano again.

Once upon a time he had been a good player. The music was seemingly a source of comfort and pleasure for Pavlína. She sang in a quiet, slightly hushed voice, yet in tune.

He set off on tip-toe, secretly snuck to the kitchen door and opened it a crack. Despite his caution, he assumed she would be startled, and indeed she was.

'What are you singing?'

'A meadow song. Girls yodel them from one side of the mountain to the other.'

'Please continue.'

'No, not now.' She was terrified that he would force her, and so he didn't.

Many of her songs captivated him and he attempted to play them on the piano. He could distinguish two types of mountain melodies: drawn-out sad ones and brisk ones with a wild rhythm.

Pavlína sang only the melancholic ones.

She liked to sit in the room when he played. As for him, he

was not shy in front of her. Sometimes though, when the piano refused to obey him, he would grin at her, but he met only admiration in her eyes. He wondered whether she would listen to him with the same enthralment if he were rhythmically beating a stick on a stump. He thought she probably would.

'The parish priest is a genius of a musician,' he would sigh.

Pavlína was of the opinion that the engineer played just as well, and that the difference only stemmed from the diversity of instruments.

On Sunday she would go to church, her head bowed both on the way there and on the way back, but it brought her relief. He was interested in what her God was like.

'I'd be curious to know how the priest speaks to you.'

'He never talks to me,' she replied with sincere surprise. Her eyes flashed.

'I mean at confession.'

Blood rushed to her face.

'He says that God is merciful ... and that He will grant me strength ...'

'To do what?'

'I abide in sin.'

She licked her lips.

'He says that?' he insisted, 'That you abide in sin?'

'No, he doesn't. I confess to it.'

'Every time? The same thing?'

'Yes.'

'And he? Every time? The same thing?'

'Yes, sir.'

The parish priest is wise, a rare wise man.

'I'm a heathen, Pavlína. I've never done penance. I'll be damned for sure.'

She shook her head.

'God is merciful.' Her cheeks flushed.

So she talked to the priest about me. She even prays for me. It wasn't an unpleasant thought.

He loved her; he was sure of that. No one else in the world mattered more to him. He would think of her on the clattering cart in the mine shaft; he would think of her in his office; he heard her voice; he saw her face.

His love even survived the hardest of tests – one hysterical scene.

They came running to him one night. Some calamity had befallen the Anna Maria mine. He quickly dressed, and as he was coming down the stairs Pavlína ran up to him. She barred his way. She did not call him 'sir'. He was astonished.

'You mustn't go to the Anna Maria! It'll kill you! That mine is damned!'

'Pull yourself together, woman, nothing'll kill me! I don't even know what happened there!'

'That mine is damned!' She summoned tremendous strength to stop him.

'Be reasonable! I must go.'

'Take me with you.'

He had never known her like this.

'Come.' He stepped back. Time was of the essence, he had no choice.

Had it been anyone else, this scene would have been unbearable for him. Any other woman would have forever disgusted him with such an outburst.

Now he felt confusion, anxiety and admiration. The creature trembling in his arms didn't disgust him.

'Pavlína,' he repeated helplessly, 'oh Pavlína!'

'The Anna Maria will destroy you!'

'It won't destroy me, if you're with me.'

He wasn't deriding her, nor did the matter seem at all laughable to him.

She waited for him several hours in the dark. There had been a small cave-in. When he went down into the pit, he thought of her and was nervous the whole time.

When he returned with wet hair – he had first showered – she was numb but calmer.

Without a word he started up his old car. She touched his hand. 'It was nothing,' he answered her. 'Everything is all right now.' Because he read another question in her face, he added, 'No one was hurt.'

She took a deep breath.

She never again forgot to call him 'sir'. He urged her to drop it, but she wouldn't be swayed. He liked to tease her. He would loosen her apron; he would tousle her hair; he would nibble her ear. She would laugh at it freely. It seemed she considered him a child in those moments. Yet when he loosened the lace of her blouse – she would tie it so tight that it would cut into her neck – she blushed. He only stopped when he saw tears in her eyes. Then he hid her in his arms and hugged her silently for a long while. She considered this the culmination of happiness.

Sometimes she worried that she had irritated him. She would throw herself down at his feet like on that first day.

'Don't be angry, sir.'

He already knew that he could only do one thing for her. Laugh and say, 'Don't be silly!'

He reproached himself, but couldn't help himself: from time to time he challenged her incredible sense of shame. In the summer heat waves they went swimming at night, and he swam naked.

Pavlína wrapped herself up in a ridiculous outfit which resembled two aprons. The pieces were held together with buttons which he would unfasten. The water in the river was cold: it burned the skin and drove them into the night air, which seemed mild in comparison.

He liked to carry Pavlína from the water and out onto the shore, which was quite a feat because the banks were sheer and slippery, even hollowed out in spots. The water from the aprons would run down his body. She would dry herself in the bushes and emerge fully dressed, her collar laced up tightly.

Then they would wander around, skirting all Želary flooded in cold moonlight. They had dreamlike images before their eyes. For a moment Pavlína would be torn from her own life, emerging from it as from the river, free and intoxicated by the beauty of the world created for her by the presence of her beloved.

Seconds crackled and Jan Šelda, who reigned even over his own heart, was aware of each of them, in their purity and transience.

3

Some people quite correctly assumed that Pavlína was in Šelda's villa only for a trial period. They believed that the engineer would soon come to regret his hasty decision.

Therefore Michal Lipka was in a hurry: he wanted make the most of the engineer's momentary madness. He stopped by, almost sober and shaved, all of which gave him quite a strange appearance, since along with the stubble he had removed the dirt from half of his face. Šelda allowed him to babble a few sentences about Pavlína being his wife, and then he suddenly cut the conversation short.

'Get lost, before I mop the floor with you!'

Michal took these words to heart. He reckoned he was lucky that he saved his skin.

Old Jireš went about it more circumspectly, but just as unsuccessfully. He put pressure on the priest to intervene, but the latter just waved him off. Pavlína was properly employed and was even getting paid for her services.

'But for what type of services, reverend father!' whined Jireš.

'She manages the house and takes care of the little one,' asserted the priest firmly. He didn't grant Jireš the right to judge, but neither did he have the sense of humour to remind the man of the fourteen-year-old gypsy girl who gave Jireš his nickname, and to ask him how much he had paid her, though she had not lifted a finger in the household.

According to public opinion, Pavlína had jumped at the offer the engineer had made to her in the Želary tavern like a fish gobbles up a fat maggot. This wasn't so. Compassion drew her to him, and incomprehensible regret that he just sat around in the tavern, stinking of liquor and staggering. With the irrationality of those who embrace their abasement too eagerly, Pavlína considered it her offence. For he had told her: 'Come with me' – and she had not gone. The engineer was honest with himself. As soon as he had seen her at Látal's and recognised her, he had admitted to himself that she attracted him. She bore her disgrace like a queen bears a crown.

He addressed her.

She recognised him too, and was scared stiff.

Her presence in the stinking tavern started to irritate him. Never before had he heard the voices of others. Then he started to hear them and they slashed at his temples. He drank, unable to get drunk.

Pavlína wiped a table on which he had spilled a glass.

He overcame the urge to grab her wrist so that something would happen.

It was morning. Pavlína was still cleaning the floor and Látal bared his thin yellow teeth.

'We're closing, Mr Engineer.'

Smash his face! But the engineer's movements were feeble; he could barely get up. Three steps from the threshold he collided with Pavlína.

'You're ruining your life,' he whispered urgently. 'Come with me.'

She drew away and disappeared into the darkness.

He walked alone on the sandy road, where he was flogged by the wind.

A few days later, again in darkness, she had rung at his door. He didn't know what to say, so he took her by the hand and led her over the threshold. Without his help, she probably wouldn't have crossed it.

He led her into the kitchen, where the stove warmed the room and where Líza was sleeping in the crib. When she leaned over the child, he put his arms around her shoulders. He was cold, calculating, he knew exactly what he was doing, he behaved like a scoundrel and wouldn't stop himself. This is the card he bet on and he knew he'd win, because Pavlína Cigošová is a wretched player.

In a few days, I might throw you out.

The servant's chamber was open: in any case it could not be shut. He realised that the iron bed was narrow and that the sheets were of different fabric than his own upstairs. He had never noticed such things before.

He buried his fingers in her hair and touched an unhealed wound. His designs were thwarted by this.

'Who did this to you?'

'A wood chip struck me when I was chopping wood.'

Right.

She spoke with some effort, but sounded calm, almost as if she were passing on simple information. He turned her face to him.

It was then that he saw her as she really was, and in a single instant it dawned on him, that with a single move or a single word, he could lose her forever.

'Tomorrow, I'll take you to the doctor.'

He knew he would not be taking her anywhere.

'No. It's already healing.'

'Let me see. I will clean it up for you a bit.'

He brought peroxide and gauze from the bathroom.

'Does it sting?'

'No.'

'Let me cover it so that it doesn't get infected.'

For the first time in his life he uttered unnecessary words, just to hear the sound of a voice, or rather for the meaning they concealed.

'How old is your father?'

He wasn't interested in the least.

'Fifty-three.'

'And you?'

'Nineteen.'

She wasn't of age.

'There. Tomorrow we'll change the dressing.'

His brain, which was keeping watch, was sending frenzied signals. You're babbling! Babbling! You're babbling like an idiot!

Nonetheless, he pursued the conversation. He experienced the sweetness of rebellion.

Before he had started going to the Želary pub, he considered babbling a women's vice, although with his mother he used to play chess for hours on end without a single word. Somehow, he didn't count his mother among women.

In the tavern, he learned that men's babble is no different from women's. The only small difference stemmed from the fact that women usually whined and shared secrets, while men bragged and put the world to rights.

That is why he came to like Vilém Svojsík. He sat in his corner by the stove, got drunk and never spoke a word.

He talked and talked and Pavlína answered. This is how they reached for each other, each out of their own solitude.

The conversation was about nothing, of course.

In the morning Líza started to grouse: it was necessary to begin a new day.

Before he retreated upstairs, to doze for a bit at least, Pavlína managed to whisper to him: 'God bless you.'

A few days later, she followed him upstairs. He accepted it as a gift and never asked her for an explanation.

Soon they became so close that he could no longer remain in his upstairs study: he would sit by her in the kitchen when she washed the little one, cooked or sewed. And, in snippets, he learned of her calvary.

She was old Jireš's only child, or rather, his only child to survive infancy. When she was fifteen, her mother died and Jireš became infatuated with the gypsy girl. He met her at the river, where she was fishing for trout. Because it was hot, she was standing in the water naked.

Jireš proposed to show her a hunting shack and met with her understanding.

They then visited the shack daily. Jireš brought her gifts there, at first cheap ones and then more expensive ones. On the day when the gypsies were clearing out from their site in the village – the county would allow them only a short stay – they were surprised by a scruffy granny who declared that she was Magdalénka's mother. She launched into a lament, accompanied with jerky gesticulations. Jireš began to grasp that by Magdalénka she meant his bronze beauty, though she had introduced herself as Gita.

I guarded her like a gold coin and now she lets herself go at barely fifteen!

Any grey-haired lady-killer would have realised what type of mess he'd got himself into, but Jireš missed the mark. He paid for Gita like one pays for a sheep.

The gypsies moved off. Magdalénka Gita moved into his place. She liked Jireš's carpentry business, his spacious house and the young handyman, Michal Lipka.

She would service the old man as she wished: he could barely keep pace. But he was happy.

It was only when he heard the insult Cigoš the Cuckold that he paused to reflect, and unable to resolve the quandary in any other way, married his daughter off to Michal, without asking her opinion.

The gypsy tolerated him for a little while longer. Twice she ran away and twice she returned, always welcomed with open arms. Finally, in her place appeared a svelte gypsy man, made of only muscle, and with him two equally muscled and moustached friends.

'You must pay, daddy-oh, you slept with my wife.'

'Move out,' ordered Jireš, but the gypsies just smiled amicably, showing their flawless teeth.

'Then we talk now, man to man, oh.'

Jireš considered his odds, and let the conversation drop.

According to the village folk, he had got off easily.

The visit was not repeated.

Michal Lipka turned out to be an exemplary brute. He treated his wife in a way that even sickened his faithful friend Štěpán Gryc, whom Lipka kept as a lodger, mainly to have a partner in cards.

Flight was the only salvation for the half-killed Pavlína. Štěpán was ready to lead an orderly life on her account, but because he was short-tempered and quick with his knife, his good intentions capsized. He and Pavlína joined a pair of tramps from the mountains, and within a few months resembled them to a T. Šelda already knew all this from his sources in the pub.

Pavlína did not mention Michal at all and Štěpán only briefly. He was rash but nice, was her judgement. Her description probably captured his essence best.

The engineer wasn't interested in Štěpán, or in Floryšek, or even in Michal. He was just fulfilling Pavlína's need to talk herself out, which she considered her duty towards him.

Before his very eyes, she was emerging from troubled water.

Of all the names, she most often mentioned Floryšek. A tramp of unknown age and unknown nationality. He had lots of papers and lots of names. Beneath his constant facile joking yawned a dangerous abyss.

He called Sefka his mother and Pavlína naively asked whether she was really his mother. The old whore indicated in her crass way that Pavlína had a long way to go to learn her multiplication tables. Otherwise she didn't disclose anything.

Floryšek treated Pavlína with more courtesy than anyone had ever shown her. In his own way, he coddled her. In his presence she felt safe, as if he had power over everything in this world. When she couldn't fall asleep long into the night, he would come and sit by her.

'Why aren't you sleeping, my lamb?'

He called her sweetheart, honey, every time something different.

'I'm afraid, Uncle.'

'There is nothing to be afraid of, precious.'

She felt that there really was nothing to fear.

They used to talk about the most ordinary of things and all were important. However, Floryšek wouldn't lower his voice and Pavlína was on edge, fearing that Štěpán or Sefka might awaken. By day, he was an old tramp, dingy in face, hair and voice. But now the dark would wipe away the darkness and his face shone.

She knew he was capable of anything.

He spoke Czech well, but from time to time he stumbled over a foreign word.

He doesn't get drunk. What would he blurt out in drunkenness?

What is his real name?

She never asked either question.

Štěpán feared him and hated him. Floryšek scorned him.

Every one of his sentences is half-truth, half-lie. Should I cling to him or should I fear him?

They lived off his magnanimity.

By the carousel behind Šádova Huť they met a foreign circus man. Floryšek recognised him and they spoke together in a foreign tongue.

The circus man reeked of depravity and laughed disgustingly, showing the debris that were his teeth. He wanted to invite both of them into his caravan. Floryšek refused and in a flash caught the hand that was just about to touch Pavlína's hip.

They looked into each other's eyes, and there was a bolt of lightning.

Such a look would have knocked Pavlína to her knees.

The circus man merely pulled his right hand from Floryšek's grasp and shrugged his shoulders. They chatted a bit more, and although they spoke in Czech now, Pavlína didn't understand them.

'We worked together a bit,' Floryšek said afterwards in explanation.

'You are not at all like him, Uncle.'

'Really, Pavlínka?'

He looked amused. What she had discerned in his eyes before was no longer true.

'What were you doing in the circus, Uncle?'

'I was a clown, sweetheart. Nothing else suited me.'

Least of all was Floryšek a clown.

'I'll take you for a ride on the swings, my darling, do you want to?'

She did and didn't.

The swings were, as she had predicted, fearsome. Her stomach lurched every time her head was upside down.

And suddenly it was intoxicating.

The owner stopped them.

'Are you crazy, for crissake? You'll fall out and then who'll they stick in jail?'

Floryšek told him a few foreign words and the guy nodded in understanding. Once on firm ground, Pavlína's heart constricted and she was sure she would vomit. Floryšek took her by the hand. As if on command, her stomach began to calm down, but her legs started quivering.

'Let's sit down, my pet. Here, at this table.'

He pushed a chair under her and called the cafeteria waitress.

'Two sausages in a roll, beautiful lady.' The fat waitress started blushing. He was a charmer – Floryšek had it in his blood.

'He provided for us,' moaned Pavlína: it pained her even today. 'He provided for us for two months.'

'With what?'

'I don't know,' she admitted. 'He carried around this little stand like the Bosnian tinkers, but he usually gave out all the stuff to kids.'

She looked at Šelda bewildered, as if she had only now grasped this discrepancy.

The engineer laughed.

'When the Anna Maria went on strike, Štěpán signed up as a strike-breaker.'

Šelda didn't let on what he thought of that.

'That was our downfall ... He and Floryšek had a fight over it.'

The engineer tried not to express his amazement.

Štěpán raised a ruckus – and Floryšek just kept silent. When he had said his piece, he shut up, and his arms sunk by his body. Pavlína's voice is colourless, the words barely leave her lips. It's as if she were spitting sand.

He only moved when Štěpán pulled out a knife. He said 'You're crazy!'

'You don't have to tell me this,' said Šelda, because he saw that her forehead was drenched with sweat.

'I want you to know.'

'He flung the knife out of Štěpán's hand so easily, that it was almost unbelievable. He had just, just barely touched him ... when he grabbed his wrist and threw him to the ground.'

Pavlína had whimpered a plea, embracing Floryšek's legs. For a second he couldn't extricate himself from her. Štěpán took advantage of it. He knifed him a couple of times. Floryšek stood rigid, and then leaned over, as if to pick something up.

Sefka's eyes grew blank. She had grasped what had happened.

Štěpán stood, legs astride, the knife in his hand, and relief on his face.

After a minute, two, he started shaking with fear.

Florýšek sat down on a rock. Blood was pouring down to his legs.

He dropped his hands down alongside his body as if he were tired.

'Get out!' he said, but he was not looking at Štěpán. He was looking at the mountains.

'I said, get out!'

He bowed his head and keeled over.

'You're not going anywhere,' Sefka started screeching, 'If you disappeared into the ground like a mole, I'd find you.'

Štěpán wasn't planning an escape. He let himself be led to the police station like a lost child.

'I killed them both.'

'It's not your fault,' Šelda said as firmly as he could, and took Pavlína's hands into his.

She smiled at him with a terrible smile.

4

Pavlína Cigošová disappeared from Želary as suddenly and as mysteriously as Šelda's wife. Her disappearance was linked to the arrival of a foreign abbess, who flashed through the village, most likely only in the imagination of two frightened young kids. No one else saw her.

Lízinka did not remember her nanny. Her memory only

recorded one Christmas long ago, when she received an embroidered little outfit – and then she had cried a lot and her daddy had cried with her. She didn't trust that memory very much. Her daddy never cried.

But the embroidered little outfit was there, carefully saved away – and almost new. She knew that she mustn't dirty it, it was somehow valuable. Sometimes she unwrapped it and wondered at how little she had once been.

She also knew that the woman who had embroidered it was called Pavlína. The name meant nothing to her.

Neither could it. At the time, she had called her 'mama'.

Christmas is forever linked to an incomprehensible fear. She considers it the saddest holiday of the year. Despite her being allowed to decorate the Christmas tree, and build a Nativity crêche, despite her receiving many presents and singing carols with Berta, while Daddy played the piano.

She senses her father's strange sadness, which he tries in vain to conceal from her. She doesn't understand him. He grows distant to her – and all night long she feels alone at his side.

When they put her to bed, she can't fall asleep for a long while. She knows that Berta will leave for Midnight Mass and that Daddy will leave shortly after her. It has always been so.

She is not afraid of the solitude. Faithful and familiar things stay behind with her, and she invents all sorts of interesting games for them. She just touches them – and at once they cuddle up to her. The dark, polished furniture, the curtains, the paintings but above all the furry carpet.

She takes the mirror down and walks on it barefoot. Her feet are stepping on moss, and everything is upside down. She is rising afloat in the bedroom ...

'Líza,' Berta whispers through the open door, 'Are you sleeping?'

Líza doesn't budge an inch.

The door to the sitting room opens, and a tongue of cold air licks at her. Berta didn't close her room. She's in a hurry.

She waits with baited breath. She cannot shake off the suspense until she hears the long steps of her father in the sitting room. It's taking forever.

After hearing them, she would usually fall asleep.

Today she cannot sleep.

Apart from the cold, a long drawn-out note squeezes its way towards her. The night watchman raised the shepherd's horn to his lips.

She gets up and presses her nose to the windowpane. She sees her father walking towards the gate.

What's happening to her?

The irresistible melody is luring her outside. Anxiety seizes her, and it grows and grows until it is as big as Líza herself: it's now bigger than her, it's now filling up the whole house.

The strength of the forbidden is cracking: its shackles burst asunder. Šelda's child is opening the front door and is exposing her face to the dirty wind. She turns back, and throws Berta's woollen shawl over her dressing gown; the shawl is too long and so she winds it twice around her body. She crosses the threshold and steps out into the snow, guided by a distant flickering – windows are alight across the sleepy snowdrifts – tonight not only Líza but the whole village is keeping watch.

The night-watchman is sounding his horn near the communal well on the village green, at the centre of gravity formed by the triangle of the church, pub and school. The deep well sings with him. In the village no one is listening to him. He has finished playing the horn and is singing carols. He is singing for himself. He knows that this blessed night needs his song. When he has finished singing every song that his old memory has left him, he heads to the church, but his legs take him to the pub.

'Just passing by, Látal, so I thought I'd drop in.'

'On credit?' the innkeeper snaps at him, reading his mind.

'Have you forgotten the sixpences that you pulled out of my pocket when you were a snot-faced kid? I'm actually heading to the cross, you heathen, to pray for your sins. I only landed upon your wreck of a shack because it stood in my way. I'm not interested in a gulp of your pig slops.'

'Don't blather, old man.'

The night-watchman sits down on a bench, Látal brings him a glass.

Here you go, you louse-infested lout! If it were any other night, I'd throw you out, but today you are a godsend. Tonight, the pub belongs to you and the engineer. You didn't even notice, did you? How he's sitting there and getting drunk like a pig? You don't care; you have no one; no one's waiting at home for you with supper. Drink, swear, curse! Like I myself am cursing inside!

He's here mourning for Pavlína, for the whore Pavlína, remember her? The one the abbess stole from him, like he had once stolen her from me. Bitch of a life!

Látal is polishing the glasses, his hands as tense as if he were touching a live wire. Without knowing it, he is moving his dry lips.

The old man is looking in the direction of the foggy window, beyond which snow is falling.

White rings are gently settling down to earth. By the morning all tracks will have vanished. Even the tracks of the knitted slippers that are completely soaked by now.

Líza has reached the clump of cottages in the middle of town and is peering through people's windows. She becomes the invisible witness to the joys of others. Presents with green branches are unwrapped.

'I'll get a gigantic doll,' Alenka Svojsíková had boasted.

Indeed, she does get one, from her uncle, the one who gave Líza the willies. She had met him once, on the way to school; the wind was combing his black hair into his face. She had greeted him and Vilém had looked at her in surprise. The wind lifted his shirt and underneath it appeared a crimson, raw scar. She continued seeing that bloody scar on the sunken chest for a long time, whenever she shut her eyes.

Líza is on the look-out for Alenka's terrible uncle.

When she finds him, he doesn't seem that terrible to her. In his face she sees happiness, a child's happiness, exuberant and clamorous. Happiness on an adult's face delights Šelda's child more than any Christmas tree or all the festivity surrounding it. Probably it is because this window attracted her so much, that she dares to do something unpardonable.

Her eyes are glued on Vilém Svojsík. Dark, unkempt hair, ailing cheeks, a chin with dark stubble ...

Alenka says that her uncle will die soon.

She gets goose-pimples.

Vilém takes his coat from the nail in the wall, and is getting dressed.

Footsteps.

She jumps away from the window and finds herself face to face with the man she had just summoned. With his threadbare coat buttoned to his neck and his hands in his wide pockets, he oks as though he has no arms.

'What are you doing here?'

Líza's whole body is shivering. Her answer gets stuck in her throat, she turns around and is now dashing across the freezing snow.

By Lipka's cottage she dusts off her slippers. As she stands there, holding the fence, she feels a hot breath on her face. Lipka's donkey is observing her, panting by her head. He's willing to befriend anybody; his heart is filled with faith in humankind. He lets himself be led by the frail little girl cuddling up to him. By the well they cross the footsteps of Vilém Svojsík in the snow. They're aiming for the pub.

'Mr Engineer, I met your child outside.'

Šelda's lids abruptly rip apart. He shakes his head, as if trying to shake off some sort of weight.

The half-poured glass lurched in the innkeeper's hand.

'Líza? What would she be doing outside?'

'I don't know. But it was her.'

An impatient order resounds in Vilém's voice.

With difficulty, Šelda gets up. 'Very well, I'm going.'

The old man by the stove starts singing. His chin is shaking. Wisps of green-lit dust are dissolving above his head. The shadow of the lamp divides his face.

Látal puffs up his chest and turns red.

'You too, old man, get out!'

He drags him to the door and throws him into the snow. Then he wipes his hand in his apron and sets out to the door, behind which Christmas candles are still lit. The clock on the wall reads ten minutes before midnight.

Vilém sets off towards the church and mingles with the latecomers hurrying to Mass.

5

Líza lay down in cold down covers, jiggled her legs several times to get the blood flowing, pulled the cover over her head and breathed with all her might, so as to warm up her little nest. Her fingers still sensed the softness of the donkey's coat. She smiled into the darkness, infinitely happy that she had petted something so soft, warm and alive, and that she carried the sensation with her.

He had accompanied her all the way to her gate. He looked back at her in the same way she looked back at him. He darted back to her again and let himself be tickled behind his ears. He nuzzled his long-eared head against her hands.

If he were hers, she would make his bed on the rug beside her bed and place an old blanket beneath his head.

Blissful images rocked her to sleep.

Something clattered. She sat up abruptly. What if she had forgotten to lock up?

Heavy steps. Daddy. She was awoken by the creaking of the keys, but it was a terrible sound.

The footsteps stop by her door. The door opens. Líza presses her eyelids shut with all her might.

Did he figure out that she had been outside?

He's leaving. He didn't figure it out.

The second time she is awoken by Berta. The darkness in the room is grey. Behind the window it is still snowing heavily.

'I bring you coffee, sir.'

'Get out, you old witch!'

A blow. Something falls.

'Jesus Christ!'

'Leave Jesus out of this, you prayer fanatic!'

'You need black coffee, sir!'

'I don't need a damn thing! And I'm a drunkard, don't you 'sir' me! Get out of my sight!'

'Mother of God!'

'Don't whine or I'll puke!'

The half-opened wing of the door flies open. Berta hits it with her elbow. Líza sinks into the pillows. Drunk again?

They eat breakfast at about noon, and when the father comes down into the kitchen, the child quakes. He has bags under his eyes and his face is ashen.

'Daddy,' she peeps.

'What is it?'

Drawn on the father's left cheek is a bloody line. Líza points to it with a hand as heavy as a rock. Bright insuppressible tears start to dance.

'You're crying? Why?' he speaks with effort. 'Child, tell me what's going on!'

'Daddy...'

'Speak up!'

'Daddy,' Líza says even more softly, though she would like to scream, 'you scratched yourself.'

He traces the scar with his hand.

'Didn't scratch myself. Must have whacked myself somewhere. Forget about it and eat your breakfast.' Líza swallows stiffly. Why is she afraid of her daddy? He had never hit her. The children from Želary are beaten and they're not afraid. They can jump up on their father's knees and hang around their necks. Líza wouldn't even consider doing something so sacrilegious. Her daddy is so different from the burly men of the village, who have curly locks instead of hair, locks just made to be tugged by children's hands.

But Líza can be proud of her daddy. Whenever something happens at the mine shaft, they ask: Where is Šelda? Often he stays on from shift to shift until he has done what is needed.

His mine, the Anna Maria, is the most productive and most treacherous of mines. He battles with trolls down there, he hews the struggling earth one black tentacle at a time. When Líza brings him her report card to sign, she does it with reverent awe. Father scans A+ after A+ and tugs her hair in praise. At that moment she would let herself be chopped up into little pieces for him.

But maybe she doesn't care for all that.

A report card is, after all, only a piece of paper.

She confesses to the reverend father: I was prideful.

'About what?'

'My report card.'

Instead of berating her, he consoles her. She's no longer anxious about the sins that torment her soul.

The reverend father is more than kind.

Because she is Šelda's, as her one and only, and sometimes traitor of a friend, Alenka Svojsíková, had once explained?

They play together, playing grocery, throwing a rag ball, jumping hopscotch, but above all, Líza likes to read.

She gets so deeply immersed in a book that she cannot stop, reading long into the night, until the letters sting her eyes and the pages become covered by fog. It's impossible for her to not finish something as suspenseful as *The Castle and the Village* or *The Exile's Daughter*.

At school she sometimes sees the same fog surrounding the small letters on the blackboard. One day, the teacher called on her, just as he was writing very finely. With cheeks as red as poppies, she read badly, terribly. Stuttering like Žeňa Zárubová, she strained her eyes to fish out at least something and grasp its meaning. The class held its breath. Every face turned to the teacher. Even the boys in the back row who were busy playing rock-paper-scissors sprang to attention. Was Líza going to get beaten or wasn't she? Her reading was an event.

But even more of an event was what the teacher did next.

Instead of yelling at Líza, instead of striking her with his bony fingers, as he would have done to anyone else, he dipped the sponge into the water-basin, and erased the whole board. Then he started to write again, with letters twice the size. Líza started to cry. She cried so quietly that no one heard her; but the teacher turned around, walked over to her bench and said, 'Come with me, Líza.'

He took her by the hand and led her outside. He had evidently sent her home, because he soon came back. A harsh struggle ensued, as if he wanted to beat out what he owed Líza onto backs of others. His bony right hand hacked away on all sides. However, his blows were not harsh enough to beat out the sensational happening from their bristly heads. This had never happened as long as school had been school. Líza Šeldová had forgotten how to read.

Would it last?

Everyone wished it to last.

Tomorrow, awaited with bated breath, brought disapointment. Líza was not at school. She only came back two days later, and while the class sounded her out, she pulled out a black case, and from it, a pair of glasses.

When she put them on and looked around, the class whooped with laughter.

She looked like a frightened little owl as she sat there quietly cowering, all bespectacled, in her brown dress. Immediately, she was transformed into a figure similar to the half-wit Brousek, whom they pummelled with rocks.

Glasses!

They had the urge to make her run, to avenge themselves for the fact that the teacher favoured her, that she was a good student, that she had nice clothes and that she brought a sandwich to school. Someone burst out, 'Owlet!'

Just then the principal entered and his eyes flashed with the intention of caning the whole class, one by one.

'Is there anything funny here?' he asked in a voice that made them break out in sweat.

He was answered by a pleading silence. He looked at Líza. The convex glasses in the dark frames cast shadows of sadness into her face. The teacher didn't express any high-spirited laughter, but even his gaze read, 'owl-face'. Glasses (worn by no one in the village, they were an aristocratic extravagance) disqualified Líza from the community of children, even though her former skills returned; even though her peers didn't dare laugh at her.

She was happiest on her way home. She would return the most roundabout way, immersed in blissful daydreams. She would imagine herself to be Snow White, who kept house for the dwarves. She would forget to watch the path, and often tripped and fell. When she painfully got her bearings, she would reach for her glasses first of all. She would examine them carefully to make sure that they didn't have the slightest crack. Despite the tribulations they brought her, they were tremendously precious to her. She would hug them to her chest.

She stopped being scared of the insult 'owlet'. The black-haired coal miner called her by the same name. He had heard the kids call her that and had laughed, saying, 'owlet, what a beautiful name'.

From his lips it sounded like flattery. This was not the word that the children yelled at her. Líza trotted by his side, protected by his nearness. She would gladly have given her life for him.

Only once in her short life does fortune surprise her with its generosity. It's on the morning when she's getting dressed to go see the doctor in town. She's getting dressed hurry-scurry, so that she won't keep Daddy waiting. As soon as she has put one arm into her coat sleeve, she grabs the purse in which Berta has packed her snack and rushes into the living room, for she hears footsteps. Instead of Daddy, there stands Vilém Svojsík.

She is so bewildered that she can't find her second sleeve. He helps her get dressed.

'Daddy had to stay in the mine,' he says as he does so, as if the world weren't turning upside down, 'a commission from the ministry arrived. You won't be afraid with me, will you?'

Líza would like to reply, but she can't emit a sound.

'Take your mittens; it's cold outside.'

The child runs into her room and brings the mittens. Without realising what she's doing, she hands them over to Svojsík. Only when he starts pulling them over her hands, does she become so embarrassed that her eyes well up with tears.

Svojsík wonders why the child is so crimson, and why on earth she is crying.

'What happened?'

She clamps her teeth. She tries to quickly swallow her tears, but it's too late. Vilém is pulling a handkerchief from her purse and is wiping her nose.

During this further humiliation, Šelda's child is trembling all over. However, the real torture only awaits her. On the way to Šádova Huť, she perks up a bit and starts answering Vilém's questions. Just then, another blow – she feels sick on the train. Svojsík leads her to the bathroom and there she throws up. He doesn't say a word; he doesn't turn away; he holds her head and wipes her face. Líza would rather die than see disgust and repugnance in his eyes.

'There,' he says cheerily, 'what was bothering us is down the drain.'

He wipes her lips, leads her through the corridor, lifts her up on the bench and sits her down beside him.

'Have you had breakfast?'

'No.'

'You have to eat a piece of bread, at least.'

He's pulling a package from his pocket, but Líza is already reaching for her bag. She unpacks her own bread and immediately bites into it. Her hands are shaking. She's so consumed by remorse that she'd like to bite herself up along with her bread.

Vilém is smiling.

'Líza, you are the most obedient child in the whole world.'

She is completely astounded by what he has just said.

The wheels of the train repeat it to her: Líza, you are the most obedient child in the whole world. She would like to be. From the depths of her soul, she'd like to be.

She pulls out her thermos flask.

'I even have tea.'

She is desperate to oblige.

'Please, have a drink.'

He takes a drink.

The wheels of the train unceasingly reassure her: Líza, you are the most obedient child in the whole world.

They reach town. Vilém takes her by the hand and leads her from shop-window to shop-window, until they come to the doctor. Líza is worried about what is going to happen. But the doctor only plays with her and with colourful spools inscribed by letters. She recognises the colours well enough, but has more difficulty with the letters. She reads badly, very badly. The doctor frowns and shakes his head. If Vilém weren't there smiling at her, Líza would burst into tears.

They get a little card and that's it.

Outside they buy glasses and Líza puts them on her nose. They act like a magic wand. The world becomes sharper, and distant objects become bigger and closer.

There are plenty of mirrors in the street and Vilém lifts her up in front of almost every one. She sees herself among hats, among clothes, among jewellery.

'You don't even know how nicely they suit you!'

She does.

He leads her to a store full of toys.

'Pick something.'

The sales lady, who looks like a painted doll herself, spreads treasures out before her: a bear, a doll, a dog ...

She brings the goods and begins to be impatient.

Líza, who until now hasn't uttered a sound, grabs the miner by the coat.

'Uncle ...'

'Pick something!'

She shakes her head.

'Don't you want a toy?'

Líza's quivering lips urge Vilém not to insist. He apologises to the saleswoman and leads the strange child out to the street.

Líza, with downcast eyes, feels that she has offended him. She feels overcome by regret that she couldn't choose, that she couldn't even touch anything, that something forced her to flee from all that beauty, too much beauty.

At last, the black miner seems to understand.

'Don't worry about it, Líza,' he says consolingly. 'Would you like to eat something ?'

'No.'

Vilém Svojsík, who usually understands children, suddenly feels at a loss.

'You must eat something, otherwise you'll get sick again.'

'I'll eat.'

'We'll buy a cake and some cocoa, how about that?'

'Yes.'

Before they finish eating at the milk bar, Líza is so unbearably distressed that she has upset Vilém Svojsík that she dares address him: 'Are you angry at me, Uncle?'

'Why would I be angry? Stop worrying and smile.'

Líza smiles with all her might; the corners of her mouth tremble. Vilém realises he's tormenting the child. They walk silently side by side, both deep in thought.

Twilight seeps into the streets.

'You're tired, Líza, but soon we will be at the train station and you can sleep in the train.'

Líza has no intention of sleeping. The city, lit up in neon lights, reminds her of fairytale beauty. In a low voice, she reads out the glowing signs she doesn't understand: UNION, CHAPEAUX, CAFÉ, ROYAL ...

She suddenly feels anxious that she might throw up again.

This time, her stomach doesn't budge.

It is a blissful ride. They sit across from each other and tell each other about everything they saw in town. They remember every important detail.

At the gate of her home, Líza musters her courage.

'Uncle, may I come to meet you at the Anna Maria?'

His eyes pop.

'Of course you can!' Touched and thrilled, he pats her hair. 'From today, we're ol' pals.'

He rings for Berta and leaves into the dark.

Behold, this is why Líza's glasses are worth all those tribulations! Like everyone else, she can mingle into the dense crowd of miners who've just come out of the shaft, and she can spot one of them and call his name.

She can do all this, but she stands at a distance, so that Vilém can't miss her.

'Líza!'

Only God knows how children recognise their mother. But they recognise her infallibly.

6

Vilém Svojsík stopped going to work.

At school, Alenka told them he would die.

Nevertheless, Líza continued going to the Anna Maria, hoping for a miracle.

It didn't happen.

One morning Alenka told her that he had died.

Líza curled up in her bench like a sick mouse.

She headed back home, her forehead burning. Along the way she encountered her dreams, just as dead, stiff and white as Uncle Vilém.

Snow White lay in her coffin and all around her, her dwarves were weeping.

Instead of going home, she walked deeper and deeper into the forest. She wanted to carry her misery off into a corner somewhere, into the shadows.

She arrived at the ravine, into which the villagers threw holey cooking pots, mouldy straw mattresses and shards. There, among the rusty wire and dirt, she saw Alena Svojsíková's doll. It lay among the rubbish, filthy and torn. In her excitement, Líza's legs almost gave way under her. She clambered down the ravine, threw herself on the tortured toy and pressed its deformed face to herself.

She lay ailing for a few days. Berta soused cold compresses and wrapped them around her head. Then the doctor came, and, soon after, the old stern wise-woman Lucka Vojničová. She gave Berta some medicinal herbs and ordered her to make a tea from them.

Being ill didn't dishearten Líza in any way. She had hidden the chafed doll in the cupboard beneath her clothes and would play with it whenever the maid wasn't nearby. She washed it in soapy water, sewed on its hands and feet and clothed it in bright-coloured clothes that she had fashioned from her old apron.

Luckily, Berta did not bother Líza. She considered her big enough and independent.

As soon as she could stand, she made her own tea. The wise-woman caught her at it once and her forbidding face lit up like the rising sun. From that moment, Líza stopped being scared of her.

The beautified doll lay in a shoebox: it was mainly thanks to it that Šelda's child was cured.

The class blustered 'Owlet' to welcome her back, and she only smiled.

They stopped calling her that.

Vilém's doll gave her so much strength that she could fight for herself, and in that battle she proved her bravery. She managed to tell Alenka Svojsíková to her face that she would never give back the doll.

Her classmates found the doll with Líza by accident. They caught her playing with it in the woods. She was leading her cloth companion along the forest paths and was talking to it. Alenka hadn't cared about the doll for a long time now, but as soon as she learned that someone had acquired her property, albeit discarded property, she was roused by childish selfishness. She exploded with anger and screamed that she had been robbed. The unsightly doll suddenly acquired immense value.

If only Líza had curled her lip and thrown the doll aside, everything would have been saved. Alenka wouldn't have picked up the doll, she would have kicked it. But instead, Líza clasped the doll and took to flight.

The children's sense of justice immediately took a stand against her.

Thief! Mangy thief!

The shrub on which Alenka tripped assisted Líza's escape. She jumped into a bush and hid there until her frustrated classmates dropped their vain search.

The next day at school, Alenka once again asked for her toy.

Líza said: 'I will never give you the doll.'

The class bristled.

The teacher had to break up the ominous crowd by Líza's bench.

'Teacher, sir!' the children shrieked, 'Šeldová stole Svojsíková's doll!'

'Quiet! Everyone return to your seat!'

There would be an inquiry and this time Líza would pay. The teacher had his foibles, but he was fair.

'Svojsíková, speak!'

'Šeldová stole my doll. I saw her playing with it in the woods. And she doesn't want to give it back to me.'

'Šeldová,' the teacher's voice softened despite himself, 'what do you have to say on the matter?'

'I found that doll.'

'Where?'

'In the ravine.'

'You found it and didn't know whose it was.'

'I knew it was Svojsíková's. She threw it away there.'

'Svojsíková, what do you have to say?'

'I didn't throw it away. I lost it. And then I looked for it. I want that doll!'

Alenka was screeching and the whole class was supporting her with subdued grumbling.

'Šeldová, do you have another doll at home?'

'No.'

The teacher thought he had understood something.

'Come and see me in my study after class.'

'I want my doll!'

'Quiet! Tomorrow, Šeldová will give it back to you. Tomorrow you will bring the doll to school, Šeldová.'

'I won't give up the doll.'

The teacher was taken aback.

'If it isn't yours, you must return it. You don't want people to say that you steal. You will get a new doll. We will talk about it in my study.'

Alenka grew quiet. She realised that she has just helped Líza get a new doll. She would gladly have shredded her own doll in spite.

But Líza didn't show any interest in a new doll, as Alenka and the teacher had assumed.

In the study, she stubbornly repeated that she would keep the old one. The teacher was frustrated. Where was this all coming from? The rowdiest lout in Želary seemed like a playful kitten compared to her.

'Tell me, why this ratty toy is so important to you?'

'It isn't ratty.'

'I'm asking, why is it so important?'

'Because I like it.'

What a reason for crissake.

'Do you want to be a thief? Do you want everyone to point fingers at you?!'

The teacher was right and Líza was starting to sweat. 'You'll get a C in behaviour. I'll call your father in to school!'

Fear of her father almost crushed Líza. However she remained determined not to give up the doll to anyone, even to him. Happen what may!

She hid it in a suitcase in the attic and covered it with a moth-eaten cloth. Daddy didn't even have to go see the teacher. Berta brought him the calamity with his coffee. The village discussed children's matters the same as adults'.

The engineer had his delinquent daughter sent in.

'Child, you supposedly stole some kind of doll.'

Líza felt like an impaled butterfly. With every movement with which she tried to save herself, she only thrust the deadly metal deeper into her flesh.

'Speak. Do you have a doll?'

'Yes.'

'Bring it here.'

Líza didn't move.

'Bring it,' the father repeated forcefully.

'I won't give the doll to anyone.'

There, she had said it. Now something horrible would happen. Uncle Vilém, the child prayed, Uncle Vilém!

The engineer stood before Líza, as if he had never seen her before.

'Whose doll is it?'

'Alenka Svojsíková's. But she threw it away.'

'Threw it away?'

'Yes. I found it in the ravine.'

'And you won't give it back?'

'No.'

Engineer Šelda started to laugh.

'Child, you deserve that doll. Keep it and don't give it to anyone, even if a whole battalion comes to claim it!'

Alenka Svojsíková got fifty crowns. The biggest banknote the class had ever seen.

The very same day, someone stole it from her.

Translated by Madelaine Hron

MAGDALÉNA PLATZOVÁ

Every Civilisation Has Its Heyday

So I've been here six months already and we haven't shot a single foot of film. Mrs K. stands by the window on the fourth floor of the luxurious building on Wenceslas Square and watches the hustle and bustle below her. It's just before nine, the clerks and salespeople are hurrying to work. Eyes fixed on the pavement in front of them, telephone in one hand and briefcase in the other, they head in different directions. Mrs K. raises her gaze and checks how much copper roofing has been added to the building opposite. From the roof, her eyes drop a little lower and, as usual, she assesses the looks of the girl on the advertising board, which covers the entire façade of the building under reconstruction. The girl stares Mrs K. straight in the face and she's not as pretty as our Eva, that's for sure. For that matter, she almost forgot. Mrs K. turns away from the window, crosses to the desk and carefully presses the eight digits that connect her with her only daughter.

'Hi, it's me,' announces Mrs K. 'So what did he say? That he stayed late at the office? And he never showed up?' Mrs K. casts a reproachful glance at the closed door where her boss usually sits.

'Did you take a pill? Well then, take a pill and go and lie down. I'll ring you later.'

Mrs K. hangs up, thinks for a moment and dials another number on the office telephone. This time the other phone rings in her apartment, which she left a little while ago. 'Hi, it's me. Did you see Eva? I keep telling her to go to the doctor. Depression is an illness just like any other. The doctor should prescribe something for her. Did you take the meat out of the freezer? Well, I'll call again later.'

Mrs K. reflects for another moment, then locks the office and takes the lift to the ground floor. Behind the window of the porter's lodge sits a woman whom she occasionally chats with, even though it's beneath her. Now she greets the woman with an ingratiating smile. No, the porter wasn't on duty yesterday, but she can look at the register. It should show the code of his magnetic card and the time he left. There's no entry. That means that the boss either didn't leave at all, or he left without using his card. There you go, the old visitors' books were so much better!

Mrs K. returns to the office and picks up the post on the way. To be on the safe side, she calls Eva right away and announces that she hasn't found out anything yet. While she's holding the receiver, she checks whether her husband has defrosted the meat. The first hour and a half of the working day passes. Mrs K. is now sitting at her desk. The pens and paper are all stacked up. She checks her email, she has even learned to do that, and she waits for the boss to arrive. She's bored. So she calls her sister-in-law at work and tells her what happened in front of Květa's mother's building. Some scumbag stole a woman's wallet right there in broad daylight. They caught him and it turns out that he was an Albanian from Kosovo. 'We're already up to our necks in it! Here on Wenceslas Square they've all got jack-knives in their pockets and those eyes of theirs, like wolves! And last night there was a huge puddle of blood on the pavement in front of the building! Be careful, Líba, Jarouš doesn't let me go anywhere alone any more!'

Someone knocks on the door to the office. Mrs K. hangs up quickly, grabs paper and pen and acts as if she's working. A wizened little man enters. He shuffles over to the desk, greets her and, excusing himself, sits down. He's one of the boss's protégés, a fellow ex-pat. The boss slips him some money from time to time and chats with him about the former Yugoslavia, reminisces, philosophises: 'Every civilisation has its heyday, followed by a fall,' says the boss. 'Yugoslavia, that was an empire that had no equal. And that's exactly why it had to fall apart, just like Egypt and Rome.' The old man agrees and adds: 'When Emperor Diocletian wanted to build a palace, he looked all over the Mediterranean, but no place was good enough for him. Until he found Split. He didn't hesitate. He pointed his finger at the map and said: "We'll build it here."'

Even in the heat the old man bundles up, as if he had ice in his bones. Mrs K. makes some coffee for him, and the old man, to thank her somehow and while away the time, starts to tell a story. 'I've always been fascinated by human fate,' he rattles on. 'Why, for example, did Eva Braun become Hitler's mistress and die with him? Fate, none other than cruel human fate. I'd like to tell you the whole story, which is fascinating. In 1925 ...' Mrs K. nods off and prays that someone will come and rescue her. The telephone rings. At the same time, the door opens and Mrs K.'s boss marches in, followed by his omnipresent henchman and gofer, Zoki.

Behind them is a tall, bony man with an olive complexion.

Probably one of them, from the south. Mrs K. says hello and answers the phone. She speaks discreetly because it's Eva calling and she wants to know if Mrs K. has any news yet. 'He has just come in,' Mrs K. whispers, her hand shielding the receiver. 'I'll call you later.' As she sets the receiver down, she feels a strange tingling on the nape of her neck. She turns around. That emaciated man is staring at her, his eyes like burning coals. Who's he? A hypnotist? The boss, who appears to have had his beauty sleep, calls out, 'Mrs K., make some coffee for us.' Mrs K.'s blood boils. This boiling is always triggered by a request for coffee. How many times has she told them that she's an assistant, not a secretary? How many times have they promised to hire someone to answer the phone and make coffee because that is one thing that she, Květa, will never do? And certainly not now, when she has three years left to retirement. She wanted to work in film because that's her line, after all. She used to be an actress and it's not her fault that she never made a name for herself. She remembers with nostalgia the years she spent in the provincial theatres. The parties, the flings, the other actors. Some of them are famous now.

Art is art, says Mrs K. A person is born an artist. An artist is simply a person kissed by the Muse, someone who isn't cut out for office work. I didn't go to the conservatory to learn how to make coffee and answer the phone, complains Mrs K. Promises, promises! In the end, after all that talk about art, Mrs K. saw a diagram of the organisational structure of the office on the boss's desk and she was listed there as the secretary, in the same box as the cleaning lady! She wanted to hand in her notice right then and there, but Eva talked her out of it. 'Where are you going to find another job at your age, mum?' she said.

The gentlemen shut themselves up in one of the offices and leave her with the little old man. Mrs K. now has to think up some trap for the boss. She has to find out if he was here last night or not. She thinks about it but she can't concentrate. What are they talking about behind that door? Sometimes they burst out laughing, then it's quiet again. Bloody bad habit, always shutting doors. Mrs K.'s desk is located right in the middle between the boss's office and Zoki's office. Their constant running back and forth and shutting of doors has left her head spinning more than once. As if they had to hide something from her! They were probably discussing artistic matters and closed the door on her because they took her for a silly secretary. The little old man continues to tell the tale on which he embarked before the arrival of the boss. He's already made it to Eva Braun's first date with Hitler, the fateful poison is already brewing. But Mrs K. is not interested. She's got an idea and she's so pleased with it that she has to smile. She'll be nicer to the old man and while they're talking she'll ask him if he can wheedle out of the boss where he was last night. The old man is flattered by her heightened interest. He thinks that he's charmed Mrs K. and subtly he shifts from Hitler's lover and turns the topic of conversation around to himself and his heroic feats.

Mrs K. believes him. Mrs K. believes anyone who wants her to. Not to believe, that would involve comparing and putting together various bits of information in her head, and that is a lot of work. In addition, it complicates matters unnecessarily and then people don't like you.

There's dead silence behind the office door. At that moment, the door opens and the man with the fiery gaze exits, holding a divining rod. The boss and Zoki follow close on his heels. They skirt around Květa's desk and vanish into the other office. They close the door. Mrs K. and the old man wait. Then the door opens again, the strange gentleman is obviously departing, the boss says goodbye. But before he leaves, the stranger approaches Mrs K., gives her a searing look and presses a business card into her hand. 'Call me!' he says with a thick accent, in a tone of voice that brooks no resistance. Only when the footsteps have fallen silent in the corridor does Mrs K. open her sweaty palm and read, 'MB Damian Rosco, acupuncture, acupressure, psychokinesis, rhabdomancy, etc'. The boss appears and says that there's a vortex of negative energy in his office. That must be why he feels so bad.

Now it's the old man's turn. He goes through the open door of the boss's office and Mrs K. winks at him to remind him to ask. Zoki runs off to the bank and Mrs K. finds herself alone again.

Jarouš has to stand on a chair next to the freezer. When something is right at the front, he can still reach it. But this meat is sure to be hidden way at the back and Jarouš is now too short to reach that far.

The freezer is bursting at the seams. There are heaps of bags and boxes with various labels: spaghetti sauce – 3. 4. 99, meatballs – 6. 6. 98. As Jarouš digs deeper, the dates go back further. It's like uncovering layers of sediment in a former seabed: the Cretaceous, the Jurassic, the Triassic. In the Permian, he finds the labelled leg of pork. But if he foraged on, into the Ordovician, or even the Cambrian, he'd be sure to find a few blood sausages from the communist era. But he's not up for that kind of thing any more. He closes the freezer, sets the meat on the kitchen counter and sits down to rest.

Klára the dog runs around and whines piteously. Jarouš sighs, lifts his body off the chair again and goes to look for the leash. Finally, he finds it under the shoe cupboard, attaches it to the dog and they leave the building together. These are the first hot days of spring. The first spring days of Jarouš's retirement. He can finally see for himself what this whole spring business is actually about. The dog runs over the pavement, mopping up spittle and stirring up dust, and Jarouš checks out women. Some of them are already pretty tanned – who knows how they do it. They probably go to those sun-beds that cause cancer. Eva goes there too. Perhaps to impress that guy who is only a few years younger than Jarouš and treats Eva so badly. They're a dishonest bunch, those Slavs from the south. All riffraff, mafia. Go into any restaurant or bar in Prague and the owners are always their kind or Arabs. They launder their dirty money there. And now those Albanians are streaming in here too and starting up their gold rackets. Jarouš clenches his little hand into a fist. If only he could! The mobile phone in his pocket starts to twitter.

It's Mrs K. She asks if he has taken the meat out and what he is doing now. 'I'm taking Klára for a walk,' Jarouš answers truthfully. He says nothing of his bloodthirsty musings. That's because Mrs K. thinks that the boss is an excellent catch for Eva. With the help of God and Mrs K., who can keep an eye on the boss at work, they'll manage to pull off a wedding. Then Eva will march right into the major league of film. Yes, for a young actress, a film producer like that is best. In the long run, it's worth a few tears. Mrs K. can already see her daughter on a luxurious yacht, the *White Flag*, in Split. She smooths over quarrels, sends Eva to the psychiatrist and anticipates every wish of the boss.

Jarouš says goodbye, sticks the phone back in his pocket and continues on his way. On the corner stands a girl, belly out, chest out, short little skirt. Jarouš looks the other way.

With that film of theirs, he prefers to continue with his bitter reflections, it's also strange. Maybe the boss used to make films. They say that he even used to be famous. But that was under different circumstances – and what is he now? A man without a home goes to ruin, Jarouš's mother used to say. But maybe she was wrong. Maybe everything is just like his wife says. There will be a film, there will be a wedding, there will be money. They need the money in particular. So why does he always have the feeling that something large and terribly dangerous is hanging over his head?

He heads for the building where Eva lives. He rings the bell, but nothing stirs inside. Jarouš takes out his own keys. He can have a little look around, at least, and see if the kid has anything in the fridge and if she's watering the flowers.

It's quiet in the flat. The windows in the kitchen are boarded up. In the living room, which also serves as a bedroom, the blinds are drawn. Jarouš opens the blinds and looks around. His gaze falls on the colourful cover of a video cassette, lying at his feet as if someone had dropped it there. 'That girl of ours is going to seed,' Jarouš shakes his head and bends over to put the box back on the television stand. Since he has it in his hand, he looks to see what kind of film it is, rummaging in his pocket for his glasses. He gapes at the photographs and for a long time he is stumped.

Jarouš is already retired but in all his life he has never seen such smut. He wipes his glasses, which have suddenly steamed up, and studies the pictures carefully. That blonde is smashing alright. And that brunette is familiar – where on earth has he seen her before? Behind his back, something squirms. Eva is lying in bed. She has kicked off the blanket and flung one hand over the bed panel. The cover drops from Jarouš's hand.

Cautiously, so as not to wake his daughter, he walks through the kitchen and out of the flat. He sits down on the bench in front of the building. He takes out his mobile and punches in the number of the office.

Mrs K. sits at the desk and studies the doctor's business card. She has a feeling that this piece of paper is alive, that it emits some kind of magnetic vibration. When she runs her finger over it, the finger goes numb. She rests her hand on the receiver, takes a breath and at that moment the telephone rings. In a muffled voice, she announces the name of the production company. 'It's me,' says the strangely hollow voice of her lifelong companion. Then silence falls. Mrs K. is frightened. 'Is everything alright? Is Eva alright?'

All of a sudden, Jarouš realises that his wife won't believe the simple truth that he has discovered. It doesn't fit in with the dream about white yachts and the red carpet at Cannes. Jarouš says nothing, overwhelmed by his sudden solitude. Then he spits out: 'I defrosted the meat.' 'But I know that already,' his wife says with relief. 'What are you doing now?' 'Not much, taking a walk. See you later.' 'I'll call again,' says Mrs K., but Jarouš has already hung up. A tear trickles over the green display. Jarouš smudges it with his finger and puts the phone in his pocket.

'What's up with him?' Mrs K. wonders. She dials the number again but in vain; her husband doesn't answer. She unbuttons her collar. Heat like this at the beginning of April, it isn't normal. The world isn't what it used to be.

Once again she gazes at the telephone number of the hypnotist. There's no one in the office. The boss has had his chat and gone out somewhere and the old man went with him. Where he was yesterday he didn't say. Or did the old man forget to ask him?

She could do it now. A sweaty finger slides over a button. Again. 'Is that you?' says the deep voice with the accent. 'I knew it would be you. When can you come?' 'But why?' whispers Mrs K.. 'I'll tell you when you get here,' says the man. 'This evening?' 'I can't today,' I've got thawed meat at home, Mrs K. wants to say, but she stops herself. 'I have to work.' 'Tomorrow might be too late.' That voice ...! Mrs K. trembles all over. 'Alright, today.' She notes down the address and says that she'll be there after five, she'll leave the office early, but she's got to be home by seven at the latest. 'We'll be done by then,' says the man. Květa puts the receiver down and all of a sudden she feels calm. She'll tell Jarouš that she had to run an urgent errand for the boss.

It's hot out today. Drops of sweat trickle down from under the little Tramp's woolly hat. He's already covered the whole of Wenceslas Square, eaten all the leftover sausages, looked in all the bins. Now he'll rest for a while here on the low wall at the metro entrance. The boy sits down on the grey wall and bakes in the sun. He rolls up the sleeves of his jacket, held together with an old belt, but he won't take off his hat. On the contrary, he pulls it down even further over his ears. Then his slightly slanted eyes carefully explore the new terrain, penetrate the space and make note of its crannies, which are his only source of sustenance. The melody of the foreign language and the noise of traffic pierce the thick fabric protecting his ear drums. They blend together into a single sound, a droning wind. The Tramp listens for a moment. This is a different wind from the ones they have at home. This one puffs about here and there. It hardly ever leans into him, and then only briefly, tiring quickly. This wind could never level a steppe. The boy gets up and sets off on another round.

Vladimir, Mrs K.'s boss, left the office early in the afternoon. Now he's sitting at a little table in the café of the Jalta Hotel with a young, well-known journalist whom he bumped into and invited for coffee. The journalist has a nice bum and that's something Vladimir always appreciates. He likes to explain to anyone who cares to listen that a woman's breasts are of secondary importance.

Only the infantile are fixated on them. A true woman can be recognised by her behind and her intimate triangle. That's the zone, says Vladimir, that radiates the most energy. A woman's character is revealed there. In this respect, he is satisfied with the girl. He'll have to note her telephone number. Vladimir likes to stockpile. It pleases and comforts him. He has a fridge full of cheese, a freezer full of meat, a cellar full of wine. In the kitchen cabinet, there are bottles of oil, olives and pickled capers, which he brings back from the south. It's good to have a few women in stock too. Each one has her uses and a man can be sure that he'll never be alone. 'We owe everything to women,' says Vladimir and he means it. Yes, fortunately a woman who can take care of you always turns up.

The journalist says goodbye. 'Drop in at my place tonight at six,' says Vladimir. 'We'll have some wine. I have some good bottles.' The journalist laughs raucously and agrees. Then she accepts one of Vladimir's cigarettes and allows him to light it. Her hand shakes.

Vladimir watches her go with a smile. Once again, he's satisfied with himself. He admires the retreating backside and relishes it until it disappears in the crowd. What a beautiful, charming day! From the raised terrace, Vladimir blesses the world and smiles even at that flat-faced boy in the strange, dark green hat who is loafing on the pavement. The boy studies Vladimir with his slanted eyes. He doesn't return the smile.

Jarouš retreats to the furthest corner of the pub. He stares into his pint of beer. Almost from the beginning of their life together he's been listening to his wife telling him that he, a clerk, could not understand art, which she had to give up. Every day she served up some sort of artistic mush along with his dinner. For Jarouš, the word 'art' acquired an ominous sound. When his daughter, egged on by her mother, decided on an acting career, he said nothing. He even paid for a private school. He knew that he would have to make some sacrifice to that god with the menacing, painted face. And truly, the god began to look more beneficent. The spurned mother fixed her eyes on the future where not she but her daughter would ascend the staircase of money and fame. The reproaches morphed into a tirade of expectations. Wait until she graduates! Wait until they discover her, until they notice her!

Well, they'd noticed her, Jarouš nods his head bitterly. He orders another beer. He has a right to it today.

Mrs K. looks at her watch and her pelvis stiffens. 'I shouldn't, I really shouldn't,' she says and undoes yet another button. Then she takes a makeup kit out of her purse. With a wet finger, she wipes the smudged contours of her eyes and paints them over. She powders herself again and sprays deodorant generously on her blouse. There. She shuts off the computer, which has been purring calmly behind her back all day. She stacks up the coffee cups in a plastic bin and leaves. With any luck, her boss won't check up on her today.

She's already hurrying up Wenceslas Square. She passes the Tramp, giving him a wide berth. He is leaning against a tree and listening to two young gypsies playing accordions. He has even pulled his hat up a bit over his ears. That little gypsy is no bigger than his accordion. He has such a serious face, not at all like a child's, Mrs K. reflects.

Half an hour later, she rings at the doctor's door. The man has been waiting for her. Silently, he extends a bony hand, leads her through a lobby and into a room where a large, framed diploma and thank-you letters hang on the wall. There's also a bed, two armchairs, a desk and a cabinet with some little bottles. Without further ado, the doctor asks her to take off her blouse and lie down on the bed. Mrs K. obeys, under his piercing gaze. First, he lays his hands on her head. The woman feels how his palms warm up and a tingling heat flows into her skull. She closes her eyes. Then she feels those burning palms on her chest, on her stomach. With slow, circular movements, they slide down to the lower abdomen. Květa is excited, dissolving in a kind of thick, hot fluid. She shifts her pelvis and sighs softly. It takes her a while to realise that the hands have vanished somewhere. Through a red mist, she hears the words, 'You can get dressed.' 'How come?' Mrs K. opens her eyes. 'When I saw you in the office,' says the man, 'I knew immediately. Now I can see that I was not mistaken.' Květa sits up on the bed, her heavy breasts tumbling into her lap. 'At the hospital they'd tell you it's incurable, but I say that it can be cured. If not completely then at least I can prolong your life a few more years. Now let's talk about it calmly. The first steps of the treatment can begin immediately. Would you like something to drink?'

After her mother's last telephone call, Eva rolled over on her other side and fell back asleep. She didn't wake up until four o'clock. She lay there a moment and remembered where she was. Then she got up and had a shower. With her hair still wet, she sat down by the telephone and called her mother at the office. She wasn't there. She called her father at home, he wasn't there either. Where had they all gone to? She lit a cigarette and dialled the number of Vladimir's mobile.

Sweat runs into Zoki's eyes. He crawls up the steep steps to the boss's flat, carrying the sea in his arms. The boss instructed him to fetch it from the antique shop. He already has at least fifty seas in his flat. Wild, oily, open seas, bays, ships ... All the antique dealers in Prague know him by now. As soon as they see him in the door, they announce: 'We've got a sea here for you', or: 'We don't'.

Finally, he reaches the landing. Vladimir unlocks and Zoki, with the last of his strength, manoeuvres the sea into the living room. Vladimir sits down and lights up. He squints at the new acquisition, appraising it, and says: 'Hang it there, over the couch.' In addition to seas, Vladimir also collects saints and in the corner next to the red, mock-leather couch stands a larger-than-life-size statue of Saint Wenceslas, his best piece. One wooden hand clutches a standard, the other points at his chest. He has pink cheeks and eyes painted blue. Wound around his neck is a string of colourful electric lights left over from Christmas. 'Put that sea over here,' Vladimir waves his lit cigarette, 'and that one there.' The telephone in his pocket beeps. Vladimir glances at the display and waves a hand at Zoki. He knows instantly what he is supposed to do. He sits down next to the boss and makes noises imitating the rumble of an engine. 'Hi, baby,' Vladimir answers. Eva asks if they are going to see each other this evening. 'Can't make it today, my darling. Zoki and I are in the car right now on our way to an important meeting. I'll call you this evening.' The electromagnetic waves transmit Eva's sob. 'We're going into a tunnel now, sweetie,' says Vladimir. 'I'm losing the signal.' He hangs up.

After five, Zoki is finally done for the day. Vladimir prepares for the anticipated visit. He takes a long shower, massages himself and puts on after-shave. Then he wraps himself in a loose dressing-gown, gets a bottle of wine from the pantry and two glasses from the kitchen and turns on the lights above the couch.

The waves on the new painting gather and crash in a golden-brown spray under the dull gaze of St Wenceslas. On the horizon, there is a black ship's keel, pointed at the sky, and the white bodies of the drowned phosphorescing in the blue-green depths. Vladimir stands in front of the painting and stares. Where is he? All around it's dark. He doesn't hear anything. He doesn't breathe. Now something moves him. The pressure of the water carries him and pushes him down a narrow, wooden corridor, then through an opening of some sort. He is out in the open. He bobs up and down and turns gently. Below him he sees the black wreck of the ship, which sinks to the dark bottom. Here, where he is, the water is motionless and totally silent. Rigid strands of seaweed hang on the rocks and fantastical beasts parade before the dead eyes of Vladimir.

Mrs K. drags herself to the tram stop. She got a little drunk on the doctor's liquor, but even through the padding of alcohol she feels the sharp stab of some terrible thorn. Limply, as if after an electric shock, her brain tries to start the habitual trains of thought, but somehow it always loses momentum. 'The tram is coming,' Mrs K. says to herself. 'Jarouš must be waiting. Did he take the dog out? At home the meat is thawed. I have to roast it.'

The Tramp sits on the stone railing of the ramp in front of the National Museum and watches the lights of the big city come on below him. He throws his head back. How far away those stars are! His eyes strain at the sky until his head starts to spin. The wind is rising.

Once again, the Tramp looks down below him, over the head of the bronze horseman. He sees the buildings come apart and the grass cover the pavement. The stars float down above his head and hang there quietly. The wind drones and ripples through the silvery clumps of grass. A strip of land starts to rise from the bottom of the square, up through the centre to the place where the boy is sitting. Higher and higher. That's not a square, it's a horse! Huge and wild. It charges in the blistering wind under the black sky, where the low stars flicker. The Tramp straddles its back and shrieks with joy.

'You bastard, you! Beat it and fast, before I blow the whistle on you and your dirty deals. I know what kind of porno flicks you're making, you producer, you! If you're not out of this republic in a month, I'll turn you in. They'll lock you up!' Jarouš finishes his beer, folds the letter into his pocket, pays and staggers out to the pavement. He wonders if he shouldn't put it in Vladimir's mailbox immediately, but then he decides to sleep on it. His wife must be waiting.

He stumbles down Wenceslas Square towards Můstek. On the corner of Vodičkova Street he feels sick. He leans on the railing. Once again, he is overwhelmed by the feeling that something sinister is hanging over him. But what can it be? He leans his head back and looks up. And then he sees it. A few feet above the head of Saint Wenceslas, above the kiosks and department stores, above the neon lights, the prostitutes and pimps, above McDonald's and Bata, above the entire Wenceslas Square hangs an enormous, shapeless, stinking piece of shit.

Translated by Kathleen Hayes

TERA FABIÁNOVÁ

How I Went to School

My mother said to me: 'You must go to school, or they will lock up your father.' There were five of us children at home, four girls and one boy. The eldest was my sister, then me, one year behind her. But I was stronger than her. And naughtier. So my mother said: 'You will be the one who goes to school, because at home you only make trouble.' My sister was to stay at home with the little children. She carried them around on her back, washed their nappies, wiped their noses and their little bottoms, and swept and cleaned the house. Everything had to be done by the daughter who was at home, because mothers went into the village to work for the *gadjos*, and only came back home at night. That was what our mother did, too. Our father went to make bricks. If there was no work, he would work for the *gadjos* for some food.

In the morning, my mother woke me up: 'Get up, Little Bighead, go down to the stream and have a wash.' A little stream passed by about thirty metres from our house. That was where we went to wash, every morning and every night. At night, I would run down to the stream on both feet, but when I came back I hopped on one foot. I never had shoes, and so I wanted at least one of my feet to stay clean. In winter and summer we went barefoot. I only had one set of clothes, which my mother had begged from the *gadjos*. As for knickers and petticoats, we did not even know what they were.

I went to the stream and washed my feet and my face. My hair was full of feathers, because Romani beds were nothing but feathers and straw, which came out of the mattress and the dirty old quilt. I went to school. I had no bag, I had no readers, no pencil, no exercise book – nothing! I had never had anything of that kind.

I went through the village, and the village was still sleeping. There was no one outside, only two or three *gadjos* going to the fields with their horses. No one even looked at me, it was as though I were not there at all. I knew where the school was, because when I used to go into the village with my mother, she said to me: 'This is where you will go to school, so I will have some peace and quiet, Little Bighead!'

I pushed hard to open the heavy school gates. It was dark and cold, and I was half-naked and barefoot. No one was there at all. Only one old *gadjo*, who looked at me and said: 'What do you want here?'

'Well, I've come to school. I want to learn things.'

'You?' He started to laugh. 'Look at that skirt on her! Why haven't you washed? Why haven't you combed your hair? Where's your bag? You have nothing, you don't even have a bag! How will you study?'

'I will study! I will come to school, I will!'

The old man laughed, and he shoved me into a classroom. I sat in the front desk. I looked all around me. I was alone, all by my little self. The old *gadjo* started to sweep the floor. I just sat there, thinking to myself how I was going to be *somebody*! I would know everything. All knowledge would come into my head if I just sat in school – that was what I believed. But then I looked at my bare feet, and my heart sank within me. How could a poor Romani girl become *somebody*? I closed my eyes, and saw myself in a pink satin dress, embroidered with gold roses. Then I believed again that I would be that clever woman who would pave the way for other Roma. Already as a little girl, I knew that we Roma were the last of the last. No one said a kind word to us. If I wanted to go out from the settlement, my mother said to me: 'Don't you dare go into the village! The other children will beat you up.' And so I only dared to go into the village when there were several of us, or when the older boys came with us, to stand up for us.

It was half past seven, and the bells rang in the church. One after another, the boys and girls filed into the class. Their mothers brought them. Two or three mothers came into the classroom, and seated their little girls in the front desk. They looked askance at me. But I stayed where I was, because I wanted to become clever. I was just waiting to become clever. More and more *gadjo* boys and girls kept coming in. They were finely dressed, everyone had a bag, and the little girls had ribbons in their hair.

At long last the teacher arrived. She saw me in the front desk. 'Who put you there?' She dragged me up, and sent me to sit at the back. 'That'll be your place.' In the first desk she sat the rich little *gadjo* girls. Then came the poorer ones, and the very back desk was for the Romani kids. 'The gypsy desk.' Next to the cracked window, separated from everyone else. I felt like an orphan. Why did I have to sit there all alone? It was hard for me, when there was not a single Romani child with me, and I was afraid. I would have felt stronger, if only someone had sat next to me. But I was alone, all by myself.

The first day in school went by. I learnt nothing. None of that knowledge went into my head, the only thing that forced its way into my mind was how poor I was. When I arrived home, no one asked me: 'so how was school?'

'Mummy, the teacher said that I needed a reader, an exercise book and a pencil.' My mother slapped me. 'Run away! There isn't enough to buy bread, and you want a book from me! Just keep on going, so they don't take your father and lock him up.'

The next day, I washed my feet again and I combed my hair and put on my old clothes and went to school. And that's how I went to school every day. A month went by, and the teacher did not ask me anything, but just looked to see that I was there. She did not know that I was listening to all that she said. When she asked one of the other girls or boys, in my mind I said along with them what they were supposed to say. I liked doing maths. The seven-times table was my favourite. At night, I was unable to fall asleep because the seven-times table kept dancing in my head. I raised my hand, and the teacher called on me: 'Go on, count!' And I counted very well. Again, the teacher asked: 'What do they cultivate in Hungary?' I knew. Peppers, melons.

'You are not stupid,' said the teacher. 'If you had a reader and an exercise book and a pencil, you could learn something. Why doesn't your mother buy you a reader?'

'My mother has no money.'

'Why do you go around so dirty? You don't even have proper clothes!'

'There are many of us at home, and there is no work.'

Then, one day, I did not go to school. 'Where were you?' asked the teacher when I returned.

'You told me that my clothes were dirty, so my mother washed them for me.' The teacher's eyes popped out. 'I couldn't go out of the house until my clothes were dry.'

Then the teacher bought me an exercise book and started to give me little pencils, which the other children had thrown away. My fingers hurt from holding them, but I was glad to have them.

One day an order was given that all 'gypsy' children must go to school. That's what the village mayor said. Among the Roma there was great horror, great panic. They ran up and down, the women tore their hair, what will they do with us? What will they do with us? The village guard came to the Romani settlement and began to drum, and the men ran out of their huts, half-naked, their hair full of feathers, and the women were screaming at the children: 'Go to school! They'll lock up your father if you don't go! Who'll support us?'

The children went. They all put on their 'very best' clothes – their mother's skirt, their father's trousers – and off they went to school. The village official went on his bicycle, and we chased after him. 'Go on, run, you gypsy rabble!'

He took us in to the headmaster. I had never seen the headmaster before. He was short, fat-bellied and bald. He had onion eyes and a big moustache, which jigged up and down above his lips when he spoke. He only had two teeth, and God knows where the other teeth had gone. When he looked at us, his big eyes bulged out. He started to tell us off for being lazy Roma, who did not want to learn anything, who did not want to become real people! He cursed us, but you could see that he was a good man. 'How will I divide you up? Filthy rabble! All the teachers are scared of you,' he said, kindly. So he started to count: one, two, three, four, five. There were fifteen of us. He said: 'You go there, you there, you there' So he divided us up among the classes. My sister Beži, who was a year older than me, also had to go to school. My mother cursed and cried that there was no one to be with the children when she went out to work.

We went into the classroom, and the teacher was scared of us. 'Where will I put you!' At the back were three desks, and she sat us there. We were separated from the *gadjo* children so that we wouldn't fight with them. We couldn't study.

Once, I was very hungry. It was just when there was a fair in the village. The *gadjos* were baking and boiling – the Roma were hungry. The teacher asked each of us what we had eaten, including the Romani children. Black Pot said: 'I haven't eaten anything since yesterday. We only eat when my mother gets home from the village.'

Bango said: 'We don't eat in the morning, either,' which was true. Our first meal used to be in the afternoon, when our mothers came back from the village and brought potatoes, cottage cheese and milk, which the *gadjo* women gave them if they chopped firewood, cleaned the manure out of the stables, or wiped down the stove.

The teacher said to me: 'What have you eaten?'

'Wow!' my eyes opened as wide as stars. 'If you could see what I ate! Biscuits with cottage cheese, soup, buns and cake ...!'

'How is it that you have eaten, while there was nothing for your sister to put in her mouth?' the teacher interrupted. 'Why are you lying? Stick your tongue out! You'll get something to make sure you don't lie next time!'

I stuck my tongue out, and she hit me across it with a ruler. It hurt so much, I could not even speak. But when I came to myself again, I said to her: 'I was not lying! I was eating all night long! I dreamed of eating, I ate in my dream.'

The teacher went red, said nothing and walked away.

A year went by. Everyone said I was not stupid. I did not fail. They let me move into the second year. I received my school report. There wasn't a single C grade on it. And I was very proud!

I ran home, jumping up and down for joy, and shouting from far away: 'Mummy, I only have As and Bs.'

'I'll give you 'A's! Do you think we can live off your A grades? A grades, A grades – at home you do everything to avoid working! At home you couldn't care less about work!' That's how she cut me short. It was hard for me. The little *gadjos* got books, watches or money for good school reports – but what was there for me? Cursing. There was no one I could pour my heart out to.

Three Romani boys went up with me into the second year. I became friends with those little boys, and the Roma said of me that I was stronger than a boy! Whatever the boys said, I said it too, and what they did, I did too. When they were beaten, I was beaten too.

One time the circus came to the village. I was mad about dancing. I knew how to put my leg around my neck. And so Šulo and Bango and Tarzan – those were the names of the three who went with me into the second year – said: 'Listen, you go to the circus – and whatever you see there, you can tell us about it afterwards!'

I said: 'How can I go, if we don't have any money?'

And they said: 'Don't worry, we'll get some money somehow. Come with us.'

We went over to the church. In front of the church was a statue of Saint John. In the morning, when the *gadjos* walked by the church, they threw money at it. And Šulo said: 'What does a statue need money for? You can keep guard, to make sure the priest or the verger doesn't come, and we'll collect the money.' They made some clay with slime and spit, and made a kind of sticky paste, which they put on the end of a stick, then they poked the stick through the grating towards Saint John. They wanted to raise the money from the dead. 'Bango, do a wee in the clay, wee in it, it will be better,' said Šulo. And sure enough, he caught a sixpence on the stick. But the priest was coming!

'The priest is coming!' I shouted. The boys stuck the sixpence in my mouth. 'Swallow it! Get it down!' I swallowed, and started to choke. I choked, retched, spat, turned red, and the boys were thumping me on the back.

'What are you doing here, you devils?' said the priest.

'We came to pray to Saint John – look, she almost choked,' lied Bango.

Of course, the priest did not know that I was choking on stolen money, and he said: 'Come here, let me give you a bit of holy water.' He poured some into my palm, and so I washed down the stolen money with holy water.

Bango said: 'We need to think of a way of getting the money.' But how? What? Where? I used to go to work for one *gadjo* who had chickens. 'Do you know what?' the boys said, 'You go into the hen-house, take the eggs from under the chickens' bottoms, and we can sell them to the Jew.'

I did not know what to do. 'Bango, you go!' I said.

'Alright,' the boys said. 'You go up the tree, up the pear-tree, and you can pick pears. Bango can go for the eggs.'

I climbed the pear tree – the dog didn't bark, because it knew me. The boys were in the hen-house, and the hens made no noise, because Šulo and Bango knew what to do. But who should be coming? The *gadjo*! And I was up the tree! He came straight for me. 'Is that how you thank me for giving you work?' He picked up a big stick, the kind you use to knock down nuts, and he went for me! I looked to see whether Bango and Šulo would run out of the hen-house. I saw them jump over the gate, and then they were gone. The *gadjo* saw nothing. Good, now I could come down from the tree. So I jumped, straight onto a nail. Luckily, it didn't go into my leg, but it tore my skirt at the back. I ran for it, and the torn skirt flew in the wind, while my naked bottom shone out like the moon.

The boys were waiting for me. They turned me round and round. 'We need a patch to sew it up!' said Bango. But where could we get a patch from?

'Do you know what,' said Bango, 'you walk in front of me, and I'll walk right behind you, and then no one will see your bottom.' So that is how we walked. My mother was watching from a distance. 'What on earth is that? Look! She's with a boy! Stuck right up against him! Does an honest girl walk like that?' (I was about seven or eight years old.) As I came nearer, my mother said: 'Is that how you go about, my girl?!' She beat me until I could not get up from the ground. My mother was wailing: 'You have one set of clothes! And you've torn them up! How can you go to school?' We never had cloth for a patch at home. My mother said to me, 'Wait, we'll do it somehow.' She took a kind of apron, which was supposed to be tied to my front, and she tied it behind me. My naked bottom could not be seen.

As soon as my mother had tied the apron to me, we went to sell the eggs. The Jew said: 'What kind of chickens do you have?' Their shells were very thin. 'You can see straight away that it's a Romani chicken.' The Jew would not buy the eggs from us.

Now what? How could we make money to go to the circus? I said: 'Oh! I am so disappointed! I'll never go anywhere. I'm going home.'

'Aha!' said the boys. 'So you swallowed the money and now you want to go home!' Šulo caught me by the ear. 'Have no fear. Wherever you try to go, we'll follow you, because that Saint-John sixpence is not just yours! It's ours, too.' But what use was the sixpence to us anyway, when the circus cost one crown twenty!

'Let's go and see what we can do,' said Tarzan. We went to the place where the circus was, and it was already full of circus wagons. Bango went to ask whether he could go and carry wood, or help in any way. What the circus manager said was: 'Yeah, I need nappies washing, and you can wash them if you want.' Bango ran for water, Šulo washed, and I just stood there as if I was their princess. Bango said to the circus manager: 'Let her go in! She can go and see the circus!'

The circus manager pushed me forward: 'Hop in! Run off, then!' I went inside, and the boys went on and on washing the nappies.

I was inside the circus! The acrobats swung on the bars, walked on the rope, and the clowns fell off bicycles – most of all, I liked the snake woman in the golden skirt, who did somersaults in the air and walked on her hands. In my mind, I did everything alongside her. I'd show the boys a thing or two!

I went home, glowing like a star. I was beaten by my mother for gadding about! I went to sleep in tears and hungry. As soon as I closed my eyes, I imagined myself as that circus lady, jumping through the air, walking on my hands, with the golden skirt shining on me like the sun.

It was not yet light when I got up secretly and disappeared off to the cemetery. There was a large lawn there, beautiful and soft, so that I would not break any bones. I did a crab. I could do that. I put my foot around my neck. I attempted a handspring. I fell crashing down on my back. No sooner had I recovered a little than I tried to do it again. I spun through the air. Good, now I could do a flip, as well. There was one thing I couldn't do – I could not walk on my hands. I fell and fell again. I was broken and bruised. Everything hurt.

The bells were ringing in the church, and I fled to school. My first lesson was catechism. The priest came into the classroom, saying: 'You were at the circus, weren't you?'

'Yes, I was.'

'You go to the circus, but you don't go to church!'

I said: 'The floor is cold in the church, and I don't have shoes.'

'Tell me how our great God was born.'

'I can't tell you how God was born, but if you want I can tell you how my little sister Ili was born.'

'Come out from behind your desk! You'll get your bottom smacked for having no manners!'

'Oh no! I can't have my bottom smacked!' I cried. The priest pulled me out of my desk, the apron flew open, and my naked bottom glowed like a full moon. The boys started to laugh. The priest sent me home. And finally my mother brought me some worn-out clothes from the village.

A week later, when I was not so bruised, I said to the boys, during a maths lesson: 'Come with me.' I put my hand up and said I needed to go to the toilet. The boys did the same thing, one after another. We had a modern school, with three flushing toilets and a corridor in front of them. In the corridor, I began to show them what the circus was like. The teacher started to wonder where the Romani boys were. Where had they gone? No one had come back from the toilet. The teacher came after us. And when she saw us, I was walking on my hands, spinning through the air and twisting my face like a clown.

'So that's what you're doing! You're teaching them circus acts. Wait here!' I was beaten again. How many times had I been beaten for one circus! And what had I gained from it? One swallowed sixpence. When it came out of me again, I hid it in the cemetery. It's buried there to this day.

A new teacher came. He was tall and young. He looked at us. 'Are those all the Romani children? Are there no more of you?'

'There are more of us, but the others don't come to school. If there were more of us, the teachers would be scared!'

'So I will take all the Romani children!' said the new teacher. 'But none of you will interrupt me or disturb me!'

The next day, what should we see but the new teacher, riding his bicycle into the middle of our settlement. He had come among the 'gypsies'. Not a single *gadjo* had ever visited us, apart from the village guard. The teacher called out: 'Every child who is supposed to be going to school, come outside!' He even said '*aven avri*', 'come outside', in our own language!

We ran out of the shacks – the teacher had a stick in his hand. 'Get going, get going, run along to school!' When we got to the classroom, he asked: 'Hands up if you haven't combed your hair.' He didn't need to ask, he could see that none of us had combed our hair.

'Why haven't you combed your hair?'

'We don't have any combs.'

'Have you washed?'

'We don't have any towels.' One after another, we started to tell him everything that we did not have.

'Good. Tomorrow you can come to school one hour earlier! If not, I'll give you what-for!'

The next day, we really did come an hour early. The teacher was already waiting for us. He had brought towels, soap, a washbowl and combs.

'Who hasn't eaten anything?'

We all put our hands up. The teacher sent Bango for bread rolls. He bought a roll for each one of us. Then he said: 'Well, now we can start learning something! Today you can all stay in school for the afternoon, too.' At midday, he bought food for us again, bread and margarine. He asked us: 'What do you want to be when you are older?'

'I want to dance and sing!' I said.

He slapped me. 'You won't earn a living that way. You need to study, then you can dance and sing.' Then he grabbed the boys by the hair. 'What do you want to do?'

'Me – a blacksmith.'

'Good, you will be a blacksmith.'

'I want to be a musician like my dad.'

'That's all fine, but you must still know how to read and write.'

Then he gave us pencils and exercise books and we really did start to learn something.

There was a fair in the village. The teachers chose good pupils to recite poems. So our teacher said:

'Just wait and we'll show them what you can do!' He asked me: 'Do you know how to sing?'

'I do.'

'Sing, then!'

I sang a very amorous lovesong from a film. I must have been about eight years old.

'Who taught you that?' the teacher asked.

'My father sings that to my mother at night,' I said.

'Which of you can recite a poem?'

'Meeeeee!' I shouted. I recited a patriotic poem which I had heard from the *gadjo* children. My face was red and my eyes shone – he stared at me.

'Good,' he said, 'you can recite a poem, and then you can all sing and play music.'

The boys brought violins and basses and whatever they could from home. But we had nothing to wear, we had no smart clothes. The teacher said: 'Oh my God, if I was not so poor! How I could help you all! Look what beautiful hair you have! Would you like ribbons in your hair?'

'Wow! I'd love that.'

'Look, boys and girls, you have to study so that you won't be stupid! So that the *gadjos* can't do whatever they want with you. If you study, you will be cleverer than your parents. You will hold your heads up high, you will know how to find your own place among the other people. Study, and pay no attention if I shout at you, or if I box your ears. I cannot get angry with those who treat you in such a way, so I have to vent my anger on you. Oh God! When I see how the *gadjo* children eat so well and bring bread with dripping, and you eat your hunger, how the anger rises in me! How am I supposed to help you? Grow up good and honourable, so that the gentlemen see that your poverty is not your fault but theirs.'

And we took an oath that we would never again be naughty or bad, that we would not steal money from Saint John, and that we would study.

We went to the celebrations. No one expected the Romani children there. The *gadjo* children were there with their mothers and fathers. They put on a play about a princess and a cobbler.

Then our teacher stood up. He said: 'Now let me introduce my pupils to you.' The boys began to play. The old men started pulling at their moustaches big and small and started tapping their feet, it made them so keen to dance! Then I recited the poem. The *gadjos* were astonished. Then I took a plate, as my teacher had told me to, and went to collect money. 'We want to study, too, but we don't have readers or exercise books.' Everyone gave some money.

I did not go to school for long. The war began, and Roma were not allowed to go into the village. They did not allow us to go to school. I did three years of school.

Translated from Romani by David Chirico

All the Colours of the Sun and the Night

It all began on a Friday. Sometimes you remember unimportant little things. It was a Friday in the spring of the year 1952, and I had spent the whole afternoon working on the slope of a small park in Prague. Suddenly I recalled a well-known and oft-cited verse of a Czech classic by Karel Jaromír Erben:

Pátek nešťastný je den,
Nechoď dceruško k vodě ven ...

'Friday's an unlucky day,
Don't go, daughter – keep away!'

Just three weeks previously I had been categorically instructed, without any further explanation, to take note of the immediate termination of my employment contract with the broadcasting service. Since then I abruptly found myself with an abundance of free time. As if no one in the whole world needed me for anything anymore. For no job, no task, nowhere – for nothing. In the whole country, the era of dismissals ordered 'from above', with no right of appeal, had dawned. Whoever was affected by this was fatally marked, became suspect. One also heard of arrests, but the rumours were vague, and one could not gauge the danger one was in.

All of a sudden our home telephone hardly ever rang, and nearly all acquaintances I met by chance in the street were in a great hurry. Only exceptionally would anyone stop to talk to me. I was too nervous to read, and writing was pointless. Who would publish anything I signed? And so the leaflet requesting participation in a voluntary work brigade, 'For an even more beautiful Prague', came right on cue. Finally, at least for a few hours, I would feel normal again. At least for an afternoon I would simply be among other people.

Only a few women appeared in the park where the flowerbeds were waiting to be planted. A group of giggling girls, two hard-working grandmothers and myself. It was a hot day. The girls soon removed several items of their clothing. Suddenly one of them, a merry blonde in black shorts and a blue and yellow striped vest, called out: 'Look over there quick, that's a warder from Pankrác prison marching by. The one in the green uniform with the lilac shoulder stripes. That has to be a great job. After the war my mother cleaned the flat of a judge for a few weeks. The things he talked about! Incredible things, really!'

The girls laughed, the grandmothers didn't seem to hear, I felt disconcerted somehow about the whole thing, I didn't know why.

I was picked up in the early evening of that day. My husband and child were not at home. They didn't tell me why I was arrested. To all my questions they just answered: 'You yourself know best.'

Friday's an unlucky day,
Don't go, daughter – keep away!

When I was arrested in Paris, shortly after the war began in September 1939, it was summer. From the window of the car that was taking me to police headquarters, I saw chestnuts tumbling down from the trees at the side of the road. They bounced on the pavement, and it was so comical that I had to laugh. The officer next to me looked at me in surprise, grinned uncertainly, but quickly reverted to his expressionless police face. The arrest was disconcerting; it made me nervous, but not bewildered. War is war, I said to myself, all kinds of things can happen. The chestnuts apparently couldn't care less. This was comforting to me – the colours of the sun?

It was spring when I was arrested in the year 1952, in my home town of Prague. I was first taken to a cellar in the villa of the security authorities, which was located in the middle of a garden. Probably the trees were in blossom there. I could not say. The day was so terrible that it couldn't leave any comforting memory – the colours of the night.

My husband and I had tickets for the cinema for the Saturday after that ill-fated Friday. They were showing *The Girl with the White Hair*, a story I had already seen on stage. It tells of a common Chinese girl called Si-'r, who was pursued by a brutal landowner. She succeeded in running away and hiding in the mountains. But overnight, fear and suffering turned her hair white. In the morning it was like snow. Then, when the revolution broke out, the landowner was hauled before court by the angry villagers.

In the first hours of my detention I was preoccupied by the ridiculous concern about whether I would be freed in time for the film. As if this were important now. As if I didn't know that I would miss a lot more than just a film screening.

The first interrogation dragged on from the day into the night and from the night into the next day. My exhaustion took several forms. I hardly felt hunger or thirst, but I couldn't concentrate at all. Thoughts ran independent of my will, and at the end of each one gaped the abyss of boundless helplessness. Would I ever get away from here? And at home? Is Duško there? Who is with our child? What is being played at here is pure insanity, and all efforts against it are pointless. If the man standing guard at the door had a longer nose, he would be a vulture and could peck out my eyes. Cigarette ends glimmered in a glass ashtray on the table. I constantly had to look at them. I was suddenly interested in whether the cigarette end on the left would go out first, followed by the one on the right, and only then by the bent one in the middle. The bent one – like a tree stump over the crater of a smouldering volcano. Oh Mexico, volcanoes and palm trees ...

The man on the chair behind the table reached for the ashtray and emptied its contents into the waste paper basket. Then he poured a glass of water over it. It hissed, and a hideous stench spread out.

Suddenly, the interrogating officer looked like an angry Chinese man. His wide gold-coloured belt and the green uniform contributed to this impression. And he talked and talked. With a raised voice that screeched in my ears, then again under his breath, so I could hardly hear him. No wonder! Evidently he was speaking Chinese at me. Was he the evil landowner from the fairy tale?

I panicked. What if my hair had also suddenly faded? Was it already white? I ran my hand over my head, as though colour could be determined with a touch. But I have always liked to check things with my hands.

I do that often. Many years ago as a very young thing I joined a demonstration of the unemployed, out of solidarity. I was brought before a police commissioner for the first time. There I had to wait, and I felt with my fingers a tiny hollow in the wooden banister that separated the arrested from the officers, and gently ran my hand over it. How many anxious people, guilty and innocent, had clung on here in their misery?

In Paris, during the interrogation in front of the examining magistrate, I often clenched my fist. Secretly, in my coat pocket or under the table, where no one could see it. This wasn't an empty gesture of rebellion. The more tightly I clenched my fist, the more I felt my blood pulsing. This calmed me. I lived, wanted to, and would live.

But now, at the mercy of an incomprehensible situation, I wasn't capable of determining whether my hair hadn't turned white. I let my hands fall back to my lap. The menacing man with the gold belt, the feared landowner, was still talking. He didn't know that he was exerting himself in a language that didn't make sense to me at all.

But what was there to be understood? The questions that waylaid me like traps hidden in the thicket? Or the monstrous suspicion that, even though not clearly pronounced, stifled the room so much that I couldn't breathe? The dark accusations they tried to pin on me were outrageous. The drooling words stuck to me like cobwebs, I tried to free myself from them without avail, perplexed, horrified, in the first hours already hurt to the core.

A bottomless swamp – and you can't move, because with every movement, with every word, you sink even deeper. But what, for heaven's sake, was this supposed to mean? Why this insane attempt to align me with criminals? This was unfortunately a logical conclusion, they told me.

A conclusion? Of what? I was told such was the requirement of the times. But when had the epoch started that called for lies to become truth? Why did they demand such unconditional lies?

For one month I was held in an improvised cell in the cellar of the grand villa. Then one morning I was blindfolded, put into a car and taken away. Without a word of explanation. After a while the car stopped, and I was brought out – still blindfolded – and led into a building. I could smell the stale air. A gate creaked; I was shoved into a room, and then came the command: 'Take that thing off your eyes!'

I stood in a prison cell, at the beginning of my solitary confinement. No one told me that this institution was the notorious Ruzyně.

The interrogations that started now were irregular but frequent. Mostly during the daytime, but sometimes I was also brought before the interrogator at night.

Outside was spring. People were looking forward to their holidays, were making plans. Sometimes it rained, then the sun shone again. Good days were followed by bad days, everyday joys followed by everyday worries. Yet in the middle of the beautiful, calm town stood buildings before whose heavy, hermetically sealed gates the seemingly quiet, everyday life had to stop. It had no admission here, other laws ruled.

After a sleepless night I sat in the corner of the badly aired office again, tired, unwashed and sweaty. The interrogator tried irritably to get hold of a typist by telephone. After several attempts the door finally flew open, and a young blonde pranced in wearing a pink summer dress with a plunging neckline outlining her fresh, suntanned skin.

'Don't be angry at me, comrade,' she called cheerfully from the door, 'I was so terribly hot, I just had to drop by the swimming pool. Josef was driving into town and took me with him.'

'You should have been here on time,' the investigator growled, while at the same time eyeing her with pleasure. 'Did you at least bring something to drink?'

'Of course!' Out of a white bag she produced a few bottles of raspberry-red lemonade and stowed them in the sink. The man let a jet of cold water run over them.

'So don't be angry anymore,' chirped the girl and pouted her lips, 'the heat is really unbearable. But at least now we have something good to drink for the whole day.'

I sat in the corner on a narrow metal seat and was thirsty. The two ignored me, as though they were alone in the room with a table, two chairs, a typewriter and a prisoner on remand. I ran a sweaty hand over my damp forehead. The man downed a whole bottle of the raspberry-red drink in one gulp. In the meantime the girl sat herself down at the typewriter desk, fished a little bottle out of a drawer and daubed the back of her neck and her armpits with Eau de Cologne. Then the interrogation began again.

On a different day, still quite at the beginning, I was brought before a stout man 'in his prime'. He had an oafish face and beneath his nose a smart little moustache.

'So this is you!' He greeted me and looked at me with curiosity, but not exactly with sympathy. 'I thought you would look different. Well, that's by the by. Let's come to the point: why are you denying everything? We want to help you, haven't you figured that out yet? You're an intelligent woman, aren't you?

We're showing you the right way here, because we believe you don't belong to the worst, you just slipped a little, so to speak. But you have to help us, otherwise we can't do anything. So do we finally get your confession today?'

'But what should I confess?' I asked, and for the first time in an interrogation I almost had to laugh. The guy with the smart moustache, the well-meaning voice and the self-important gesticulations, all were really funny.

'What should you confess?' he repeated. 'Well, my goodness, your crimes of course. High treason and espionage for the class enemy. Contacts in the West. Activities in Yugoslavia, all that. So come clean, I will take it down, you will sign, and we will send you home. Is that clear?'

'Why are you saying such a thing? It is pure nonsense!'

'As you wish.' He turned red in the face, and the smart moustache bristled indignantly. 'You'll have yourself to blame for the consequences.'

The man turned his back on me, reached for the telephone, dialled a number and said into the receiver: 'Hello, is that the club? The club, yes. – Listen, Alois, is that you? Good.' He lowered his voice a little, but just so that in my corner I could still make out what he was saying. 'I left my revolver there yesterday. Please send it to me. Where? Here of course, but soon, I will probably need it.'

He turned around. I looked into his face and said quietly: 'What's all this play-acting? Aren't you ashamed of yourself?'

'Blindfold her,' he shouted. 'Guard! Lead her away! Unbelievable, such impertinence!'

'We're representing the Party here for you,' bellowed the gold-belted official, the landowner from the Chinese story, and puffed up until the back of his neck turned almost purple. The Party?

Which Party? Surely not the one I had belonged to since my rebel years, not the one that had promised all the oppressed a full right to life. He was representing it? As investigator of a violent police system. As enunciator of insane accusations and perilous lies. Who gave him such a right? Was this still in the realm of the intelligible?

The man planted himself close in front of me, breathing heavily into my face. I sat in the corner on the narrow metal seat and couldn't even turn my head away.

'We are a huge apparatus,' he boomed. 'You can't do anything against us. You are completely alone. Nobody is helping you. Will you finally realise this!'

It was hot and sticky in the room. Suddenly the man ran to the window and slammed it shut. I felt nauseous.

Perhaps I'd never been really this abandoned, without any legal assistance or contact with my closest. Without any advice, without a single friendly word. The difficult years of my youth I'd spent surrounded by like-minded boys and girls. When we were barely twenty years old we plunged head-first into the dramatic, for us fascinating times, filled with colours, sounds, light and shadows, music and noise, interwoven with threatening disaster, but also the dream of a better future. We felt drawn to the creation of a socialist order that would put ideas of liberty, equality and brotherhood into action. Standing aside wasn't an option for us in those turbulent and exciting years. That was the only danger that didn't threaten us.

When the National Socialists took power in Germany in the early thirties, thoroughly imbued with the false doctrine of a superior race and longings of martial conquest, there were few people in Czechoslovakia who weren't aware what this meant for our small republic. The radio broadcast previously unimaginable diatribes from the neighbouring country. In the border region, but also in Prague, Brno and other towns, fascist youth groups 'for order and change' promised: 'The day will come!' Even before then, the spectre of expanding Fascism cast a shadow over our young years. It spread throughout Europe and crept into our heads as nightmares, but not into our dreams of the future. For the time being they stayed untouched.

Of course, we feared the loudmouths in the brown, black or local grey shirts. But we knew them, scuffled with them. In the street, at meetings. We knew they were repulsive and capable of any misdeed. That is exactly why we were not prepared to tolerate them.

It is indeed strange to belong to a generation that doesn't seem to have a beginning or an end. 'It is our lot, and you belong to it, whether you want to or not. Being a little younger or a little older makes no difference.' Who had said this to me? It had to be someone out of my close, my closest circle. One of the people I was involved with as a young girl, eager to absorb everything that could give meaning to my days.

Looking back, I can observe almost with amazement, but also with relief, that in Stephan's Secondary School in the eventful thirties, there were no frictions, no spiteful outbursts as a result of nationalistic or even racist fervour. In my class and in all the others, sons and daughters of German and Jewish families sat next to each other, were friends, spent Christmas or Easter holidays in the 'ski chalet' in a village school on the Keil Mountain. Maybe less peaceful things were to be heard in the homes of some of the pupils. In the Stephansgasse we felt none of this. In that time of social crisis, our minds were on another kind of passion; my first and last love poems were written there.

The generation I belong to. Such were its beginnings. Like all generations mine also felt the desire for change. That's why we left the beaten path followed by those before us, and along which they continued to scamper. That's why we despised everything forced on us as obvious and necessary. Our need for action predominated. Sometimes only to scream, sometimes to fight, just never to be content with passive acceptance.

Maybe it was these beginnings that made me join the ranks of the generation that doesn't seem to have an end.

Translated from German by Nicole Balmer
Erben's verses are taken from
Susan Reynold's translation of Kytice

Kateřina Rudčenková

The Forest

My childhood was filled with sounds that came from behind the thin walls of my room covered with birch-tree forest wallpaper. I lived in a birch forest. At night I looked at the ceiling criss-crossed with moving streaks of light from cars passing in the street below my window. I listened to those sounds and tried to imagine their monstrous meanings and the actions they accompanied. I listened to the stories with which my mother entertained her guests when Father no longer lived with us, when there were often parties in our home with her colleagues from work, loud music, dancing, laughter – activities I guessed at from their voices.

In my dream Mother became seriously ill and her whole body had to be amputated so that only her head remained. I was put in charge of the head, and somebody advised me that I should read to it from Werich, which I find infinitely dull.

Father on my left, Mother on my right. Divided, incomprehensibly, irreconcilably, and between them in my head lies a road on which I stand alone.

'Take a seat.' Where? At the table with newspapers? Mother is guilty. Or Father. How many times did she die in my dreams? Once I flattened her with a bulldozer. And still she survived. 'Give my regards to your mum!' 'Why?' Mother is guilty, not Father, because she was the stronger one. In my memory I try in vain to find some explanation from him: his words, a good-bye – nothing of the kind. And so, from now on, I am forever going to feel ashamed about what I do.

'Arguing again?' I am standing in the doorway, the child witness of their conflicts, who, in their view, understands nothing, and who is therefore never consulted about anything.

How to settle their dispute, how to reconcile those voices which I was not capable of reconciling? I just wanted them to be quiet, to stop antagonising each other. I wanted both of them to be here.

How do you decide which part of you remains at home and which follows him to others, where he becomes grafted, indistinguishable from the original branch, while to me he appears entirely inappropriate, incomprehensible, perverse?

Destructive dreams about Mother, erotic dreams about Father. We walk down Kamenická, our street, which in my childhood led either to the park on the left or to Auntie Věra's in Dejvice on the right.

We stop on the pavement by the launderette, one of the few places that has survived throughout my life without changing, with the terrible roar of machines and the melancholy scent of wet washing.

He leans with his back against a car and I squeeze his member under my bent knee and rub it until he spurts on the windscreen between the wipers. Our action is scandalous, the police appear from somewhere, I run into the doorway of an apartment building, one of them catches me and presses a pair of handcuffs between my teeth. And him? Where has he disappeared to?

The infatuation of a child. Caressing his face: 'You have grass growing here', she laughs at the rustling of his stubble.

Father and I are walking silently through night-time Lidice where he is living with his second wife – all news has been passed on. He spits on the asphalt, a stranger; in vain I search in him for the person I have lost. A wasteland. An abrupt severance. End of an enormous certainty, trips to the zoo and the fairground where I was allowed everything, where he bought me everything and forgave everything.

The ceremony of handing over money remains like an empty symbol of an old relationship. He offers it to me every time we see each other after a long while. I take it from him with a mixture of shame and shamelessness and quickly pocket it so that the terrible proof, the reminder that he is a stranger of whom nothing is left except an outstretched hand and a guilty expression, is obliterated as soon as possible and we can pretend again that nothing has happened. The things we talk about, things we have often discussed, are never important. How are my studies going, what about his business, small talk drifting in a closely guarded space that we must not break out of.

I am travelling from Krems for my graduation ceremony. Mother had said that she didn't want Father to be present at the lunch following the ceremony. She could not watch him gloat over our achievement in front of the family. She was the one who had brought me up and had taken care of me. My degree was therefore her pride.

I arrive home and she asks again: 'What will you eat? What time will you get up before leaving?'

'Why do you want to know?'

'Because I want to fry up some schnitzels you can take with you.'

'But I don't want your schnitzels.'

'And can you tell me why?'

And I am silent, a long silence, unbearable for me, because to say why would mean I had to say it all, from my birth to their divorce and up to this very moment. I am silent, I don't have a short answer. I don't want her schnitzel because schnitzel means further violence, those elongated fingers that have forever been pulling the strings of my life.

While I remain silent, she walks into the room, sits down and says: 'Is it because of Viktor?' And I say: 'Maybe because of him, too, but not only that. It's mainly because I don't want to live here anymore.' 'But who is forcing you? No one wants to live with their parents forever.'

Then we discuss Father again, the usual things, his constant and unconcealed infidelities during their marriage, the nights of drinking, the fact that he had joined the Party to advance his career, the betrayal of his colleagues that, in the end, didn't work out the way he had expected, and how he became unpleasant. And last but not least the fact that he beat my brother. An image of Father has stuck in my memory: chasing my brother around the dinner table with a broomstick in his hands, shouting. I, on the other hand, was spoiled by him. Whenever I wanted to take revenge on my brother I just waited for Father to walk past, I did something to my brother and he got the beating. 'It's possible I was stricter with you, but he was so unfair towards him,' says Mother now. If it were not for her 'higher' authority, I would have grown into a monster and my brother into a poor little wretch.

When my brother was fifteen, he said to Mother: 'Why don't you just divorce him?' And Mother said: 'You're right! Why didn't I think of it before?' And when Father came home, she told him: 'Viktor, I've had enough, could you please move out?' 'Of course,' he said and the next day he was gone. Nobody told me anything. I was seven. 'Where is Daddy?' 'He has moved out.' (Where, why, is it my fault?) 'And he's not coming back, he won't live here any more?'

'No.'

'I just don't understand,' said Mother, 'where this anger is coming from and why you are so unfair to me. And I don't understand why you define yourself so negatively in relation to me instead of relating positively to the world. Didn't I always admire your attempts to embark on something new? You could have moved out a long time ago.'

Father rings the next day. What about the celebration? For a long time I can't tell him. I understand Mother's point of view, but why do I have to deal with it? Yes, she did say that if I were to miss him she would overcome her resentment, but who wants to watch her aggrieved expression? 'You see, Mother is not exactly favourably inclined to your being there,' I say, my voice trembling. 'I can't understand why,' he says, 'but don't worry about it, I don't know those people anymore anyway.'

Mother realises, however, that it's not possible *not* to invite him because she has already invited Grandmother who would find her son's absence difficult to understand. So she is forced to phone him that evening and persuade him to come after all.

I am seven. I walk into our dining room where they are in the middle of an argument. They both stop in their tracks and go quiet, stare at me in surprise. Then they pick up the argument again, as if I weren't there at all. So it is therefore not in my power to silence those voices and stop them provoking one another. I have no influence. I can't be that important to my parents if I am unable to keep them together. Who knows, perhaps my brother might have had that power.

When I step from the light of the street into the darkness of the corridor, I look at the phosphorescent hands of my wrist watch and the second hand silently circling the luminous face.

Seated at the head of the graduation lunch I cast my eyes down the length of the table surrounded by guests. A mirror in a gilt frame is hanging opposite and I see myself sitting there, with short hair, wearing Mother's graduation dress, mother engineer, daughter engineer, the degree is in the pocket, I am satisfied now, you can go out into the world. I nodded at myself ironically in the mirror.

We both sat there, me and my reflection, looking at each other with amusement, we both found the celebration entirely inappropriate, as there was obviously nothing to celebrate. I had finished my studies but would never be an engineer, under no circumstances, and what I hate most of all is the celebration in my honour, because I have long become used to feeling like a person on the margins and that is why I cannot shake off the impression that all those present are part of an ironic joke. Next to myself in the mirror I saw my parents. Father came with his third wife and Mother's face was red because she had cried all night. 'I have nurtured a snake in my bosom all my life,' she told me the night before when she cursed me. 'I have brought up a monster!'

In my dream I saw Mother devoured by flames. Lying on a grassy hill, she kept sinking through the earth. It was terrible. Her body convulsed and disintegrated. The dream pinned my gaze to the thighs that had produced me. And all that burned to ashes, turned to dust and became one with the earth. I was left alone and I said to myself that now I would have to work and I would never have the time to go to the theatre in the evenings again.

Translated by Alexandra Büchler

Kateřina Sidonová

A Day in the Half-life of Class 4D

BOULOGNE

'Hi crew,' yells Suchomelová as she rummages through her bag for a smoke. Finally finds one. 'Burn me up, bitch,' she says and takes the flame. 'Thanks,' she adds. 'I'm smucked. Old man locked me in last night. No going out.'

'Poor you.'

'Hi crew.'

'Look who it isn't. Slush and Llama.'

'Hi.'

'Is life boring, or what? Has Llama got a new lighter?'

'Roboš gave it to me.'

'Just what I need to light my own fire.'

'I'll have to think about that.'

'Scrof you, you slummock. I'd rather use my own matches.'

'Hi crew,' we hear from behind a bush. Now it's Ryvolová hitting the scene. 'Good to see you, swine.'

'Can't say I'm glad myself. Whenever I see you something tells me I'm at school.'`

'Too right, Soda Pop. You should join our banjo'd band. Then you'd know us as partners on the piss,' says Revolver as she lights up.

'Look who the cat's brought in. Ackermannová.'

'Hi crew.'

'Hi. Coming for a cig?'

'That'll be the day,' Acorns shakes her head and throws in an ironic smile. 'You addicts just can't do without it, can you?'

'Too right, vicar.'

'Look out, it's Martyš!' Slush screams and squats on her haunches to avoid being seen.

'If I had the habit, I wouldn't hide myself to feed it,' Ackermannová continues her sermon.

'Hey, do you think we'll get a history oral?'

'From Mrvová?' Suchomelová thinks about it and adds: 'No way.'

'Oh yes we will.'

'I'm saying no way so no way,' Suchomelová closes the debate. 'We'll make sure we don't.'

'Don't you think we might be pushing it ever so slightly?' Timidly I'm coming out with my concerns.

'What do you mean, pushing it? Tests turn you on, or something?'

I shake my head.

'You see, no limits to pushing.'

'What are you burning, Slejšková?'

'The usual. Rothman's.'

'Flash the ash, babe.'

'Well it's not exactly my pleasure but out of kindness to a fellow human ...'

'Forget it, I don't want one.'

'Latch on, lummox, I'm really letting you have one here.'

'No, I was just kidding.' Suchomelová is playing hard to get.

'Take one, Mellow.'

'No. What do you think you're doing, airhead, embarrassing me like this?'

'Please yourself, then. All the more for me,' says Slush with a shrug of the shoulders.

'Look who's scurrying over. Bureš.'

Burger sneaks off to the Bois de Boulogne with a gasper in her gob and a blow torch in her hand saying 'Do I have time for one?'

'Loads.'

Burger shifts her attention to Llama. 'So what's the news?'

'What should it be?'

'Come on, Roboš stayed at your place, didn't he?'

'So?'

'So – robust?'

'So – nothing.'

'What do you mean, nothing? Must have been something.' Now Acorns is getting really wound up.

'So what do you want me to tell you? All right, we had a shag.'

'And you still haven't come?'

'No.'

'You prannet, I'd like to know if there's one girl in this class who's actually managed an orgasm.'

'My guess is not a single one of us. Welcome to classus frigidus.'

'This is getting on my tits.'

'Time?'

'Five to.'

'Better be going.'

'Christ, I've only just lit up.'

'Finish it on the way.'

'Haven't got the nerve for that.'

'Stub it out, then.'

'Hey, crew, why don't we just turn up late?'

'Oh sure. I'm keeping that tactic for when hard times hit.'

'You're a greebol.'

'You're gimboidal yourself.'

'Come on, we don't want to be late or we'll only get more shit from Corsair.'

ENGLISH LESSON

Miss Kořenová enters the classroom and ascends her throne.

'Right. Any volunteers?'

'None,' comes a chorus of replies.

'Don't be silly, girls. There are some very bad marks here in my book.' She is looking at her police files and without lifting her eyes from them names Llama.

'But Miss Kořenová, you picked on me last time. It's not right.'

'I know I did, but you got a paltry F.'

'You know what, Miss Kořenová, you pick on her nearly every lesson.'

Llama turns to the rest of the class and conducts the chorus. 'Help me, crew! Try to talk her out of it.'

'It's not right, Miss Comrade ...'

'Langmilerová is going to be tested. Come on, Eva, up you come.'

'I don't want to, really I don't,' Eva protests. She turns to me. 'Katka, do something, for God's sake. I'm as hollow as a bamboo.'

'Did you see that film on the television yesterday, Miss Kořenová?'

'No, Kateřina, I did not see it. Eva, take the stand.'

'Oh, that's a shame. Wouldn't you like me to tell you what happened?'

'No I wouldn't. All right, Eva. The History of the United States.'

Nothing to be done. Victim approaches board.

Revolver is hugging the desk in apparent boredom. Mellow is adding colour to her face. Slush turns round. 'Tom-toms, Katka.'

The knocking resounds through the classroom. No response from Corsair. Tom-tom reprise.

'Please Miss Kořenová, there's someone at the door.' The pirate pays no heed. Knock, knock for a third time.

Without even glancing in my direction Corsair responds in her usual way. 'Leave it out, Kateřina.'

Boring. Mellow turns to me. 'Do a frog.' I make a face and croak. Revolver moos. Mellow starts to cluck. Quietly to begin with, but then more and more voices join our menagerie and soon we are barking, mooing and clucking at full throttle. Corsair doesn't so much as bat an eyelid. It's as if she doesn't hear us.

'She must be deaf,' Šustrová chimes in with a shake of the head. We're getting fed up with it now. Llama goes back to her seat with another Fail. She slams her exercise book down on the desk. 'Frelling brill. You cowbags cackle and cluck and you don't even fart me a prompt.'

'You should have done some work, birdbrain,' says Revolver
with an air of indifferent superiority.

'Right, who's next?' says Corsair, stirring the pot. 'So far
as you're concerned, Eva, it will be just the same next time.
Right then, girls, who's volunteering? No one? Again?' She acts
amazed.

'Right then, we'd better Eenie Meeny Miney Moe it.'

'Heavens no, Miss Kořenová,' the class screams in unison.
'How about a lovely conversation class? We'd be happy to sing
you a song.'

Nothing helps. Eeney Meeney Miney Moe it is.

'Looks like it's Eeney Meeney Miney Monika.'

'Me again?' Pařízková objects. 'That's not fair.'

'Don't blame me.' Corsair shrugs her shoulders. 'You think I
calculate my eeney mineys at home beforehand and then feign
surprise when it falls on who I've chosen?'

Shoe String eager beavers, Revolver sounds like she's snoring
and Mellow is out of it. I make myself at home behind my desk
and prop my legs up on the radiator. Under the desk I've got a
pouch of Drum baccie so I'm rolling my own. It's my little idyllic
moment. If it were summer I'd open the window and drink in the
view. Revolver throws me a dreamy gaze. 'Look at you, you've got
it all. You look so cool. All you're missing is some gum.'

'Get me some, then.'

Revolver rummages for gum in her peniscil-case. Finally she
passes some across and I start chewing so as to look even more
cool. Llama's got over her ordeal by now and turns to me.

'Gizza slap.'

'Sure.'

'Thanks.'

I nudge Shoe String. 'Get me Revolve.'

She does so.

'What's your problem, prannet?' says Revolver in her usual terms of intimacy. 'Can't you see I'm listening? Here I am trying to follow the orals and you're dragging me away from them.'

'Sorry, pet. Coming for a cig?'

'Sure.'

'To the changing-rooms?'

'You must be mad. That's miles away. Don't freak out, baby, it's the toilets for us.'

'All right. Wait for me.'

'Bring some matches, Soda Pop.'

Corsair has finished examining and gets ready to start on a new lesson. In the end we deign to open our exercise books and put pen to paper: *So the President of the United States is elected every four years for a four-year term and can be elected ...*

'Sidonová, where do you think you've got your feet?'

Obediently I take my feet off the radiator and slide them under Llama's bum.

'Hey mudsucker, stick them up your own.'

'Yours is more comfy.'

'Yours is two metres wide.'

'*... the president has the right to veto legislation, in which case the bill can be passed ...*' we write full-on till there's smoke coming out of our ears.

Mellow is the first to object with her well-known, 'This is just too much.' Other voices start to join in: 'Enough Miss Kořenová, enough!'

'My hand's falling off.'

'My head is too.'

Corsair shakes her head. 'Just look at you, girls, such a feeble little bunch.'

Enter Brabec with more police files. No sooner is she through the door than she announces: 'Martyš is in a foul mood today.'

'Is she going to give us orals?'

'Naturally.'

'In what?'

'The poet Horký.'

'Holy slut!' Revolver is swearing off steam. 'I'd been revising Majakovsky.'

'Serves you right, you little boff, you could have spared yourself the swotting.' Slush sniggers at her.

'That's enough, Jana, off you go.' Corsair looks up from the class attendance book. 'Girls, get out your sick notes.'

I stand up together with the others. 'Shoe String, cross your fingers for me.'

'She won't be able to tell.'

'I'm not so sure.'

I move past Vestal. 'Been shirking, have we, Soda Pop?'

'I was on my deathbed, dumbo.'

I show her the sick note. 'You signed that yourself, didn't you? What's this? More menstruating pains?'

'I'm always really sick, Miss Kořenová,' I answer, playing the penitent. If only the poor thing knew how I'd dragged my father out of bed that morning in order to get the note. Dad had thrown me a sleepy glance as he said: 'Playing truant again?' 'I just don't feel like going to school today.' 'Mum knows about this?' 'No way.' Dad heaved a sigh and went to make coffee. He called out from the kitchen: 'But don't start thinking I'll sign it for you.' 'No worries, I'll sign it myself.' Time for another paternal sigh. There's nothing he can do. His daughter's cut loose.

Corsair gives us a show of indignation. 'I told you I wasn't going to accept excuses like this.'

Now Llama is the one to protest. 'So what are we 'sposed to do? We might come to school and collapse right here.'

'Knowing you, you would.' Corsair smirks and I realise that I'm going to get away with it.

'Yeah, and that Grauová girl,' Revolver chips in. 'What about her? She's allowed to spend years visiting the gynaecologist, isn't she?'

'Isn't the gynaecologist her uncle?' Mellow's pushing the envelope.

'And all the time she's sitting in the Klementinum library and cramming for the university entrance exams.'

'Is your mouth on overtime?' Corsair is really getting mad now. 'You're a terrible bunch. You skive off, you smoke – yes, Slejšková, don't give me that look, it's your smoking that gets to me most.'

'Why me in particular?'

'I don't even know. It's simply that I mind it in you the most. Who are the other chimneys?' She turns to the class. ' Uři, what about you? Got your cancer sticks, have you?'

Uři pulls out something low tar. Corsair wails 'Veselá?'

'Left them at home.'

'Langmillerová!'

'I'm a fan of the Czech Sparta.' She takes out her coffin nails with pride.

'Good God! Don't show them to me!' She clasps her hands to her head. 'I'm not supposed to see them.' She continues her interrogation.

'Kateřina.'

'Roll my own.'

'Yuck. Šustrová.'

'Don't smoke.'

'You don't say.'

'No really. I don't smoke, do I, crew?'

We mumble agreement.

'Ryvolová.'

'Got them.'

'Good God, Karla. You're supposed to say: "I haven't got any".'

'I've got some right here.'

'That doesn't matter. You're supposed to say that you haven't and tomorrow you won't.'

'But you wouldn't want me to lie, would you? I have got them and tomorrow I won't.'

'Alright.' Corsair starts to calm down. 'As of tomorrow I'll be checking your bags for narcotics.' She gives Revolver another look. 'You've spent the whole lesson slouched over your desk. Show me your exercise book. I bet you haven't got anything written down.'

'I beg your pardon Miss Kořenová, you're not doing me justice.' She shows her the notes she's taken.

'Goodness me, Karla, I owe you an apology,' she says in an ironic tone.

Revolver dismisses the remark with a condescending wave of the hand. 'No harm done.'

The bell rings. Bliss was it in that dawn to be alive, but to be smoking in the toilets was very heaven.

BREAKTIME

Ciggies up their sleeves and matches in their pockets, a file of girls abandons the classroom and heads for the gents. They pass Plastik and Liška in a huddle of gossip, while the sound of the chattering twins from 3C reverberates in the distance. 'Pavel, keep guard for us.' Mellow appoints Winking Málek to be the look-out. They open the door of the Gents where they're welcomed by clouds of smoke and rank odours.

Jaroušek shouts in delight. 'Jesus, girls, who's got one for me?' Vráťa, who has come with the need loos were designed to satisfy, gives a resigned shake of the head. 'It's a bit much when a guy can't even come here to urinate.'

'Hey, what would we do if, say, Kiss of Death turned up here?'

'Unzip and make out we're pissing too.'

'Ha ha ... that would be a laugh.'

'I couldn't. I've got a skirt on.'

'You could hike it up.'

'Boys, has Kiss of Death ever caught you in here?'

'Yeah. Once. He hardly looked at us. Just walked past us and then out again. As if he hadn't seen us.'

A knock on the door. Pavel sneaks a look. 'Girls, it's Kiss of Death!'

'Great Zot!'

We all fall over one another in a scramble this way and that, now for the door, now for the urinal. We succumb to total panic. We scream at one another, stub out cigarettes, clasp our heads in agitation. Finally we all pile into the only cubicle, each with a hand over the mouth of another so that no one gives us away. Someone knocks on the door. 'Come off it, girls. Get out of there.'

'He left?' we ask in a whisper.

Out we come. The boys enjoy the picture we present. It hadn't even occurred to them to stub out.

'Kiss of Death?'

'Never came.'

'Why did Pavel say he was?'

'He never said that he was coming here.'

'Fokken Hail. Frag it to boggeration. To think that it made me climb into that stinking loo ...'

The bell rings. We emerge from the black hole of Calcutta. It is the ...

HOUR OF PHYSICS

Swab is already at her station in the classroom.

'So sorry we're late, Mrs Švábenská, we were with Mrs ...'

'It's quite obvious that you were smoking. Sit down.'

I can smell the stench of nicotine weaving its way through the classroom.

'If only you'd follow your form teacher's virtues rather than her smoking. Do you think it looks fashionable or what?' Swab sighs. 'Right, Sidonová, up you come.'

'Fuck a duck, who gets the luck,' I sigh to myself as I make my way to the board. It's not long before I'm back at my seat with a Fail.

Now it's Burger's turn to sweat it out at the blackboard.

'Right, Burešová, remember the formula.' Markéta does remember it, but a moment later she doesn't know what to do with it.

'For goodness' sake, Burešová, there's not even a smidgin of physics in this, it's pure maths.'

'But we're students of the humanities,' the class cries out.

Swab looks out of the window in disgust. 'So when you have children and they want you to help them with their multiplication tables, are you going to say "I can't. I'm a student of the humanities"?' She turns to Markéta. 'So, what do we do with this '1' in the formula?'

Markéta gives the blackboard her undivided attention. It even looks as though she's thinking. After a long period of reflection she comes up with an answer: 'It's the numerator.'

'No, definitely not,' sighs Swab.

'No!' Burger strikes her forehead with the palm of her hand as if she'd at last worked it out. 'The denominator!'

'That, Burešová, is the only other option.'

At last the grilling is over. 'Right, Sidonová, come up here with your presentation.' The command comes from our bored physics teacher. Llama and I respond by rising enthusiastically from our seats. The class tears itself away from books, schoolwork, noughts and crosses and other sources of entertainment, and lends us its ears. They have been primed with planted questions which they can be called upon to ask when the time is ripe.

Once we arrive at the board we are overcome by paroxysms of laughter. We calm down and begin to read out our masterpiece. It is called *A Journey to the Stars*. But when Llama reaches the sentence: 'At the age of ten little Konstantin Ciolkovsky caught scarlet fever and went deaf as the result of a complication,' we explode into uncontrollable giggling. We try to go on reading, but the sentences that follow merely raise the decibel level of the raucous laughter, which now comes not just from us but from the whole class. All that we could manage in the end was to stammer out in a halting and disjointed manner: 'Every minute of the life I lived with other people was a form of suffering,' he later sighed, 'I felt that I was isolated, excluded and humiliated among them.' We successfully loped through Ciolkovsky's life of suffering and left him to expire. We move on to the next man of destiny, Yuri Gagarin. At this precisely predetermined moment Markéta raises her hand in order to put her question. She braces herself against the desk with her hands, assumes the expression of an imbecile and starts to ask in a tone of mock simplicity: 'So tell me, this Mr Gagarin guy, when he was in this outer ...' She gets no further, in view of the fact that half the class has collapsed in fits of laughter. After a few vain attempts to complete a whole sentence she at last succeeds in doing so. She asks whether he could live a normal life when he was always stuck in Star City with the cosmonauts.

'Gagarin,' we reply, 'was a man of many interests. He went swimming and skiing, he spent his free time playing basketball, he sang in a choir and he played games with his daughter.'

Another hand flies into the air. Swab looks a little riled, but is unable to head off another question. 'How much did his space rocket weigh?'

With the air of true scholars we look at our notes and provide precise figures for the weight of a rocket both with Gagarin in it and without. Mrs Švábenská raises glazed eyes heavenwards. Our presentation ends with a consideration of whether there is life in outer space.

'The answer to that lies in the stars – in this case literally in the stars. Human beings have fastened their gaze upon them and have prayed to them for thousands of years. We are the ones to conquer them.'

The lesson begins after our presentation. The class takes no notice of Swab. Communication is in full flood. At the back Andrea is talking in a low voice to Regas, Katzová is reading forbidden literature under the desk, Zvolánková is combing her locks, Bláža is squeezing her blackheads, Uři is reading Nezval, Llama is putting her face on, Slush is plucking at her eyebrows, Vestal is cutting something out, Malenická is boffing for biology, Revolver is scoffing, Mellow's bored, Shoe String is raving about Pavel, Macek and Brabec are writing me a note, Grauová is catching up on her homework, Bamboo is copying marks into the police files, Pablo and Víťa are playing Mastermind, Ludicrous is mugging up English, Acorns is writing a note to Revolver, Edgar is sitting dejectedly contemplating Marx, Hyba is snacking, Gaspipe is gossiping with Ilonka, Pařízková is moistening eye-liner with her tongue, Neumannová stinks, Tereza is translating something from Polish, Halka is absent, Saša is motionless. Přibylová is chatting with Galaš, Daniela and Mikeš are actually paying attention.

'By now you can see that this will be a straight line,' says Swab more or less to herself, 'at this point I will try to bisect it.'

'Just you try, cowbag,' I hear from Llama behind me.

Without turning round from the board, Swab remarks: 'I can do without your advice, Langmillerová.'

Llama stiffens. But nothing comes of it and on we go. Shoe String nudges me. 'Hey, Pavel hasn't found that condom in his pencil-case yet.'

'He probably hasn't opened his pencil-case,' is Vestal's view of the situation.

'We can ask him for his eraser,' it occurs to me.

'No we can't, he'd know at once what was going on,' Shoe String observes quite correctly.

'Ask Ludicrous.'

'Luďka!'

'What do you want?'

'Ask Pavel for an eraser, but don't say it's for us.'

'You what?'

'Go on.'

'Are you soft in the head or what?'

But she does as she's told. Pavel opens his peniscil-case. We take an inconspicuous peek at him. He sees IT. We in turn see his ears turn as scarlet as the Red Flag. He looks around the classroom and his gaze comes to rest where we're sitting. We are taking a very close interest in our exercise books, which is precisely what gives us away. He passes the condom back to us. 'You left something with me, girls.'

Now it's our turn to go scarlet. Vestal and the girls behind us start a chorus of giggling. Then the boredom sweeps back over us. No new note from Macek and I've got nothing to do.

'Luďka, lend me that bag you keep your writing gear in.'

'What for?'

'I need an ink eraser.'

'I haven't got one. Besides, you use a ballpoint.'

'Never mind, I'll borrow something else.'

Shoe String treats me to the same look of incomprehension as Ludicrous. I already have the bag. Holding it inside the desk, I carefully remove the writing gear. 'Shoe String, you've got a sanny, right?'

'Are you on the rag or something?'

'Frinx off, I just want to borrow it.'

'What are you doing with it? Ho capito!'

She pulls out the sanitary towel and we end up shoving it into the bag together. 'Thanks, Luďka.'

'Don't mention it.' She grabs the bag. 'What did you put in here ... you pigs!' She chucks the towel into the air. It touches down on Halka's desk. 'Yuck!' Take-off time for the towel again. Viktor turns round and his eyes start out of his head. He taps his head at our madness and goes back to the Mastermind players. Finally that pilchard Endrštová places the towel in front of her on the desk and writes on it with a red felt-tip: 'The Sanny of Sanity.'

GEOGRAPHY LESSON

'The United ... States of ... America ... has abund ... ant reserves ... of what? ... of mineral resources...' Mrs Šmídová talks in a monotonous voice that seems designed to send us to sleep.

'And where do they drill for oil? Anyone? Hm? Ryvolová?'

But sweetly a-slumber Revolver is not in response mode.

'Revolver, wake up!' Mellow nudges her.

'Jesus, what's got into you?' snarls Revolver. Then it dawns on her that she's in class. 'Who, me? All right, I'm on my way.' She gets up and heads to the board.

'No, you gimboid,' gasps Mellow.

'What? What the flup's going on?' Revolver is getting narked.

'Where do they drill for oil?' Mrs. Šmídová repeats the question.

'Sorry?'

'Where do they drill for oil, you numbskull?' prompts Mellow in a low voice.

'Ah yes ... oil ... oil ... yes, drilling ... boring ...'

Mrs Šmídová turns to Probs. 'Přibylová?'

'In the Gulf of Mexico.'

'Well done. Sit down.'

'In the Gulf of Mexico, I knew that too,' recalls Revolver with a sleepy sigh that takes her head back into its position of contentment on the desk.

The boredom is insupportable. The projector drones on. Meanwhile something begins to pong in the classroom.

'Can you smell it?'

'What?'

'Something stinks.'

'What?'

'Can't you smell it?'

'No.'

'You're thick as shit.'

'You're thick as shit in the neck of a bottle. Wait a minute, something reeks in here.'

And so the word spreads from desk to desk. The stench may be non-existent, but mass hysteria has been unleashed. The whole class sniffs the air before the first shrieks fill it: 'Stink bomb!'

'Gas attack!'

'No, something's on fire.'

'... and when we come to consider non-ferrous metals then we must mention zinc, cobalt, copper ...'

'Mrs Šmídová, there's something really niffy in here.'

'And these metals are to be found where? In the Cordilleras.'

'It must be the projector.'

'... then again, the United States is also home to a range of precious metals such as ...? Procházka?'

'Which one?'

'The one who's speaking.'

'But something's stinking the place out here.'

'Ackermannová, which precious metals?'

'Gold. Mrs Šmídová, I think something's happening to the projector.'

'Jesus, it's going to explode!' someone yells.

'Get some gas masks!'

'And where do we find gold? In California ...'

'We'll suffocate! We're going to be burnt alive!'

'And what else is California famous for?'

'Shouldn't someone be sent to the head's office to sound the alarm?'

'For the cultivation of fruit. And what fruit in particular are we talking about?'

'Mrs Šmídová, you haven't an ounce of feeling.'

'Citrus fruits. And now let's move on to the mining of black coal, which is important for which branch of industry?'

'Jesus, I don't want to die, I haven't had a life yet!'

'Electricity generation. And black coal is mined mainly in the central region of the United States. In which city?'

'Do something, Mrs Šmídová!'

'In the city of Detroit. And what other industry do we associate with Detroit?'

'Switch off the projector!' someone screams at the top of his voice.

Mrs Šmídová goes over to the socket. 'The automobile industry. And this city is situated in which region?' She switches off the projector.

'The Great Lakes,' the whole class replies in a single sigh of relief.

CZECH LESSON

'Action stations!'

'Saints alive,' I freak out, 'you mean it's Czech?'

'Yes.'

'Get in position!' I yell too.

'Which one?' comes the quick retort from Shoe String.

'Try 69,' a few of us chime in.

'I'd prefer something more traditional,' sighs Llama.

'I'd prefer nothing.'

'So! Soda Pop doesn't like sex?'

'Definitely not with Klapr.'

'Does he still do it kneeling?'

'Yes.'

'Tell him, then.'

'I'd feel like an idiot.'

'Yeah, but this way you'll get old waiting for an orgasm.'

'Go to hell.'

'Study position!' Acorns shouts out.

'Get into study mode, Vestal.'

'That's what I'm in.' She stays standing where she is.

'Hey, don't be a prat, he'll get really narked.'

'Don't twist your knickers.'

Enter the Great Master Hoznauer. He glances at Vestal but doesn't say a word. Guiltily she sits down. We are silent. So is Ozostomia. He stares through the window without a word. Five minutes go by before he finally says in a tone full of irritation: 'So, young ladies, how many times do I have to tell you that you are the showcase of this school? That's why you have to behave accordingly.' Five further minutes of silence on both sides. We nudge Llama: 'Llama, you're on duty.'

'Jesus,' she stands to attention and announces: 'No change in the number of absentees.'

Ozostomia makes an entry in his file.

Slush nudges me from behind with the words, 'Katka, anthologies of Neruda, tell me quick!'

'Well, *Tales from the Lesser Quarter* ...'

'That's not from a poetry collection, you airhead.'

'I didn't say it was a collection of poems,' I object. 'OK, poetry, let's see, there's *Cemetery Flowers, Cosmic Songs, Plain Themes, Ballads and Romances, Books of Verses.*'

'And the sixth?'

'There's a sixth?'

We turn to Halka. 'So, Heckler, how many collections of poems by Neruda are there?'

Halka exercises the grey matter. 'Well, there's *Plain Themes, Friday songs, Cosmic Songs, Ballads and Romances* and *Cemetery Flowers*.'

Slush counts on her fingers. 'That's still only five. What's the sixth, for frek's sake?'

Master Hoznauer finally turns away from his favourite window. 'So, young ladies, we will proceed with a culture test. Take out a sheet of paper.'

'Farking iceholes, I'll get a Fail again,' sighs Slush from behind me.

'Don't tear a page out of your exercise-book,' I mutter.

'Especially not the one you use for Czech,' Shoe String completes my thoughts.

'Don't tear a page out of your exercise books,' Ozostomia continues, 'Least of all the one you use for Czech.'

Acting in unison, we all tear out the middle page of our Czech exercise books.

'Question one ...'

'Katka, just prompt me a little,' whimpers Slush in desperation. 'That Czech painter who died recently, give me his name, quick!'

'I don't know, you greebol.'

'You should turn away from your neighbours, impolite though it may be, lest you be diverted into plagiarism,' purrs Ozostomia.

'This is going to be such a pile of shit,' moans Llama.

'So, ladies, first question. List all anthologies of poetry by Jan Neruda.'

'You really mean all of them?' comes our brainless complaint.

'All means all.' Ozos closes the conversation on a severe note.

The questions are dictated while Zvolánková mutters something under the breath she is too scared to take.

'Right, Zvolánková, black mark,' declares Ozos, the muttering having come to his attention.

'But Mr Hoznauer, I didn't do anything!' comes the protest from Swallow.

'There will be no discussion. A black mark it is.'

'Yes, Zvolánková, a black mark,' – the class oozes *schadenfreude*.

A few minutes later Ozos glances around the class. 'Put down your pens and hand in your tests.'

It's all over.

'Shambles is not the word for this,' comments Shoe String, summing up the feelings of the rest of us.

After a short period in which Ozostomia allows us to let off steam, we return to the topic of the day. 'Which of you has not read *Notes from the Gallows*?' A forest of hands goes up. An expression of disgust etched onto his face, Ozos demands: 'Give me your names.'

'Pařízková.'

'Miss Pařízková, tell me what mark you want to get in Czech. Fail for NŠ (*Nikola Šuhaj The Bandit*), Fail for BM (*Ballad of a Miner*) – just what do you expect?'

Next victim.

'Suchomelová.'

'You can't be meaning this seriously, Suchomelová. Fail for NŠ, Fail for BM, Fail for PC (*The People come to a Crossroads*) and now a Fail for NG.'

'Please, Mr Hoznauer, I have read *Nikola Šuhaj* by now.'

'All right. What about the others?'

'I will read them all.'

The expression of disgust becomes visible again as Ozos turns back to the window. 'What do you know about Fučík, Prooocházka?'

Viktor gets to his feet. 'Julius Fučík was a Communist.'

'Anything else?'

'He edited the Communist Party newspaper Rudé Pravo and was a member of the illegal central committee of the Communist Party of Czechoslovakia. Then the Nazis arrested him, imprisoned and executed him.'

And what would you say of him, now that you have read *Notes from the Gallows*?'

Viktor shifts from one foot to another, evidently with no idea what to say.

'Prochááázka?'

Edgar stands up at his desk. We are waiting for another blunder. We don't have to wait long.

'Julius Fučík was a Communist,' Edgar pronounces in a firm voice that doesn't waver.

'We've already heard that from Prooocházka. Please sit down.' He offers a bored wave of the hand. He goes on to inform us that he will read to us some article published before the war. It is about how a poor working man is happier than a rich one. 'Even the washerwoman finds a song to go with her work.'

'What a frakhead that Fučík was,' comments Slush from behind me.

'What else would you expect from him?'

Shoe String weighs into the discussion with 'It so happens that *Notes* is not such a bad book.'

'Wouldn't know. Haven't read it.'

'I didn't see you at confessions with your hand up, Soda Pop.'

'I know about the book.'

'It's not so naff. It's at least readable.' Shoe String continues her campaign.

'Anyway, he didn't write it.'

'That's what they say.'

Meanwhile Ozostomia sounds out the class for reactions. He even calls upon me to give my opinion on the article. I stammer in my usual manner, so that barely a word can be extracted from me. Heckler says something like it seems strange to her that Ol' Jules would write in that way. Now Ozostomia's face lights up with a kind of pleasure: 'And what about you, Mr Prochááázka?'

'I liked the article,' Edgar pipes up proudly.

'And why did you like it?'

'I think Fučík's great.'

'Yes, but if you think an author's great it doesn't mean you have to think all his works are great.'

'I think everything he wrote is great,' says Edgar, holding his ground.

Ozostomia waves a worn-out hand. 'Pray sit down. Fučík didn't write this article at all. It was written by Karel Čapek.' He fixes Edgar with an expression of triumph. 'What do you say now, Mr Prochááázka?'

He doesn't bat an eyelid. He runs the Czech teacher through with the force of his glare.

LATIN LESSON

Mrs Brožová is at the blackboard talking something over with Uři, Šárka, Tereza, Daniela and Markéta, all taking their matriculation exam in Latin. Meanwhile I redeploy to join Revolver, Mellow and Katz in the window position, where we take over Markéta's seat.

'Hey crew, come and play Who's doing it with Whom?'

'I don't know that one,' boos Mellow.

'Yes you do, you greebol. It's the one with the little pieces of paper.'

'The ones you fold over without seeing what was written before, add a phrase, and unfold to read the whole sentences?'

'That's the one.'

We scream with laughter as we read out: Squinting Edgar and Hyba the Halfwit were in front of the windows of their shepherd's croft, discussing *Years of Crisis for the Party and the Lessons We Learned from Them*. Up came Salivator. He said to them: 'I hope that you're thinking of your class identity.' They answered: 'Where else could we do it but here?'

Farting old Llama and Slarty Sidonová were kicking arse and having fun in the bullrushes on the bonnie bonnie banks of the river, just before orgasm. They started feeling sleepy and she said: I'll sort things out here. They answered: Shut your gob and paddle off.

Robert half-sharp Redford and Yo-yo knickers Natasha were sifting through the corpses of small children during an air-raid in Kazakhstan. Up came the eternal Jew and said: Gary Glitter and Anal Spread, This is the sign upon our head. They answered unto him and said: You know what? Better push off.

Physical Kiš and skanky Blažková were squeezing each other's spots during a total eclipse of the sun in Mobi's Bar. Up came Miss

Martínková and said: Hands up! They answered: we wouldn't give you the steam off our piss.

Dirty Ozos and shitty Martyš were farting and dumping on the desks at school day before yesterday. Up came the General Secretary and said: I detect foul odours. They replied: Give us a rimming.

Edgar Little Mr Procházka 1, an individual at last, joins swotty Cáchová scavenging in the metro litterbins at five to eight in the morning. Up came Zvolánková and said: Give me vouchers to shop in the Tuzex shops where the vanguard of the proletariat buys decadent western goods. They answered: Bloody 'ell, not her again.

Shagged out Eddy and washed-out Snow White were engaged in sexual intercourse of the 69 type at dawn on the floor of the head teacher's office. Up came a good friend who said: Stop it, you pigs. They answered: We'll learn it by tomorrow.

A pizza-faced Russian radical and a slutty caretakeress were having a noncommittal flirt in Hollywood on the eve of the GORE (Great October Revolutionary Explosion). Up came Pavka Korčagin the communist legend and said: who's been eating my gingerbread? They said: Yet you wouldn't risk your neck to find out, would you?

We're having so much fun that for once the bell comes as a troublesome interruption. We pack our things.

THE CLOAKROOM

Screams ring out: 'Hanka, when can we have a peek at your history essay?'

'What's the homework for English tomorrow?'

'Shit, I've got to get coal for my grandma.'

'Are you off to Mobi's?'

'Anyone lend me dosh for fags?'

'Hey Galaš, couldn't the class fund run to lending me ten crowns?'

'You owe thirty already. When you give some back, you can borrow some again.'

'Hanka plea-ease!'

'You heard what I said.'

'You scrof. Hey crew, who can slip me ten crowns?'

'Time for a sharp exit.'

'Where's my scarf, you slummock?'

Constant din and confusion go with us as we graduate to the cloakroom which has already burst into song. Everybody's yelling. I'm yelling too. 'Week ending, la la la, week ending, la la la, week ending, weekend sta-a-a-arting!'

Someone's full-throated roar adds to the mayhem. 'Tomorrow I'm free all day long, how am I going to get along?'

'Coming to Mobi's, Katka?'

'You bastich, where are my shoes, where have you put my shoes, you little slitches?'

Andrea sways her hips as she slips on her jacketsky and sings 'Nománě, dount jú uant mý, bejby ...'

'Give me him to hold, I'll kiss and blow ...'

'Nománě, dount jú uant mý nááááu.'

'You whores! Wait for me, you wassock!'

'This toothbrush.'

'I can't, I've got to get coal for my grandma.'

'Just lend me enough for a coffee.'

'Is Beanpole hanging around for you?'

'Gott im Himmel, where are these shoes of mine?'

'He's not going to wait, Love soon goes out the gate,' sings Andrea.

'Try Class C. You might find them there.'

'Puckernuts to Class C.'

'Come on, who can I cadge from?'

'Forget Granny and come to Mobi.'

'I can't, I just can't.'

'Owwwch, stop treading on my hand.'

'Who's got their jacketsky on my peg?'

'What are you doing throwing my coat on the floor?'

'You shouldn't go hanging your cast-offs on my peg.'

'Christ, come on, I'm in a hurry.'

'What are you doing Sunday?'

'No idea. Shit, what's this?'

'What's what?'

'My hug-me-tight's coming apart.'

'Hardly a surprise if it's got to hug you.'

'Got your shoes?'

'Yeah. They were next door with Class C.'

'Fraz those mudbloods.'

'Ohhhhh they stink.'

'The week's over!' The lone scream is heard.

The crew makes its way out of the school. Some head for Mobi Dick's, others go home, out to a date, in to swot, up to the mountains, off to their cottages, and so it goes on – possibilities are infinite.

CLOSURE

Translated by Mark Corner

Elegy

Who could have given her such an idea? Such a slender long neck and she goes and cuts her hair so short.

She held her satchel by the strap, the clasp gradually coming undone.

In the end she took the burden under her arm.

The shimmering air swayed sleepily in the dark. In the tiled house a window clicked and the risqué rhymes of a favourite pop hit spilled onto the pavement.

She stopped and lifted her head.

A couple walking past her did the same. When they didn't find anything remarkable in the sky, they burst into hiccupping laughter: 'We used to do that too, but we ...'

The tired maple trees were dozing off, shaking off leaves like open hands. She crushed them with her heels and inhaled the end of summer. A worried fox terrier approached her from the shadows. She didn't seem in a hurry.

I looked old in that chignon. It's so stifling hot I can't wait for the autumn its smell is the best and one can see the farthest in autumn. What time is it I wonder past eleven I guess. Not a single star but those clouds they seem so low if the chimneys weren't stabbing them they might come all the way to the ground. Warm summer fog. Warm summer fog. It's fuggying. Those clouds are so that's what the sea must look like. – What are you laughing about you two what was it you used to do too? – The leaves smell nice smell best when you step on them. Of earth and rot. This bothersome bag can just. Smell old-fashioned and bitter. Like a forgotten cemetery for children born November 1893 died February 1894. Or like when you bite into a fallen chestnut. Look at the shadow. I look so different with the haircut what will he say. Good thing the street is so long one two three four every fifteen steps a tree what are these trees called.

At the corner the dog sniffed her. He was obviously satisfied with his findings and decided to follow the girl.

She walked faster.

The heat made the dog weary but he stepped up his pace. When she looked over her shoulder, he pretended nothing was happening and took an intense interest in the lowest part of the tree trunks. He didn't want to bother the young lady. He had a clear opinion on loyalty. But a lost master is a lost master.

She was nearly running.

In the end she broke into a desperate sprint.

The dog in full speed hadn't the time to properly feign his concern for the dried-up yellow puddles. He didn't like half-done jobs and moreover now was no time for fun and games. Oh no. My master got himself lost at dusk and I can hear the last tram rattling in the distance.

After this brief reflection the dog elected to lay all his cards on the table. He was not going to take any notice of the young lady's indignation. He was true to his word. He stopped observing the moist landmarks and shamelessly scampered after the young lady with his tongue hanging out. The whole scene resembled an extremely hurried dog-walking.

He was brave. But the look in her eyes when she saw he was still on her heels was difficult for him to bear. – Just you frown, madam. I don't care. Night is upon us and I wouldn't mind a bite to eat. You'll just keep me overnight and in the morning I'll set everything straight. You don't agree? Oh but you will. I'll look at you like this and that will be it. It's guaranteed. Not the first time they lose me. – Such were the thoughts the dog entertained while he ran with his head turned to face her.

Well look at you! You got lost where is your master where is he then? Hungry aren't you and I don't have anything on me right now. Furry doggie. Silly doggie. No don't do that please no. You can't follow me stop it. They won't let me bring you home I'm so sorry don't look at me like that look here. Hm? A trace? See you'll be fine. No? Ah, just a puddle stay by the puddle. There. No don't do that and don't hide among the trees I can see you. Listen I live far away I have to take the tram can you hear it and then you'd never find your master. Once I brought a kitten home and I had to take it back out to the street that very night I can't run anymore please just understand I feel really sorry for you but I can't help you. I cannot and don't you with your eyes puppy sad as if you didn't know what kind of dreams I've been having.

The tram slowed at the bend. The girl jumped onto the platform. The panting dog stiffened his tail in surprise. He slowly turned around and nonchalantly wandered back. He was clearly

offended. – If I knew how, I'd step with my left paws first and
then with my right, to show you how I couldn't care less, madam.
– A white lump enticed him to the pavement. – Well well well,
what have we here? Wouldn't mind a drink after that marathon,
but all things edible be praised. We'll eat the bun and then see
what next. –

A closely cropped head was catching its breath in the tram.
She looked out the grimy window until the dog disappeared in
the warm blackness.

*Look a number nine I've never jumped onto a moving tram I'm
terribly scared but I'll do it now otherwise I'd never get rid of you
rid of you. Today's been a bad day for you like me. It's at the corner
already you'll find your master tomorrow for sure. I know Mrs
Conductor but there was a dog running after me this window is
so dirty where is he I have a stitch so hot there he is. Why are you
looking at the ground you are sad me even more. And it was such a
sweet smelling evening.*

Two bow-ties were bobbing on two Adam's apples. The boys were
kneading pairs of sweaty gloves. They were confiding to each
other excitedly in croaky voices and then shrieking with laughter.
A well-wrapped granny was guarding a basket of gooseberries.
In the corner a railwayman's head was dropping down onto his
chest.

When the girl jumped on, the bow-ties slid down, up, and
exchanged a knowing comment. Then they immediately returned
to their previous worries.

The elderly woman shook her head and popped a berry into
her toothless mouth. Her dry cheeks puffed out and deflated only
when the last pip had been spat out.

The new arrival did not wake up the sleeping railwayman.

A coquettish redhead with a hen-like expression raised her blue eyebrows and glanced at her wrist.

But the girl stood stuck to the glass and misted it up with her breath.

The conductor was a plump blonde moulded by her uniform and decorated with clanging earrings. She sat on the bench rolling coins into stacks with the fingers of baroque cherubs. At every stop she would stand up lazily, pull the bell and send out a sleepy smile to the driver: 'All clear, František.'

A tall man in a rustling steel-grey topcoat climbed on. He fingered his ticket and folded himself up next to the old woman. 'Take some, young man, picked 'em this morning.' She slid the basket forward. The bow-ties nudged each other, the conductor arranged the curls on her forehead, and the railwayman gave a start. He recognised the street through the crack of his eyelids and stepped off with a curse. 'Don't mind if I do,' the tall man appreciated, and grabbed a clumsy handful.

The girl finally tore herself away from the window. She sat down next to the neat little stacks of coins and focussed all her attention on a thick book.

The conductor leaned back slightly and squinted over the girl's shoulder. The girl jerked her shoulders and gave the podgy face a careworn stare. The earrings clinked angrily, 'What a tetchy person!'

The girl marked her page with her thumb and observed the chubby fingers counting off the coins and packing them into paper rectangles. The hands got exasperated and swept all the packets into a pouch. The girl returned to her book.

The tall man was squeezing the gooseberry between his teeth. It was puckeringly tart. He glanced at the posters above the windows and spat the berry into his hand. He watched the girl with the book.

She motionlessly devoured one page after another.

In vain he searched for the title on the spine.

The twittering bow-ties finished their confidences with 'I swear it's true, man,' and flew down the tram steps into the darkness. A cloud of strong perfume lingered after the soubrette. The granny fumbled for her basket and bumbled out with a 'God bless you folks.' The earrings floated over to the driver and hugged his shoulders.

The tall man did not divert his gaze from the cropped head.

She was oblivious. Until suddenly. The book slammed shut and the satchel swallowed it. The girl got off.

The tall man quickly got his act together. He jumped up and skipped onto the pavement.

The tram clanged, the earrings grinned at the vanishing couple and yawned melodically into the driver's back.

The tall man unbuttoned his cloak and set out after the flustered heels.

That's it. Hopefully he'll find someone else the fluffy pup abandoned this window is a pretty cool mirror why is everyone looking at me are my stocking seams askew? That granny is like mine what's that she's spitting ah the gooseberries. Wow those are some earrings Mrs Conductor we use cherries to decorate our ears always in pairs around each one. Milady I can smell you all the way over here. That railwayman is sleeping he might miss his stop what a life who would want to be a railwayman they ought to ban trains but then how would people travel. What are you staring at little boy I can see you in the window how old can you be you're wearing daddy's suit aren't you little boys should go piddle-widdle and off to beddy-

byes these days they send toddlers to ballroom dancing how can you have a normal conversation with them mademoiselle do you enjoy going to the movies yes kiddo but not with you your hands are sweaty. September it's not the season for balls yet. How does she do it I'd never manage to pack those small coins. František. So you're also František Mr Driver.

Welcome valiant knight untamed glory of the nation at least six feet ten please have a seat well done just like a folding umbrella perhaps a little gooseberry for monsieur have some it won't make you grow taller everyone is wearing this topcoat these days he must be boiling. So the railwayman did miss his stop too bad. I'll sit facing the basketball player and read. Which book? Graves and Scholars I'll never finish it already two reminders. Bother my face powder spilled into my bag I dare say that an average identity card holder can contain a fair quantity of powder oh joy of joys just my luck I'll deal with it later. Anyway that Tutankhamun must have maybe I should have taken that dog after all even though dogs may be transported only with a muzzle isn't that so Mrs Conductor is so. Why did you jerk so suddenly did you catch a cold in this weather those earrings would get on my nerves jingling like that. May I watch you packing I see you first have to catch the edges and then tap it on the side so that it keeps shape well you sure are clever if only you weren't frowning all the time. What happened to you? Oh yeah night shift never mind where was I Hammurabi that would be a good name for the dog.

Stop watching me you beanpole gawking ogling why don't you get off I don't like it burial gifts who is it jewellery vessels what if he follows me Assurbanipal he's gawking I'm scared and must go out I'd rather pass my stop. To be on the safe side. Last stop everyone off I have to go on Mrs Conductor tell František to drive very slowly or rather very fast my hands are shaking I have to get off here no further it must be past midnight!

Is he following me? He is. Help. What should I do. Run. I should have taken that dog if only there were a tram in the other direction now I have to walk back two stops and this man puffing down my neck. Past that long hopeless wall I'll go crazy I'll hit him. With the keys. In the eye. Then I'll kick him. Very hard. Immediately. Now. No. Run. Hey people where are you! Save me! Murder!

The tall man caught up with the heels at the second block.

'To address young women in the street is embarrassing,' he mumbled close to her ear, 'but what was I to do?'

She glanced at him but did not stop. 'What did you want to do?'

'I wanted to introduce myself. My name is Štěpánek. Zdeněk Štěpánek.'

'Dana Medřická.'

The tall man did not change his expression and his outstretched hand was not returning to his side. He seemed intent on the proper ritual of introduction. 'Zdeněk Štěpánek,' he repeated.

He has a nice forehead kind of square nose so-so but teeth like chisels and neat fingernails good.

'I don't like – Zdeněk.'

He was silent. He evidently had time to spare.

The girl slowed down and stabbed a fierce look in his face. He caught it with his eyes and held it. 'Potůčková. Lída,' she whispered and shook his hand.

'You're nice.'

'I'm married.'

'You are married?'

'Yes. And I have a child.'

'Perhaps you are married. But you don't have a child.'

'All right. I don't. But I am married.' She turned away and considered the conversation to be over.

But he was not put off. 'How about we meet once in a while? You wouldn't mind that, would you?'

She took a deep breath. She was surprised to hear herself answer: 'No. I wouldn't mind. On the contrary. You seem friendly. When?'

What did I just say? Like some kind of.

The tall man pulled out a packet. 'What are you reading?'

'What are you smoking?'

'Lípy.' With the cigarette between his lips he added: 'Lasht one.'

She pulled the corners of her mouth downwards.

After he had inhaled some smoke he corrected himself: 'Last one.'

'Absolutely last?'

'No. Last in that packet. I cannot offer you any.'

'I don't smoke.'

'I'd be interested to know what you are reading.'

'In the tram?'

'No. In general. Do you like Salinger?'

'He'd catch up with me faster than you, huh?'

Overlooked. 'The Catcher in the Rye.'

'He that mischief hatches.'

He was patient. 'Have you read anything by Borchert?'

'Who?'

'Borchert.'

'No.'

'And Steinbeck?'

'Escapes me at the minute.'

'Do you like exhibitions?'

'I don't like exhibitions. There's nothing better than a bare wall well white-washed.'

He was onto something. 'What do you think of art in general?' he persisted. 'Do you know Salvador Dalí? Have you seen *Viridiana*? What do you say of Pasolini? How did you like *Violent Life*? What about Françoise Sagan?' Ruthlessly and unrelentingly. A walking confessional.

What do I read I didn't get through a single sentence in that tram he speaks with the cigarette in his mouth and he narrows his eyes when he pulls I shouldn't have answered him but I can't act deaf it looks stupid what's his deal with the reading why does he need to know. Salinger Holden Caulfield and all that jazz but mind your own business Salinger isn't he also that sprinter isn't he. Borchert so you won't give it a rest bedtime reading. Steinbeck. You forgot Winnie the Pooh and Lassie Come Home shame you don't have a dog too. A dog. God what if he's a madman won't he hurt me in a word it's my own fault people who engage in art are fraudsters said Picasso have you heard of him? The public opinion poll and anyway is it really one already?

An unbelievably angular car was parked close to the pavement. The black mudguards shone and the vehicle sheltered a couple inside that was passionately entwined.

'It's one o'clock,' she interrupted the interrogation.

The tall man ignored it.

Not Sagan. One hour past midnight would you please attempt to make yourself aware of this fact.

She pressed her lips together. 'I realise that I have stated information for which you have no category in your questionnaire. Nevertheless it is getting late and dawn is upon us. I must make haste.'

Unwillingly, he had to smile. 'What do you think I do?'

What could you possibly be doing smelling of hospital you disinfected spindlelegs.

'Medicine.'

'Why do you think so?'

'You are steeped in carbolic, my child.'

He sniffed his sleeve. 'What about you?'

'I sell books. Can't smell that, can you?'

With a flick of his wrist the cigarette butt hissed at the bottom of the gutter. 'The colour doesn't suit you.'

'Perhaps. Your ears stick out a bit. Did you know that?'

'I did not wish to offend you. I only wanted to say that the colour doesn't suit you because it truly does not suit you.' He paused. 'Do you hate the truth?'

'Neither did I want to offend you. I only wanted to say that your ears stick out a bit, whereas they stick out considerably.'

On their left a never-ending long wall jeered at them with a huge sign CAR REPAIRS.

The tall man gazed at the girl carefully. 'Are you really like this, or is it a mask?'

'I am really like this.'

'Great. Then I'll be frank. I'd like to have you.'

What? Have me. So that's it. Must get home. Terrifying is this how one speaks to a lady who does he think he is. I'll scream.

She pouted her lower lip slightly. 'Strange.'

'I know. This is not the way it is normally said. – Do you find me attractive too?'

'Sort of. We'll see.'

Something gave way. She walked with incredibly long steps and every now and then would wrap the long figure in a scrutinising gaze. She kicked little stones out of her path with the tip of her shoe and playfully babbled with him on subjects that he promptly raised one after the other.

In front of an old single-storey house she stopped. 'This is where I live. I'm off.'

'Is your husband at home?'

'No.'

'I would like to visit you.'

'Why?'

'To see what kind of things surround you.'

'Now?'

'Why not?'

She would not understand.

'Oh I know.' He smirked. 'You haven't tidied up.'

'I never tidy up.'

'Do you take pride in it?'

'No. I just don't like clearing up.'

'Can you manage to get things done in a mess?'

'I can't. Good night.'

'When will we see each other?'

'In a month at three o'clock in front of the botanical gardens.'

A shaking hand pressed itself into the tall man's palm, then it curled into a ball helplessly for a minute before reaching to the bottom of the satchel.

I should carry the key around my neck you have no idea how happy I am to see the back of you away hurray hurray away he walked away like a daddy longlegs. Do you hate the truth? Salinger Steinbeck exhibitions that colour does not suit you I would like to sleep with you may I do so immediately in a month I'll wait. So that's that.

The distance muffled the squeaking of loafers and a key rattled in a lock.

❧ ❧ ❧

'I don't know which one it could be. I don't mingle with the ones in the higher grades.'

In this godforsaken street most of the shops had gone silent. The communal enterprise Fotografia sported a warning sign in the form of a few emotional brides and determined grooms in its glass display. Among the well-combed babies with candles between their noses and the cakes stood a pensive bearded man with a pipe. Despite the deep issues he was considering he did not forget the camera and presented his face in the best light.

A red scooter speeded down the middle of the street. The rider had been held up somewhere and was making up for lost time. At the corner near the pavement an inebriated character was tottering. He decided to stop the rolling wheels. The scooter screeched in a panic and only just managed to brake in time. The drunkard shook his fist at the cloud of acrid smoke. 'Watch out, you contagious disease! I'll send you to the reformatory! Together with my mother-in-law.'

'That guy overdid it.'

A diffident six-year-old with a school bag on his back carefully steered clear of the teetering figure. Then he stared at the man from afar with his mouth open.

'What are you gawping at, you halfwit!'

'Yesterday they brought us something like that. He had fallen into a pit where the pavement was dug up and broke his skull at the temple.'

The little boy turned around hesitantly and continued on his way. He diligently carried his gym shoes in a bag in front of him. He stepped on it and fell over.

'Did he – die?'

'Of course. They tried operating on him but there was no point.'

An elderly street sweeper was pushing a pile of colourful leaves in front of his broom.

'He was over sixty and still had all his teeth.'

In front of a wooden wheelbarrow the old man straightened his back and fumbled in his pocket. He fished out half a cigarette and lit up with gusto. 'Where are we heading, young ladies?'

'To the autopsy room.'

He pushed his torn cap back and laughed uneasily.

'Surely not.'

'We are indeed, grandpa. Want to come with us?'

He bent down to the dry heap and filled the cart. 'There's always enough time to put that one off.' His eyes were sky blue. 'On we go, buddy.' He gripped the handles and clattered along the pavement.

She was shortish, chubby, and had soft hands like brioche. Ringlets of light hair cascaded over her collar. On her forehead and at the temples it gave way to white downy fuzz. Little forget-me-nots in gold nested in her earlobes. She trod softly like a bunny. Were she to fall, she would keep her hands in her pockets. The scent of cloves enveloped her. The cropped head had to lean down: 'Why did you tell him that?'

'Tell him what?'

'About the dissecting room.'

'What about it.'

'I don't know. He's old.'

The fair head shook. 'You're so naïve.'

A spiky green ball fell off a tree and delivered a moist chestnut.

'Last week we had a four-year-old. They brought him to the hospital with poisoning. He exed out by the morning.'

'Exed out?'

'Exited. Died, you know. Just imagine, he didn't even want the mushrooms. He didn't care for them and the father saw red on account of the kid being too picky. They stuffed it into him by force.'

'They must be going crazy now.'

'They sold him.'

'What do you mean?'

'For the skeleton. Two thousand crowns. Our group did him. He was done in an hour. He had such terribly tiny bones.'

She slowed down. 'I don't think I'll go, Marta.'

'What's the matter? Nobody ever fainted there.'

The wind grabbed an acacia branch and threw a bunch of coin-shaped leaves in the girl's face. 'And doesn't it – smell bad?'

'Unbearable. We suck mints.'

'What of?'

'Formaldehyde. That's what they're preserved in.'

A van rattling past startled a flock of sparrows. A load of

sleds poked out from beneath the canvas. After it was gone the flock returned to the heap of horse droppings.

'Hey Marta do you remember how you were sweating over the entrance exams and meanwhile you couldn't even bear to see a cut?'

The fair head laughed.

'You must have stopped being afraid of it all at a certain point.'

The fair head tilted toward the shoulder.

'I mean. Didn't you sort of. For instance – an amputated arm. Chopped off at this spot. The stump.'

'You get it soaked. Kind of mushy. It looks like boiled beef. At the canteen we gross each other out with it.'

'But the first time!'

'It's hell. The assistant comes, tells you what element he wants you to dissect, goes off, and you have to poke around for it.'

A queue of twenty shoppers stood in front of the greengrocer's. Their hands fingered limp carrier bags while waiting and then brought them out swollen and full of vitamins. Potatoes drummed on the bottom of tin buckets and coins tinkled on the counter. 'He seems to think men don't have to wait their turn!' It smelled of earth.

'And what do you wear?'

'In lab coats. They have a belt in the back and boys hang muscles on it. You walk around the lab and you have muscles floating behind you. Mum didn't want to wash the coat afterward so she burnt it. But I'd have to buy a new one every week.'

'Muscles?'

'Like long fibres. Worse is when he wants something flat. Would you isolate the *planta pedis* for me please, Comrade Čtrnáctá. In that case you have to wait till he turns his back or

someone has to distract him. Then we pat it into shape some
way or another and spit on it. They want it completely clean and
that's impossible.'

The girl looked at the palm of her hand and moved her thumb.
'What about – the stomach?'

'The stomach is the worst. You always cut through something
you're not supposed to. And that's where most of the fat is.
Disgusting.'

'Marta. Do you understand what I'm saying at all? The process
of getting-used-to-it!'

''Cause it's tricky scraping the fat off.'

A perfumed dandy emerged from the barber's.

'What kind of people are they, the ones you dissect?'

'All sorts. Mostly those left unclaimed. They're fine. It gets grim
when they come from the path lab. Blood still dripping and stuff.
Pathology. When you have to investigate the cause of exit. Horrible
stench. These are on the contrary sort of dried-out like. When you
pass your nail over the skin it crackles like parchment.'

A cocker spaniel ran out of a house pulling behind it an upset
lady in a short fur coat. Her hair was the same colour as the dog's.
'Harpagon! Harpagon! Stand still!' She tried to compel the dog to
behave. 'Quiet. Mummy must put on her gloves.' It calmed down,
stood straight respectably for an instant before dashing off at full
speed. The lady affixed to the other end of the string jolted and
hurtled after the animal with long leaps.

'The boys keep taking bones home with them. Once they were
carrying a knee bone in the tram and there was a dog there that was
going berserk.' She stopped. 'Here we are.'

The girl looked through the open gates. Students were shoving
each other and shouting Latin words.

'I'd better not go, Marta.'

'Don't be silly. It's nothing. You'll see.'

'I don't think so.'

The fair head sighed. 'As you wish. But you needn't have dragged me out here.'

'I'm sorry.'

They walked away. 'Then let's go to neurology. I'll show you pictures of schizophrenics.'

❦ ❦ ❦

A thin wind bitterly nagged the pedestrians. They turned their collars up and avoided the puddles. Children splashed their numb hands in murky streams of rainwater.

A tram disgorged a file of nuns. The wind ruffled the black and white habits. The flapping of the cloth was lost in the splashing of the rain.

Terrible weather I can still go back would serve him right the snob what if he doesn't turn up oh he will for sure but god knows what I'm doing here. What if we bump into. We have to sit down somewhere. Yes I am also getting out would you like help with the pram that kid looks like it needs changing. Brrr it's freezing I can still go back I still can but what for.

A tall man was walking back and forth fretfully in front of the botanical gardens. He held a briefcase by its corner. It reached down to his knees.

A bright red fluffy sweater approached him from across the street.

He swung in its direction. 'What are you doing coming so

late? Look at the time,' he tossed his head toward a street clock. 'And how come you don't have an umbrella?'

'I'm short-sighted,' she sent out a cloud of white mist toward him. 'But I recognised you. Because of the coat.'

'Then why don't you adjust your eyesight with lenses?' He leaned over her.

'You must mean glasses.'

He sighed. 'Is something the matter?'

'Where do you want to go in this weather?'

'I wanted to excuse myself for today. I forgot that I have a commitment to a friend.'

I couldn't care less about your friends but I cancelled Russian class.

'You forgot. Or you didn't know about it a month ago.'

'I promised and I keep my word.'

'Far?'

'In Smíchov. I have to bring him a doctor's note. He put himself on sick leave.'

So they're already lending them official stamps not bad.

'That's it?'

He put on a stern expression. 'That's it.'

'Will you stay long?'

'No. I'll just hand it over. Why?'

'If you want I'll come with you.'

'You'd come with me when it's raining cats and dogs?'

They looked around.

'I don't like walking,' he remarked.

'We can take the tram.'

'Not necessary. It's round the corner from here. But afterwards.'

'We'll find a café, no?'

'We'd do better going to my place. I'll light the fire.'

Yes certainly young man no. Visit postponed indefinitely.

'No.'

'Why not?'

She didn't answer.

'Look here. This is silly. I don't see why you couldn't come to my place for a cup of coffee.'

'So. I don't want to.'

The tall man was exasperated and veins popped up on his forehead. 'If you don't want to come to my place because it is not proper for young women to visit men, then in my books you are a bourgeois pure and simple. And I can't stand bourgeois pettiness.' He behaved as though he were alone in the street. He stood and gesticulated in the middle of sentences.

Just you talk all you want I'm not going. So a bourgeois? You look ridiculous when you get angry like a rag doll with badly sewn arms come on they're looking at us.

She waited till he had finished his indignant lecture. Then she said: 'Bourgeois or not. I just don't feel like it.'

He spat out an imaginary speck of dust. 'I won't crawl to you if you don't want.'

Disgusting idea like raw flesh what were you testing my general knowledge for.

They stepped onto the bridge. Waters dark as ink angrily scurried

out of the way of a thousand little sharp gusts and broke into
wavelets.

*The river smells of mud quite pleasantly what are these ducks doing
here in this cold and what do they eat.*

He stopped insisting. 'Tell me something about myself.'

'Twenty-two.'

'Bid higher.'

'I'm talking about the ducks. Don't you have some bread?'

'No. But I wanted to hear something about myself.'

'I have a pretzel. – What? About yourself?' She looked at
him as if he were a cactus that bloomed overnight. 'You have an
ugly nose.'

He shifted his briefcase to the other hand. 'And?'

'And I don't know. I don't care.'

'It could be just a pose,' he thought to himself and said it out
loud.

'So what if it is a pose? I don't care about that either.'

'Explain to me what you are trying to delude yourself
about.'

'I can't say I understand what you are insinuating.'

'Stop acting and we'll understand each other.'

'I'm not acting anything,' she cried out and looked
exhausted.

He took her by the hand.

*The two of us will never find the same wavelength but luckily that's
not what it's about don't hold my hand Prague is a small place.*

'Show me. You'd need some Papparevin Atropin or some jabs.'

'What for?'

'For those fingers. It's –' and he uttered something that she forgot immediately. 'Why aren't you wearing gloves?'

'Sometimes my fingertips go white when it's cold. You think?'

'Don't mess with that. I can show you what it can lead to. I'll bring you photos.'

'Don't bring anything. I'm going to the clinic. I already have an appointment.'

'As you wish. But those photos would move you.'

She jerked.

'What is it?'

'Nothing.'

'I'll be right back. Wait for me at the corner.' The tall man left the girl and vaulted into a house.

She leisurely passed shop display after shop display. She didn't seem impatient.

I'll wait and wait even if he lets me wait for an hour but what if he lives here no why would he do that. Those shoes aren't bad. I'll be right back I'll just hand it over whatever you're doing do it fast because I'm turning blue out here and I have many things to tell you. Isn't that – no thank god he has darker hair. Ten minutes. What if I went away no that might be just what he wants but too bad for him I'll wait. What a funny-looking sieve I wonder how sieve production is planned how does one calculate how many to produce or graters or actually everything. I'll catch a cold for sure my feet are freezing I'm going numb it's taking ages. That's quite expensive nearly two hundred for such a creature. With blinking eyes. Metal construction set Merkur I know that one the gyrating crane TK-08 and a vacuum-cleaner bag full of little screws. That teddy bear is cute or is it a squirrel no a rabbit. Little boy don't cry mummy will buy you a no she won't you should have cried more go warm up. Locomotive engine with a tunnel a bridge and how many carriages at least fifteen. What time is it I'll kill him but I'll wait. Eye Optician I'd like to know what other kind of optician there is opera glasses what if he's spying on me with binoculars from a window no he doesn't look like the type. Campaigning centre Long Live the First of May A Celebration for all Working People nice font. I'm turning to ice. What's he up to it's been nearly twenty minutes. Do Not Bake at Home!

Just as the girl was about to enter the stationery shop he came out of the house. He caught sight of her at the glass doors and flew across the street straight into the shop as though he wanted to prevent the transaction.

She smiled and stood in line.

He grabbed her sleeve. 'Great. That you didn't leave.'

'Your coat is buttoned crooked. Missed a hole,' she scolded him.

His chin hit his tie knot. Begrudgingly he pulled off his gloves.

She halted him. 'Unless you button the extra top button to the extra hole at the bottom.'

He did not enthuse. 'It was warm there,' he mumbled.

She yawned. At least it looked as though she yawned.

At the cashier's a customer's little chin was quivering. Everyone had overlooked him. He leaned with his nose against the counter and sprinkled tears on postcards of Prague under the snow. The cashier stood on her tiptoes, wiped the stain with her elbow and pronounced in a boiled voice: 'And what can I do for you, sweetheart?' Sweetheart carefully wiped the snot over his face with his little fist and whimpered: 'One sticker.' Somebody at the back guffawed. He finally unstuck himself from the counter. The line dragged its feet ever so slightly forward. The queue moved unhurriedly and premeditated every step.

'What do you want to buy?' frowned the tall man. 'Do you know how long we're going to stand here?'

'It's warm here.'

'If you want to speak in metaphors, then be aware that I shall soon fall by the wayside. I had to erase something because they gave me the wrong dates.'

'Look. That pen. The eternal blue.'

'That's what you want?'

'No. A pencil-sharpener.'

'Pencil-sharpener? What the hell for?'

'I don't know. It looks good in the cup of the hand.'

'I'll wait for you outside.'

She tilted her head and wiped her face on the thick damp collar. But she didn't say anything.

He turned to the exit. He staggered around the pavement wrapped in the metallic coat and smoked.

He grumpily stepped on the cigarette butt, glanced at the glass doors and clambered into the telephone booth opposite.

He hung up. The receiver clicked and a quarter-crown unexpectedly fell out of the box. The tall man dutifully reinserted it into the slot and reversed out.

He mingled with the crowd of on-lookers at the food store. Rushing passers-by were tripping over something. He felt a tap on his shoulder.

'I'm here.'

'With the pencil-sharpener?'

'I needed a guiding sheet. I don't know how to write in straight lines.'

He politely announced: 'I don't know how to write straight

either.'

'You should have said earlier. I would have bought two. Now we have to borrow it from each other. But it's mine.' She took out a blue eternal pen and signed the corner of the sheet of lines with care. 'There.'

'You comedian.'

'Close your eyes and open your hand.'

He obeyed.

'I bought you one too.'

A lemon-coloured pencil-sharpener sat on the tall man's palm. 'Thank you. And what should I do with it?' He asked pleasantly.

'Sharpen pencils. Remember that the basic prerequisite for success is a properly sharpened pencil.'

'Did Picasso also say that?'

'No. Daddy did.'

They moved on slowly.

The tall man's fingers played with the pencil-sharpener until it slipped from his hand and splashed into the gutter. He wrapped it in a handkerchief.

'So where are we going?'

He shrugged.

'You know what? Let's go to some church. To the Maltese,' she suggested.

'You believe in God?' he asked.

'No. Why?'

'So why there?'

'It smells nice in churches. Of incense. And there are terribly funny prayers in frames,' she described.

His forehead wrinkled up.

'Do you believe in God?' she asked him.

'... No.'

'So what's the matter?'

'You don't have to make fun of it all. For some people faith means everything.'

'I'm not making fun of faith,' she defended herself, 'only of silly prayers with spelling mistakes.'

He was silent.

She stopped in her tracks, her jaw fell open, and she let him advance three or four steps. Then she gathered her wits and caught up with him. She exclaimed in amazement: 'You are – praying, František?'

He jumped.

'Sorry,' she whispered.

'František!' he hissed mockingly. 'We'll go to the college. The classrooms are heated and one of them will be empty. It's awfully cold in churches.'

❧ ❧ ❧

The spacious hall was loaded with silence and with dry warmth. Endless rows of slanted desks with tip-up seats stretched from wall to wall. A huge blackboard and a grand piano in the corner.

They sat down at the edge of the front row.

'This is where you study?'

'Why are you whispering?' he laughed loudly.

She leaned back and set down her head on the desk behind her. 'Classroom.'

'Lecture hall. Don't you like it?' he was unfastening his coat.

The milky glass globes of the lamps followed their conversation with the obliging stiffness of butlers with serving trays.

'Like in a bank. Or not. Like in a railway station where no train has ever run.'

'That's because of the impossibly high ceiling.'

'Won't somebody come in?'

'Play something. Didn't you learn to play the piano?'

'My hands are freezing.'

'Give them to me.' He warmed her numb fingers in his hands. 'Is it better?'

'Now the other one.'

He breathed into her cupped hands. 'Kiss me.'

'No.'

'You don't like kissing?'

'I like kissing.'

He pulled her toward him, but she wrenched herself free.

'Leave me alone!'

He moved away and looked extremely offended. 'You're only hurting yourself.' Then he returned to her at least with his eyes. 'What kind of a woman are you?'

'A monster. I don't want to kiss someone I don't like.'

'You don't like me?'

'No.'

'Then why are you sitting here with me?'

'Just because. I'm experimenting.'

'Then go on and experiment.' He got up and opened the piano lid. 'Do you know Peer Gynt?'

'Again?'

He withdrew. 'I only wanted to invite you to our club. We chose some scenes from it and we're adapting it as a melodrama with Edvard Grieg. It looks good.'

'The festivities at Jirásek's grave have already taken place this year as far as I know.'

He bent over the keys and stutteringly rapped something out with one finger. 'Won't you play?'

The swivel chair wailed. A timid melody rose.

He drummed on the top of the piano and declaimed: 'The young lady is playing Chopin. Already at the age of five Daddy and Mummy consulted and came to the conclusion that their lovely daughter is extraordinarily talented and has perfect pitch. They called for the best teacher in the country and placed their child into his hands ...'

'Humoresque in simplified style for the benefit of visitors. That's right. Why did you want me to play then?'

'I wanted to check something.'

'So you are experimenting too.'

'So I am.'

She closed the piano and slowly slid back to the tip-up seat.

He climbed onto the lectern directly facing her. He wedged his fingers together like for a prayer and put on a pious air. 'You have small breasts, don't you?'

She nodded. 'Yes. I have small breasts.' She took off her thick sweater. 'It's warm in here.'

'I thought so,' his foot kicked the stand. 'And you like to be alone, isn't that so?'

'I like to be alone very much. But I can never achieve it. Even when everybody leaves the house there's still the canary.'

'So you have a canary! A cosy little cage on the wall! Perfect! I just love that. And what about embroidered pictures, those too?'

She lay down on the desk. 'No cosy little cage. The biggest cage in Central Europe. Imported from the GDR. No hook would hold that one up. Which is not important anyway. Because the bird spends most of its time outside it. I often come home and I can't find it. Calling in vain. Usually it crawls under the couch and does some clearing up there. It only uses the cage for sleeping. Stuck to the perch like a yellow shaving brush. But I worry that it's cold, sitting on the cold thing. So I lined one of the corners of its cosy little cage with a woolly rag but it kicks it away. Naughty birdie.'

He listened to her every word.

'It pecks at everything. Even mackerels. And pigeon meat. Cannibal. But it puts on weight quickly on that diet. Sometimes it enriches its nutrition with earth from the flowerpots.'

'It'll croak soon. Canaries shouldn't get fat.'

'It's not fat. I chase it around the flat so it gets some exercise.'

'Doesn't it escape?'

'Why would it? Where would it get as good care as with us? Its name is Kratochvíl.'

The tall man slipped off the table and approached the girl.

'But I don't embroider pictures. I don't know how to thread a needle.'

He leaned over the desk, narrowed his eyes and said to her from very close up: 'You don't embroider pictures. You don't know how to thread a needle. – I'd really like to know what kind of show you're putting on all the time. You painstakingly stylise yourself and plot evasions. Wouldn't it be easier to talk directly the same as you think?'

She did not budge and answered straight into his face: 'I speak just the way I think.'

'Then explain it to me please. For instance the canary.'

She put her hand to her chin and reflected.

'Tell me, "I love you".'

She said, 'I don't love you.'

'Have you ever been unfaithful to him?'

'No.'

'But you will be.'

'No.'

'You will for sure. You'll see. But I want to be the first one, you understand? How long have you been married?'

'I am not married.'

'How come?'

'I am not married,' she repeated and placed a yellow pencil-sharpener on the tip of her little finger. 'I made that up.'

'Made it up. Why did you lie?'

'I wanted to get rid of you. It was past midnight.'

'You wanted to get rid of me,' he bristled. 'Then why didn't you send me away? Why not? You could have told me to go away. I would have gone. I swear I would have gone away.'

She gazed through the wall. 'I'd like to see you in my shoes.'

'Nonsense,' he snapped. 'In what shoes? I'll never get my head around this. Why can't people just say the truth?'

She tapped the desk with the pencil-sharpener. 'Why did you ask me about Salinger and exhibitions? Why? Did you want to show off your own knowledge or were you looking for an original pick-up line? Go on, tell me! I want to hear it! I want to know why you asked me about it when you actually couldn't care less and all you want is to sleep with me!' She was almost shouting.

'What do you mean, I couldn't care less?' he burst out. But she didn't let him continue.

'Were you inspired by my reading in the tram? But I wasn't reading, I was trying to distract myself from the fact that an annoying man was sitting across from me in a two-hundred-crown topcoat thinking how to quickly and easily get me into bed! You ... and your truth!'

He watched her intently.

'Apparently you'd prefer my announcing publicly: Ladies and gentlemen, I am not reading my book at all, don't get the wrong idea, I am just staring into it and thinking about the dog I ran away from. Please talk me out of it. And while you are at it would you prevent that beanpole facing me from harassing me at night!'

'Beanpole,' he grimaced.

'Yes. Otherwise known as six-footer, spindlelegs and daddy longlegs. Aren't you on a crusade for the truth?'

He rested his elbow on the black shiny surface. 'Come here.'

The seat clicked and the girl stood in front of the piano. 'What do you want?'

He put his hands on her shoulders. 'Nobody has yet complained about my performance. Go lock the door. I'll get undressed.'

She stepped back. 'I don't want it.'

'Why not?'

'I'd be embarrassed.'

'Don't be a bourgeois again please. Don't lie to yourself. You can't seriously start telling me now that you wouldn't like to try it with me. Why are you pretending?'

She took her red sweater from the desk. 'It might be better if we left.'

'No. Wait. I want to know. Why are you always putting on an act?'

Her heels resonated in the empty room.

He remained propped against the piano and waited.

She turned around at the door. 'Has your mother passed away?'

He put on his coat, grabbed his briefcase by the corner and walked down the aisle after the girl. 'And what about it?'

❦ ❦ ❦

Dusk was falling. It was drizzling softly. A damp chill penetrated everything. They walked in a file over wooden boards where the pavement was dug up and spoke not a word.

'I'll wait here for the number nine,' she said and hid in an alcove.

'As you want. But there's a café just there.'

Tables bedecked in white were laid out behind the big glass panes. Some people were gesticulating and laughing and others were dying of boredom. Yet all of them were sipping from delicate cups.

The girl pulled herself away from the neon sign. 'Let's go then.'

❧ ❧ ❧

A helpless fan buzzed at the ceiling. It didn't have enough strength to disperse the lazy clouds of acrid smoke.

Knots of hopefuls stood around the cloakroom with their coats open looking anxiously for an empty table.

The frozen couple gulped the stifling air and blinked their eyes.

A moustachioed man at the window was holding a wooden newspaper frame in his fleshy hand. He was staring into a women's magazine VLASTA and looked like a radish. Facing him a first love was fervently wringing her hands.

A button. Bother. He hasn't noticed. To the toilet. Where is it.

Under an art-deco glass chandelier sat a dozen fairy godmothers. They bared their porcelain teeth at éclairs with whipped cream and exchanged little local scandals for embroidery patterns. One of them incessantly wheezed and coughed into a laced handkerchief.

She held it to her pointed lips with thin pale fingers like bean sprouts.

But I'll freeze without stockings.

A veteran piano was sinking its legs into the podium in the blackened corner of the room. A violin case and an accordion lay indifferently on scattered chairs. A percussions set stood akimbo close by, ready for anything.

Empty chairs. But join which table. There's no point. We have to leave anyway. And then it will be even worse. It's slipping down already. What an awful day.

The garçon carefully trod his winding path among the tables. The tall man whispered something to him. The boy stepped on his own foot and pointed to the orchestra. The top-waiter was standing among the drums with the expression of a germinating potato. The tall man shrugged powerlessly.

Out we go then. That's the end. Lucky it's dark. Homeward-ho.

The girl pushed the revolving doors with her whole body. A draught of cold air impatiently streamed into the room.

❦ ❦ ❦

The sky grew heavy and incessantly sifted quiet rain. The wind made its way through the darkness and grumpily looked for a dry spot. The street lamps blinked listlessly. Between the chimneypots the anaemic moon was bored.

'Everywhere's going to be packed today. It's Saturday and it's pouring,' chattered the tall man. 'You're freezing, aren't you?'

The girl bundled herself up in the sweater that had gone limp with dampness. 'I'm terribly cold.'

'We could've gone to my place.'

'I'll wait for the number nine here. We can't walk around like this.'

'There's no point standing still and getting wet when no tram is coming. We'll walk to the next stop.'

The wooden boards over the dug-up pavement were slippery and squeaked a sucking noise under each step. Red lanterns stood precariously atop the cairns of dislodged cobblestones. The wind had knocked one over. Slivers of glass had spilled into a pothole.

A tram was approaching. The girl made for it. – Stop No Longer In Use.

A side street put an end to the battle against the burst pipe with a red-and-white triangular sign.

The gutters swallowed murky streams eagerly and gurgled like weirs. Water from drainpipes washed out red trenches alongside the houses.

They blundered in the mud. Shops turned their backs to them with rattling rusty shutters.

A car urgently sobbed in the distance – it had to go to a place it didn't like.

They hid in a doorway near the tram stop.

She wiped her face with a soaked handkerchief. 'Can I enter the tram in this state?'

'You don't look exactly charming,' he assessed and took out a comb.

'I'm completely drenched. Even my shoes.'

He hopped from one foot to another and shook droplets off

his cloak. 'Your problem. It doesn't rain at my place.'

'As if I'd jumped into a river. What does the doctor suggest?'

'Into bed.'

'That's all?'

He giggled. 'And something to warm up.'

'... I'm really not feeling well.'

'What can I do?'

'Nothing.'

'Yes madam. Premolar on bottom left – cavity, second molar on top right – extraction.'

The wrung-out handkerchief hung limply in her hand. 'So you're a dentist ...'

'Why are you so surprised?'

'I thought you were – a doctor.'

Someone was groping for the doorhandle on the inside. They stepped aside. The door groaned and a head like a fish bladder appeared in the opening. The smell of Saturday with its garlic and burnt buns escaped from the house. The man opened a checkered lady's umbrella and discreetly crossed the rinsed street.

'It's coming.'

She wanted to walk to the tram stop but halfway through her step she froze.

'What's wrong?'

She collapsed to a squat. '... Nothing.'

He caught her arm. 'What do you mean, nothing. What's happening to you? Are you all right?'

'Yes.'

He pulled her over to a passageway. She resisted and nearly cried. He stood her up against the damp wall and looked her in the eyes. 'Now tell me what it means.'

She bit her lip. 'What, it?'

'You know very well what. Stop playing around and explain to me what this theatre is about. Without any stupid lies. I don't understand what it is you are acting now. Give me the truth!'

She put her hands behind her back and leaned forward a bit.

'I'm fed up with this,' he muttered. 'Up to here. Do you get it? All this pretence. What happened?'

She pushed him away from her until he nearly fell over. She clenched her fist. Then changed her mind. 'The truth. All right. I'm expecting.'

He pulled his head between his shoulders. He looked like a condor. He spat out curt sentences with the expression of a Jesuit who has caught a heretic. 'So mademoiselle is gravid. Our Lady had a visit from the Holy Ghost.'

She crouched in a dark corner of the alley on the wet cobblestones. She rubbed her calves with her hands.

'You've turned out to be quite something, kitty. Let's go.'

She wasn't listening.

'Stop it. I said, let's go. We could have been safe and warm long ago.'

She stood up.

'What are you gaping at? I won't bite you. Come along.'

'Where?'

'Where. To our place.'

She bent over and straightened out something above her knee.

'What kind of an idiot was it? With me it would never have happened to you.'

'Go away. Go away or something will happen.'

'Don't be hysterical. Nobody has given birth yet. ... What's with your stockings? Your suspenders snapped or something? Then why don't you pin them up?' He graciously turned the other way. 'I'll wait at the entrance.'

A car passed with fogged up windows and splashed through a puddle of brown water.

She did not appear.

He went back in.

The corner was empty.

He went to the end to the passage, but had to come back.

It was a dead-end.

❧ ❧ ❧

The hinges screeched and the heavy door with metal fittings slammed shut.

She aimed for the aisle. The cold tiles rang out and her footsteps swelled into the space in a manifold echo. She sat down in the front row.

On the dusty shelf lay a forgotten old-fashioned spectacles holder. She picked it up. It fell apart.

The gothic windows barely let through any light. The flames of tall candles flickered in the semi-darkness. One of them died. Down the middle of the nave crawled a dark red carpet. It separated two rows of crouched confessionals. A circlet of bright yellow wax dahlias graced the main altar.

The large space of the church breathed smoke and trembled with chilling emptiness.

A distant voice suddenly moaned above. The girl jumped up from the bench in fear and looked up to the dome. The voice was coming closer and was accompanied by the acquiescent murmur of a male choir. A whiff of sickly-sweet stench floated through the church. The girl scrambled to the wall and hit her back painfully against a vessel for holy water. It was dry.

The stairs to the gallery creaked under the procession of shaven monks. The first one carried a standard. At the tip of the long thin pole dangled a black velvet rectangle.

She tried pushing the heavy gates. They were locked.

The organ thundered. She pressed herself against the last pillar and watched the descending cortège. In the wall opposite a little door opened. The standard set out on its march across the black and white tiles.

She desperately tried to come up with some sort of prayer. She wanted to get out of the way but she could not move.

The procession stopped in front of a dark painting on the wall. The organ went silent.

The first priest opened his mouth and in a zealous trance lamented incomprehensibly. The group around him kneeled and complemented him with monosyllabic whispering. The empty pews filled up imperceptibly with dark figures that motionlessly observed the holy ceremony.

The priest had finished. The organ's bellows rustled and once again the dense harmonies boomed through the church. The priest faced the girl and curled back his fleshy lips. All his teeth were of gold.

'I don't want it,' she mumbled and managed to retreat a few steps. The priest made the sign of a cross and started to chase her. The file of monks lowered their heads and followed him with their hands clasped.

The priest raised glazed eyes to another painting and continued in his monotone recital. The faithful in the benches stood up stiffly and gradually joined the black mob.

The Stations of the Cross marked every painting along the walls and pursued the girl with wailing litanies. From painting to painting, step by step, all around the church.

The last painting. The cortège fell to its knees and rolled its pale eyeballs upward. Jesus on the cross with blood at his palms and feet smiled into the deadly silence.

She opened her eyes and glanced at the Christ's face. He moved his lips.

'No!'

The cortège jumped and hissed angrily. The priest holding the standard rose from his knees and strode down the aisle. Everybody sighed Amen and slowly marched after him.

The priest lifted a stone slab from the floor with one hand and the whole file disappeared into an underground tomb.

The church stood empty.

The girl dug her nails into the wooden folds of the fluttering robe and slowly returned her gaze to the Crucified One. His head hung down and his whole body was contorted in pain. She mustered her courage and came closer.

The picture was embroidered.

She pulled herself together and turned to the way out. From afar she reached for the wrought iron handle of the massive doors. She made a few steps on the red strip.

An urgent knocking on wood made itself heard from the last confessional and the velvet curtain rippled. She stopped in her tracks. A bald head nodded through the lattice.

The confessor looked like a well-fed miller's wife. His skin was white and slimy like a wet mushroom. He gasped as he breathed and he mumbled incomprehensibly through his pink baby lips. He patted his belly with a jumble of ten maggots adorned by rings. With a crooked smile he examined the girl from head to toe.

'I WANTED TO GET RID OF HIM.'

The confessor pulled greasy eyelids over his frog-like eyeballs and the burgundy curtain soundlessly slid over the window.

Away! The carpet swallowed the sound of her footsteps.

As she passed the next confessional, a wooden bench creaked from inside.

She had to turn and she froze to the tiles.

The velvet drape exhaled a century of dust. In the dark recess a sugar loaf wobbled and took on the shape of a confessor.

The priest observed the girl with lashless and browless eyes. The white of the eyes had turned yellow and were criss-crossed by red veins. He had an egg-like head and the mouth resembled a random crack in the shell. He rubbed his hands with small gestures, as if he were counting money. His skin sounded like crumpled paper.

'I AM NOT MARRIED.'

The confessional exhaled some more dust and closed its eye.

A little dry man with a wrinkled face appeared in the next window. A close-set pair of raisins roved from left to right.

He shifted his head and turned his ear to the girl.

'I HAVE SMALL BREASTS.'

He jumped and made a cup of his hand that he placed to his ear. He was evidently hard of hearing.

'I HAVE SMALL BREASTS. I HAVE SMALL BREASTS.'

The little man wriggled contentedly and then settled like water in a cup.

The priest in the next confessional looked like a cheesecake that had fallen on the ground. Rivulets of water meandered down his forehead and temples and drops of rain fell steadily to the floor of the confessional. He was soaked and he reeked of garlic.

'I LIKE KISSING.'

He wheezed and coughed into a small white square.

The fifth confessor was nailed to the seat. A pair of crutches was propped up in the dark corner. All the tragic experiences he had been through left their imprint in the corners of his mouth. He ignored the girl.

She stamped her heel. The crutches knocked each other down and fell noisily. The priest picked them up with a smile. He looked up at her.

'I LIKE TO BE ALONE.'

He lifted his eyes to the dome. Softly the organ resounded. He slid the window open and slipped his arm though the gap. She gazed at his beautiful head. The space of the church grew warmer.

She cried out in horror.

He had six fingers.

Everything disappeared and she stood on the bank of the river. The air was heavy and the dark was yellow.

❧ ❧ ❧

The sky scattered sparse flakes of wilting snow. Rays of sun winked from frosted roofs.

On the surface of the river dirty glass crusts crashed.

A tram crawled along a never-ending wall.

The cracked plaster bulged into flat bubbles and humidity painted surreal landscapes on the wall. Deep cracks stripped it down to the bricks. A blackbird with a broken wing nestled up to the metal spikes on its ridge. It looked down indolently to the yard that spread like a small airfield. A whistling breeze roamed through the disassembled rusty cars toppled on their sides and bonnets.

The tram slowed down.

A man with a red nose carefully measured his steps on the icy pavement. His long figure was concluded with a green hunting cap. In a short winter coat gathered at the waist he resembled a capital H. He followed the house numbers with his head buried in a turned-up collar.

He stopped in front of a single-storey house.

A key rattled in the lock and struggled for a while. Then it jerked angrily and a little old wiry woman shuffled out in her slippers. Locks of grey hair escaped from under her headscarf and a greasy apron hung over her skirts. She carried a large basin full of ashes.

The tall man addressed her.

The elderly woman pouted her lower lip and then slowly shook her head. 'Din'you get the number mixed up?'

'No.'

She reached into the basin with a coal scoop and sprinkled the ashes over the slippery paving. 'Watch out or you'll be covered in muck.'

He caught her arm.

She cast a sour glance at him.

'She must be living here.'

'Not true.'

'I'm one hundred per cent certain.'

She set the basin on the ground and tightened the corners of her kerchief. 'Look 'ere. I been living in this house fifty-eight years.' Lumps of cinder scraped under her slippers. She turned back to the door.

The tall man ran after her in anguish. He clasped his hands and almost kneeled. 'It's not possible!'

Through a narrow crack in the door she bared her last two bottom teeth. 'You made it up, mister.' She slammed the door and poked around in the lock.

He tugged at the handle.

All the doors were locked.

Translated by Nancy Hawker
Karel Hynek Mácha's verse is taken from
Hugh Hamilton McGovern's translation of Máj

Svatava Antošová

Don't Tell Mum

'You're not anything like *mia* biological *madre*,' said Darka as she took a long drag on her cigarette.

'All I ever got from her was: "What are you gaping at, you knucklehead? Lie down, moron!" or "Shut up, you cow!" But since I've been with you, I've found my ... *heytchdee*.'

'Your what?'

'I mean my human dignity.'

'I see.'

'And since I've found my *heytchdee*, I'm back to being a normal human being, right?' I can get a boyfriend, lose some weight – since the only reason I used to overeat was because I was afraid I couldn't get a guy. Actually, it was *mia madre* who was afraid. I know I'd be able to hold on to him even without being submissive. Someday I could maybe even have a kid and try to bring it up differently from that never-ending struggle I was always having with *madre*.'

Darka was *mia* adopted *figlia*. It's really only symbolic, but because of that it's got even more significance for both of us.

Back then she was really lonely, with a psychiatric clinic in her past and zilch in her future. Her self-confidence had taken a hike God knows where, and her sex appeal had already sounded its own death knell. She was getting on in years, too – getting old and nobody to talk about it with. Just like me.

'So, when did you actually lose your *heytchdee*?'

Both of us were being jostled around at the bar trying to get a beer. The pub was a jumble of all sorts of characters from hoary hippies to underage hipsters to snot-nosed kids with facial piercings and their crotches dangling about their knees – everyone tossing and tumbling from nowhere to God knows where, jostling us apart from one another, all to the persistent roar of *Ramstein* thundering from the speakers.

'Probably since the time *padre* left us ...'

I looked at her quizzically. I knew she'd had several.

'*Padre numero zero*,' she kindly clarified. 'You know, my biopa.'

'Did anything ever go on between you?'

I'd simply taken a wild guess, but it had obviously cut her to the quick. She lapsed into a prolonged silence, blushed, and gnawed on her lower lip.

'Well, did you?'

'Well, yeah,' she finally managed to say. 'I sucked him off once when I was ten. Now no one can surprise me with those lingual loops. I've got them down to a tee. But then *madre numero uno* found out about it and blew a gasket, and then the bastard hit the road. Everyone said he emigrated, for cunt's sake! They had no idea what went on at home. They thought we were an anti-regime *famiglia*, but we were no anti-regime *famiglia*, we were too afraid to do anything like that. *Padre numero zero* just took advantage of me and that was it, and he was such a coward he'd never have taken off otherwise, and when he did take off, he took my *heytchdee* with him. And without my *heytchdee*, I couldn't stand up to my bioma ...'

My head began to throb. I always got a headache whenever Darka tried to hack her way through the psychological thicket that was her adolescence, and she could never shut up about it. I silently cursed myself that I'd asked her about it in the first place.

'... I couldn't stand up to that pig who'd filched my childhood and made me fuck up my youth. I used to kick and spit in her face when she came to the squat to get me with the cops and begged me to come home. Ha! Home! I'll never forget the time she was having it off with a fellow, and I could hear her orgasmic screams all over that disgusting pre-fab apartment: 'I love anal! I LOVE ANAL!' Back then I didn't know what that meant, and when I found out I cried out for it myself with my own orgasmic screams and had to have it from every guy I was with – each one had to fuck me in the arse until blood oozed from my ripped-up bowels. It's because of my parental models, that's what my shrink told me, unconscious parental models ...'

The barman finally placed two beers in front of us. Darka bought some paprika-flavoured crisps and then cut a path through the pub, heading toward two vacant seats on a bench beneath the television.

'Hey, *madre numero due*, what were your parents like?'

'Mine ... ?'

I tried to recall my relationship with my parents. It was odd. When they died, I stopped feeling lonely.

'That was a while ago ...'

'What, you can't remember anything?'

'I don't know. I don't like looking back. There's nothing back there.'

Darka fidgeted uncomfortably. She could tell I was lying. I did have a past, and it was nipping at my heels, flaying them raw. Every step I took toward the future was intensely painful. I kept hearing *mia madre* shouting: 'Don't fall! Don't get wet! Don't catch a chill!' She always said that, both out of love and out of a shortage of love. And she continued to shout these things long after I'd become an adult – when there was no place for me to fall, when I carried an umbrella with me, when I stuffed myself with vitamin C.

'Come on, or we won't get a seat,' I said and headed through the throng hoisting our pints above my head to the back where they were getting ready to show a film.

'Let's sit on the floor,' suggested Darka and made her way to the front of the crowd where she plonked down right in front of the screen. I arranged myself beside her on the floor and placed the beer in front of us. Darka ripped open her bag of crisps and offered them to me. I took a handful.

'So what's the *cinema* supposed to be today?'

'No idea.'

'Oh, a *sorpresa*, then?'

'Yeah.'

'Some *subcult*?'

'Huh?'

'You know ... subculture ...'

'Oh, yeah.'

Darka whistled with satisfaction and took a long pull of her beer. She silently scrutinised the area, evaluating the guys in the room, and then launched into a completely different subject.

'Hey, *madre numero due*, me and Otík bought this old helicon from a burnout, and he learned to play it really well, you know, the czardas, the waltz. I'm serious, he's really good. I had no idea he was so musically talented. He figured the fucker out in a couple of days. I couldn't believe it. And when I first heard him play, my *cuore musicale*, or whatever you want to call it, started hammering away, and I started singing again – you know I spent my whole childhood belting it out in the *whycee* ...'

'Translate, please.' I leapt into her running monologue and realised that Otík was probably that cool guy she'd shackled herself to when she'd regained her *heytchdee*.

'... you know, the youth choir ...'

She started rocking to some odd rhythm.

'You said you bought a helicon?' I asked without concealing my scepticism. 'How much did you pay for it?'

Darka swallowed and hesitated for a moment. Then she came clean.

'Two tubs of akin ...'

'Which is what?'

'Akineton. Dope-heads like it because it puts them over the top.'

'What do you have it for?'

'My eye rolls.'

'Your what?!'

'So my eyes don't roll back in my head.'

'I've never noticed anything like that with you.'

'It only happens when I'm at *la casa* and the beast hits.'

'Hmm.'

I was wondering if Otík was the same loony she'd introduced me to at the Už jsme doma concert.

'Is Otík still working with weapons?'

'Yeah,' nodded Darka as she lit up another cigarette. 'Why do you ask?'

I didn't say anything, and my silence probably seemed odd to her because it riled her up.

'Look, *madre numero due*, what are you trying to say?! All he does is stand behind a counter and sell guns: he's really good at it, and everything's on the up and up. Don't worry about it. So one time he pulled a gun on me, big deal. He pretended he was going to bump me off and made me crawl on the ground and beg for my life, but otherwise he's a real sweetheart. At first I thought the gun wasn't loaded and sort of laughed and tried to provoke him, but then he suddenly shot a hole through the ceiling and it was clear the game was over, that the shit was about to hit the fan, and that the next bullet would find my skull, so I let him do whatever he wanted, he tied me up, pissed in my mouth and then he even fucked me with the gun, it really hurt, but that's love too, isn't it? Later a girlfriend of mine told me to leave him, that he'd bump me off sometime anyway, but I could never do that, he's such a sweetie pie, and you know his life hasn't been all that easy, but he said I couldn't talk about it, so don't even try, he'd kill me if I told you, but there's no way you're going to convince me to leave him, no fucking way.'

It was useless. There was no point in trying to tell Darka the danger she was in. The most important thing for her was that she had a guy and wasn't alone. And that she'd located her *heytchdee*. But I couldn't help giving her a jab.

'Didn't you just say that now that you've located your *heytchdee* you could keep a guy without being submissive?'

'But I'm not submissive!'

'Letting someone piss in your mouth? Please!'

Darka wanted to object but then stopped.

'So you think letting someone piss in your mouth is a sign of submissiveness?'

They put the lights out and rolled the film. A *subcult*. It was called *Fun Fearless Family*. The adults played children, and the children played adults. No plot whatsoever, just a series of scenes and shots in which they took turns serving dinner to each other. Especially powerful was a scene in which a child in the role of the parent had his daughter suck him off. The daughter was played by a forty-year-old fat bitch. When they got to the lingual loops Darka got up and went to the bathroom. The audience was snorting, and the little shit in the role of the parent was having a blast. *A child paedophile!* went through my mind. 'Don't tell Mother', said the little shit after he came. The daughter promised she wouldn't. Then she went and told her. The mother was barely ten. She was drinking cocoa and cutting off the tits of a Barbie doll. The forty-year-old fat bitch burst into tears. 'My Barbie!' she sobbed, 'my Barbie!' Her mother knocked her to the ground. 'Tell your father to buy you a new one.' The fat bitch stopped crying and then went to tell her father she wanted a new Barbie. 'You're my shweet Barbie doll,' lisped the little shit in the role of the parent and pulled her lovingly to his chest. *Cinque anni dopo*. The little shit in the role of the parent is beating his over-grown daughter. She's been out all night. 'Where have you been, you slut?' he screeches at her. 'Nowhere!' screams the daughter with dread and horror in her eyes. 'Where have you been, you slut?' His childish voice falters, and he hammers his absurd little fists into the back of the fat bitch. 'At a girlfriend's ...' The fat bitch is wiping away tears. 'You're lying! I'm asking you for the last time, where have you been?' The mother turns up. She's drinking cocoa and her tits have been cut off. Cancer. 'With David ...'

I closed my eyes. My *padre* used to beat me as well. He always beat me when I loved somebody. When I was happy. When I stayed out all night. He didn't call me a 'slut' but a 'whore' instead. But I never sucked him off. He always concluded his beatings with the words: 'I should have strangled you in the crib. At least then I'd have a little peace from you.' It was because of those words that I hated him, more than all the beatings in the world. Back then I used to think: 'One of these days I'll kill you. One of these days I'll kill you, you bastard!' I didn't kill him. After the death of my kind *mamma* I even looked after him ... When I opened my eyes the audience was applauding and whistling, and Darka was sitting next to me again. She was baked out of her head.

'Pull yourself together,' I jabbed her with my elbow. 'Do you have to take these things so personally?'

'Look, *madre numero due*,' she retorted, 'you don't know what you're talking about, you don't know what the fuck you're talking about!'

It never would have occurred to me before, but now all I could think about was whether or not Darka and I would ever do it together. 'To sleep with *mia figlia*!' ran through my mind, 'to sleep with *mia figlia* and fuck with another taboo.' It really enticed me. Chubby Darka certainly never attracted me, but a little weed would fix that. THC works wonders!

'Hey, *madre numero due*,' whispered Darka making sure no one was listening, 'it occurred to me, I mean, don't get me wrong, but it just occurred to me that I'm becoming *una vecchietta* and I've never had any experience with ... you know ...'

I started to get the picture. It was clear we'd been thinking the same thing.

'... well, you know, it would probably be a good thing to have some experience with a woman before I get married and have kids. What do you think?'

I didn't react. Darka jabbered on.

'You should experience everything in life, right?'

There was an unbearable urgency in her voice, her eyes, and in what was left of her body, which I unconsciously resisted.

'Try a porn flick,' I said when I'd brought myself under control.

'Noooo,' wailed Darka, 'you don't understand! Look, *madre numero due*, I need your advice ... there's this friend of mine, you see, I like her and I'd like to try it with her, but I don't know how to go about it ...'

A house of cards. And it collapsed. On me.

'So, what do you want me to do? Supervise?'

I was angry. Darka instantly cottoned on.

'For cunt's sake, *madre numero due*, you're jealous, aren't you?'

Out of nowhere appeared a blue-eyed blond fellow in an orange shirt, tight black trousers, and with his nails painted orange.

'How's it goin', girls?' he roared at us.

'Hi!'

'Hey girls, why aren't you wearing a pink triangle?'

I gave him a smirk. It was supposed to be an indulgent smirk, but it didn't come off. Darka didn't say a word.

'What a retarded fascist!' she hissed and turned towards me.

'What an ancient cunt!' hissed the fascist and turned toward me.

Darka stared daggers at him and hustled me outside. She lit up another cigarette.

'A friend of yours?'

I said nothing. A sermon was the last thing I needed to hear from *mia figlia*.

'Did you hear what I said?'

I did. But I couldn't answer. Was he a friend of mine or did I just know him? Did I sense I understood him or did I simply not give a damn?

'Why do you keep going out with Otík?'

Darka flinched.

'Look, *madre numero due*, what kind of evasion is this? Otík's not a fascist!'

She paced nervously back and forth, pulling heavily on her cigarette.

'So you like those pink triangle comments of his?'

'He thinks he's being witty,' I answered, 'so I just leave him be ...'

'And that seems normal to you, is that it? Look, *madre numero due*, I can't stand those fascist jokes, do you understand? *Padre numero zero* used to pull shit like that, and he was blue-eyed and blond as well. He also thought he was better than everybody else, and he'd go around scrawling 'Blacks into the Ovens!', always scribbling a Swastika somewhere, screaming at us: 'Raus!' and dreaming of a pantry full of gats, for cunt's sake! All that while me and *mia madre* didn't have shit to eat. Look, *madre numero due*, I know it was all just a pose, that he was just fucking around, but it warped my entire life, get it?'

I got it. Utterly. She saw her biopa in every swinging dick she happened to come across. A single phallitic act and enough trauma to last a lifetime.

'I'm going back in for another beer,' I said.

'You go right ahead! Go back in and chill with your fascist friend!'

I went back in and got another beer. Darka stayed outside. I made my way to the back where the filmmakers were sitting, including the fascist. An older woman was perched next to him. I took the vacant seat across from him and gave them both a good looking over. No, that's not his mistress, I decided, it's his *madre*. I was right. She was sipping at a glass of cherry brandy, and after she'd sized me up she inquired.

'Did you like the film?'

'Not really,' I hesitated and fastened my eyes on my beer.

'What do you mean, "not really"?'

The fascist put in his tuppence worth.

'I worked on it with the directah here myself and you say *not really* ...'

'Did somebody say "not really"?'

That was the director from the head of the table. This is how it always goes: they just want to yak away and jerk each other off over how good they were.

'I did,' I admitted.

'What do you mean "not really"?'

'The film wasn't about anything.'

'What do you mean, it wasn't about anything?'

'There was nothing. No catharsis, no nothing.'

'Catharsis?'

'Catharsis?'

The directah and the fascist goggled their eyes at each other. The fascist's *madre* pricked up her ears.

'You're looking for catharsis in this nonsense of theirs?'

The *madre* gave me an amused smirk. It was clear she was above all this. But then the directah chimed in.

'Did someone say "nonsense"?'

'I did.'

'Oh, knock it off, mum,' the fascist tried to pacify her and clinked her glass. 'These days it's only *nonsense* that makes any sense.'

Then he turned to me again.

'You can't say it wasn't about anything. We were voicing a protest ...' He didn't have time to finish.

'... against child abuse,' the director completed his sentence. He was rubbing his paunch and felt good.

I was bored. The fascist was furiously text-messaging someone beneath the table.

When he had finished, he excused himself. His mother said something to me about the bastard but I couldn't take it in.

'I'll be right back,' I said and beetled off to the *doubleyoocee*.

I located the door with the girly on it, opened one of the stalls and turned to stone. Orange spots danced before my eyes. There stood the fascist with his back to me and his trousers around his ankles doing someone from behind.

'*Favoloso*,' he sighed, '*favoloso!*'

His pace did not abate. He was all quickening movements and guttural grunts. And then I heard it. Then I heard three words that made my bowels seize up. The words were wrenched out of the mouth of the creature bending over the toilet bowl with feet spread wide, the only part of which I could see was her fat, white haunches.

'I love anal!'

Those were the words. And again.

'I love anal!'

'For cunt's sake,' ran through my mind: 'Darka! The fascist is fucking Darka!' Then he turned around. His face was red, his lips grinning, and his eyes covered in a hazy mist. When he realised I was standing there he slowed his tempo a bit and shot me a conspiratorial grin.

'Come on, man!' groaned Darka. 'Come on!'

He gave me an apologetic shrug of the shoulders as if to say: '*Scusami*, but as you can see, right now I am otherwise occupied,' and then picked up the pace again. Darka bellowed in pain, the fascist in pleasure. I closed the door and backed out. 'The swine!' I said to myself.

'Is something the matter?'

The fascist's mother was simply dripping with empathy. It felt like a leech had attached itself to my face.

'Yes,' I nodded and fixed my eyes on my beer, 'something's the matter.'

'Did you see my son?'

'Yes.'

'Where?'

'In the can,' I snapped and then added, 'the ladies'.'

His *madre* rolled her eyes.

'He's mixed them up on purpose again, huh?'

'Yeah. Apparently he's going to have a sex change.'

'He's so silly,' groaned his *madre* and went into a nicotine hacking fit.

The orange shirt appeared in the doorway. The fascist. A lit cigarette dangled from his lips, and his right hand held two pints, his left two cherry brandies. He set everything down in front of his *madre,* took a seat and slid a beer and a cherry brandy over to himself. Then he took a long pull of his beer.

'*Favoloso,*' he sighed, and he looked at me askance.

'What's up with your gender again?'

His *madre* prodded, and the fascist hesitated.

'What do you mean with my gender?'

'If you turn yourself into a girl, I'll rip your eyes out.'

His *madre* simply stated this as a fact, with no emotion whatsoever.

'A girl?'

The fascist had no idea what was going on.

'Just stop going to the women's bathroom, do you hear me?'

He stared daggers at me, and I stared daggers at this *madre.* His *madre* wanted us to explain to her what was going on. The fascist blathered something to her, but I wasn't listening. When he finished, and his *madre* turned away from him to devote herself to the directah, my cell phone beeped. A text message from the fascist: 'Don't tell Mother!' I thumbed back a reply: 'Otík will kill you ...' Then I switched it off and stashed it away.

'I'm outta here,' I said and got up.

I nodded to one and all, emitted a generic 'bye!' and beat a retreat. As I was passing the besieged bar I thought I saw Darka. I turned around, and sure enough. But she hadn't seen me. She was involved in a conversation with two gypsies, holding a package of weed in one hand and a beer in the other. I hesitated for a moment and then poked her in the side.

'Hey, *madre numero due!*' Darka's eyes widened, and she raised the hand with the beer.

'You're stoned,' I said with disgust and looked around anxiously. 'Can we talk for a moment?'

There was such a din in the place we almost couldn't hear each other.

'You want to go outside, like?'

'Just for a moment.'

We went outside. Two couples were nibbling at each other, and a little further away stood a group of teenagers smoking. I pulled Darka further down the street.

'Hey, *madre numero due*, what's up?'

'Isn't there something you want to explain to me?'

'Like what?'

'Like that extempore in the can ...'

'What extempore ...' she faltered, 'in what can?'

'Stop playing dumb! How long have you been having it off with that fascist?'

'For cunt's sake!'

Darka panicked. She started tearing at her hair, kicking the wall, and spluttering. I made her shut up.

'Knock it off!'

'So you were spying on us?'

'I didn't even have to.'

Darka didn't want to answer. She put on a hostile expression, puffed out her cheeks, and started rolling her eyes.

'Fine. So let's sum up the situation: in bed the fascist doesn't bother you, is that it?'

Darka didn't bat an eyelash.

'Do you hear me?'

'Yes, I hear you! Look, *madre numero due* ...'

She swallowed the rest.

'The fascist doesn't bother you, and you love anal, right?'

Darka stood frozen for a moment and then started sobbing.

'Look, *madre numero due*, you just don't understand! You don't understand anything at all! In the bathroom he was imagining his own *madre*. He always imagines her ... Do you understand?'

Now it was my turn to stand there frozen. I couldn't believe it. I couldn't believe the fascist could find his *madre numero due* in Darka and that he was doing her in the arse only because he'd never dare do it to his bioma himself even though he wanted to very much. 'Are you playing his *madre* or his shrink?'

'Both. He needs both! Look, *madre numero due*, don't be so horrible! It's simply more powerful than me ...'

It overpowered me, too. Then something occurred to me.

'Come on,' I grabbed Darka around the neck and pulled her towards me. 'What if it's all the other way round?'

'What do you mean?!'

'What if you don't represent any *madre* at all ...?'

'But I do!'

'... what if he represents your *padre*?'

She stiffened.

'What *padre*?!'

'I don't know. One of the several ... Maybe *padre numero sei* ...'

'That's ridiculous!'

'You're right, that's ridiculous. What about *padre numero zero?* Is the fascist actually *padre numero zero* ...?'

Darka began to shudder. This time I was the one who'd stolen her *heytchdee*. Darka tried to say something, but all she could do was move her lips wordlessly, then she gave up and ran off. 'No,' ran through my head. 'We could never do it together. She wouldn't be able to. Unless I pissed in her mouth like Otík ...'

Translated by Craig Cravens

ERIKA OLAHOVÁ

A Child

She had been married for five years – and still nothing. Her relatives felt pity and compassion for her; it was not usual for women to be barren in her large family, where children had always abounded. Every woman on her side and her husband's side of the family had children. Lots of children! Big-eyed curly-haired boys and girls, in all sizes; they called her auntie, and it made her feel sick. She did not feel any hatred towards them; rather, it was the comments and reproaches of her husband and mother-in-law that had turned her into a taciturn and hardworking woman. She had no interest in chatting with the others on the doorstep. Rózka was big, strong, but nevertheless beautiful. Her hair was fairer than the rest of her kin, her skin was not as dark and her eyes sparkled with gold. This already set her apart from the others.

Rózka was healthy, so she devoted herself to her work, labouring in the fields and in the household until dark. Her husband had not yet come to terms with her not giving him a child, and drank all the more, until his tanned face stopped smiling. They lived in one room with his mother and father, and she would return there from the fields or from the cattle when dusk was falling.

Once when she came home, her mother-in-law and her husband weren't in and her father-in-law lay drunk on the bed. She asked where the others were – he only muttered unintelligibly to the effect that her husband had taken his mother to town to his sister. Apparently she wasn't well. Rózka ate her supper and went to lie down.

She was woken by his alcoholic breath and he was crushing her completely with the weight of his body. She couldn't resist in any way, not even by screaming. He had covered her mouth with his huge hand and helplessly she looked into his crimson face ... When he had finished he stood over her and told her she mustn't tell anyone – anyway, they wouldn't believe her. He slammed the door shut and she could only hear the clock clanging in time with the beating of her frightened heart.

Her husband came home about an hour later, didn't even turn the light on, lay down next to her, turned over and soon fell asleep. He did not embrace her or even touch her, as if she were not there at all. She wanted to tell him everything, but had no strength left in her, and she spent the rest of the night staring into the dark; her thoughts, fear and humiliation mingled with the tears that streamed down her cheeks.

The old man continued to ignore her just as he had before, but her mother-in-law looked on with a smile as she threw up in the mornings and as her curves grew nicely. The smile returned to her husband's dark face and he was kinder and more generous to her. The neighbours finally had something to talk about, while Rózka and her mother-in-law prepared the baby's outfits and discussed what name to give it.

One month before the birth was due she had a dream. In it she saw her father-in-law and a child that resembled him. In the dream they were very evil and hurting her. When she woke up in terror, she could still hear their fearful laughter. She broke out in a cold sweat; she already knew that she didn't want the child, that it would bring her damnation all her living days.

She gave birth to a son; they named him Karči, after the father-in-law. Rózka suppressed the strange repulsion she felt towards the baby and took it into her arms. Her son looked at her just like an adult and smirked malignantly as he narrowed his eyes. She quickly laid him back in his crib and shied away. Nobody noticed and everybody milled around and smiled at him; it was only she who saw that he was different from the other newborn babies, and that he was watching her with his coal-black, squinting eyes.

In the night, when everybody was asleep, a noise woke her. She sat up in bed and looked around: she discovered with shock that the boy was standing next to her bed with an eerie sneer on his face. She was surprised to find that he had teeth. He gave a sinister snigger and scampered back to his crib. She screamed until everybody woke up in alarm; they sleepily lit a lamp and asked her what had happened. She told them tearfully what she had seen. Her husband suspected that she had dreamed it, and her mother-in-law rushed to have a look at the baby, who was sleeping innocently. As it started to whimper and then cry, the old woman took it into her arms and comforted it. Then she came over to Rózka and scolded her for not loving her own child and ordered her to breastfeed him – the boy was surely hungry. Rózka was completely confused but took the child and offered her breast. The boy started sucking immediately. Suddenly she felt a sharp pain: the little one had bit her nipple to the flesh, and blood gushed out. She pushed him away onto the blanket at the foot of the bed and complained in tears that the child had bitten her. The mother-in-law picked up the baby and passed her finger over its toothless gums. Her daughter-in-law must be wrong. She chided her and everybody came to the conclusion that Rózka had cut herself on purpose so as not to have to breastfeed. The old woman decided that she would feed the baby cows' milk and told the young mother that she would look after her grandson herself since his mother had rejected him. The grandmother took the child to bed with her and her husband; and so that night came to a close.

Nobody spoke to Rózka in the morning. The young woman felt miserable. She didn't know what to do, how to tell them everything that had happened and that the baby was actually a sin about which she had kept silent; that he was actually the devil's little helper in a child's disguise.

Barely a week later they found the old woman dead. She lay in bed with her eyes open wide, and the child giggled next to her waving its arms and legs in the air. Rózka knew that it had killed her mother-in-law, and that it would continue to kill. Nobody listened to her; they thought she had gone crazy and was talking nonsense. They assumed the death of the old woman had been caused by a heart attack.

During the following night Rózka decided to stay awake and keep an eye on the child. When it thought everybody was asleep it slowly climbed out of the crib and scuttled over to her husband's bedside. She pretended she was sleeping but watched the creature through her eyelashes to see what would happen. The child pulled the pillow from under the man's head and pushed it down on his face. It had such strength that even when the man was kicking and trying to pull the pillow off, it still held him down and the man gradually became weaker. Rózka jumped up and tried to tear the pillow out of the baby's hands. Its strength was tremendous: it pushed her over and continued to smother her husband. She picked up a chair and hit the baby on the head. It started to squeak and made noises like a goblin.

Suddenly a light came on and the old man and his half-dead son beheld an awful sight. Rózka was on the ground covered in blood: the small child, with bulging eyes and twisted face, was tossing her around and punching her face with its puny fists. Both men rushed to the young woman's assistance. The goblin attacked them too. The younger man caught it by the legs and smashed it against the wall. It fell to the ground, quickly picked itself up and darted to the door, squealing. It turned around one last time before escaping into the darkness with a blood-chilling screech.

The young man took Rózka into his arms and wiped her face with a cloth. His hands were shaking and he was crying. The woman was barely breathing. The door creaked open and closed and she looked through it apprehensively into the dark night as though she expected the devilish child to return.

Translated by Nancy Hawker

VĚRA STIBOROVÁ

Spades

For Dáša Šafaříková

General Flemmer is my secret and yours, and if we found out the truth about General Flemmer, our secret would be over. I look at the cards and tell myself: cards and clocks and trains and trains and stations and roosters and trains and cards are things that I constantly encounter and that continually touch my circles and around which my fate twists in different ways, my fate and yours, yes, around stations, around clocks, around pigeons, around roosters, and around shoes and hats and around cards, everything is connected with them – my loves, my wanderings, my secrets, my endless and unending journey towards you.

At the beginning of August, said General Flemmer, laying down the ten of hearts, Cadorna finished the preparations for the powerful attack on the Sochi River, because the capture of Gorizia meant a stage in the occupation of Trieste, and the attack was entrusted to the Italian Third Army, which was commanded by the Duke of

Aosta himself. Flemmer's favourite subject was left incomplete. General Flemmer felt unwell, went to lie down, and died in the night. General Flemmer apparently died of the consequences of all those battles he had been through in the Great War. There were battles in Galicia and there were battles in France, and there were battles in Italy, and the general was tormented by Galician lice and French mud and Italian dust and long marches or long lingering in positions, all of which sapped the general's health and all of which accumulated in the general's body and now added up to one big sum of a problem. General Flemmer was a peculiar man; he despised all the medals that he had ever been given, and he lost them all at cards. He had always played card games like gin rummy, matrimony and stacks, and since he had moved here, which was already a good fifteen years ago, he had been playing gin rummy, matrimony and stacks with Houdek and Faltys up in the attic in a cubbyhole which was almost custom-made for playing cards, and in that nook stood a couple of smaller crates for chairs and one larger crate on which was written in black stencilled letters VIA ASMARA VIA ASMARA VIA ASMARA, for a table, and above that a bare light bulb in a Bakelite socket. And we must not forget that on that larger crate, which served as a table and on which was written VIA ASMARA three times, stood a bottle of red wine during the game. Here the three men sat and Faltys began to shuffle the cards with that expert shuffle that resembles juggling, and he shuffled them with a twitch of alertness and pleasure around his mouth, and at the same time he looked absent-mindedly at General Flemmer and from Flemmer to Houdek and from Houdek to the round dormer window, where a piece of blue sky floated like a little balloon, and then he switched, quite imperceptibly, from shuffling to dealing. General Flemmer removed the cork from the bottle in the authentic manner of a true drinker, by hitting the bottom of the bottle with his palm until the cork popped partially out. I've never in my life seen such a general's art of opening bottles, said the former teacher Houdek fawningly, in order to secure a listener for his discussions of equinoxes, solstices and conjunctions during this session of wine and cards, but despite this effort General Flemmer said more often than was strictly pleasant, Yes, in wartime a man learns all sorts of things, dear Houdek, nobody else can imagine it, especially not a civilian. Houdek didn't like being called dear Houdek, and he couldn't stand the idea that nobody could imagine something, and civilian had a whiff of insult about it, and all in all, dear Houdek and the rest of it sounded like someone was putting on airs, and Houdek never took anything as hard as when someone put on airs in front of him. In such cases, he threw himself headlong into equinoxes, solstices and conjunctions, whether one liked it or not, and said in a tone borrowed from General Flemmer, Yes, you probably don't know this, but the ancient Egyptians in Syene already showed that ... And Faltys also had his favourite subject, which was how many people had ruined themselves through card-playing and how many marriages had fallen apart due to cards and how many suicides and runaways had been caused by cards, and all the while he constantly shuffled in that casual manner, and suddenly the cards started to fly through the air in such airborne fanlike succession that neither Houdek nor the general were able to catch them, and at such moments Faltys added, Yes, dear honourable, honourable dear gentlemen, in these decisive and fateful minutes the devil himself stands with us, and he laughed, he laughed devilishly.

Many times we saw those old men, how they trudged up the twisting staircase to the attic, always with their hands full, they never went up empty-handed, they carried cards, bottles, various coats and perhaps tobacco and other smoking utensils and also a canister of water, and it took quite a while before they appeared on the next landing; it resembled an act in the theatre, they paused often, they put their coats down on the banister and speechified at great length; they continued up or retreated a step or two and sometimes someone even had to come back down all the way from upstairs, usually the nimble Faltys, who came down swiftly, nearly flying, and then headed back up to the attic two steps at a time with some paper or an envelope or a forgotten newspaper, and once he was almost running with a pole of sorts, apparently in order to win the praise of the two older men, and we looked at them from the upper level of the road, because that old building stood on a steep slope just before the turn of a sharply rising hairpin bend, so from the lower part of the roadway it seemed to us that that house was the tallest in town, it stood there alone, isolated, the last Mohican of the old houses, the ground floor was beneath the level of the lower road and always surrounded by coal-dust and garbage and maybe even rats, while the roof seemed to be in the clouds. If we walked up the bend in the road, we almost reached the level of the roof, it was full of smokestacks and chimneys, and all of them kept smoking faintly, or at least hot waves rose from them, so behind those waves a panorama of our city, all the towers and even the river and its bridges trembled and floated and one had the impression that one was looking at a big aquarium or today we would compare it to a blurry television screen, and one might be afraid that suddenly the whole capital might disappear from the screen and in place of it only a few black letters will appear, such as VIA ASMARA VIA ASMARA VIA ASMARA. So if one reached that level and looked down, the house was plunged into a dark pit and below in that pit was gloom, dampness, coal dust, and a musty courtyard full of rubbish. We often liked to stand on the upper part of the road and we leaned over the railing and we saw in that house of demons, as we called the house, we also called it the house where Dostoyevsky had lived, how in the early evening the lights turned on in the miserable apartments, and we saw women at the stoves and women at the tables, how wearily they dragged out the pots, as if they were about to drop them, that heaviness, and we saw men in their undershirts drinking beer straight from the bottle and old men staring vacantly into space under ancient lampshades and of the lower floors we could only see legs, human legs, the legs of wardrobes, the legs of beds, the legs of tables, the legs of chairs, and more human legs. At the top we almost touched the dormer windows, the round attic windows, the eaves, the pipes, the little roofs, and the little chimneys and weathercocks and weathervanes. And above those overcrowded and inadequate apartments, above those dark rooms where flames occasionally licked the stoves and threw hellish satin at the walls, Houdek, Faltys and General Flemmer sat down to gamble in their little attic cubbyhole. They played and wrung their hands, jumped up, held forth on various topics, and drank from the bottle and General Flemmer very often argued, got offended and frowned, because as soon as he lost hope, he lost his head as well.

I, he said when he lost the round and lost his head, I, who crawled through mud in France and was full of Galician lice on the Eastern Front and who choked on dust before Venice, here in this stinking den I have to lose this damned game, and he threw the cards on the floor and stamped on them and rushed for the door. And Faltys and Houdek pulled him back and said, General, we'll start everything over again from the beginning, there must be some kind of mistake, certainly not yours at all, please do sit down again, and the General sat back down and the game was declared invalid, and they played on and alongside them played the music of the Old Town and New Town clocks on all sorts of towers and it measured time by chimes and also by merciless strikes.

They played on and the general never lost, because for Houdek and Faltys it all began to be about how to spend the most pleasant time possible, and the time most pleasantly spent was time gambling in the company of the great General Flemmer. Gradually they arranged it so that General Flemmer never, absolutely never, lost, that old card shark Faltys always covered it up with a card in his sleeve or under his coat, wherever a stranger wouldn't notice it, and sometimes not even any of the locals noticed, because Faltys was an exceptionally gifted cheater, and also no one noticed, understandably, that General Flemmer should have lost. Faltys knew a lot of tricks and essentially he enjoyed bringing them to the light of day, he dealt them out and thus proved his persistent abilities, that way he increased his wealth of tricks and was – happy. It is perhaps quite rare for someone to cheat to his own disadvantage. But here from the outside it was hard to contemplate what was advantageous to Faltys, and what momentarily wasn't at all.

And General Flemmer was in an excellent mood and remarked that during one day and one night the battle at Lutsk had been decided, even sealed, and in one night 89,000 soldiers surrendered to the Russians, something General Brusilov had never even dreamed of. And when he won General Flemmer fell into his stride and explained that he intended to present the public with most interesting statistics, in book form of course, about the bloodiness of wars measured by the number of casualties per day of fighting, and he said that the bloodiest wars of all prior to the First World War were the Balkan Wars of 1912–13, with 1,941 casualties per day, followed by the Prusso-Austrian War of 1866, with 1,102 casualties per day, then the Crimean War of the

1850s with 1,075 casualties per day, then the Franco-Prussian War of 1870–71 with 876 casualties per day, then the American Civil War with 518 casualties, then the Russo-Japanese War of 1904–05 with 291 casualties, then the Prusso-Danish War of 1846 with 25 casualties per day and finally the completely ridiculous Anglo-Boer War at the beginning of the century with its nine casualties per day. They were playing for 10-heller pieces, then for matches, and finally for honour. It was all the same to Houdek how many casualties occurred in any day of wartime, because these statistics seemed somehow incomplete to him; more than anything else, Houdek had a go at the bottle, he went for it more often than the others, because as he claimed, he could only get through a teaching career at the cost of tremendous amounts of patience and he could only maintain his patience at the cost of tremendous amounts of alcohol. What Houdek liked most about playing cards was drinking red wine and the heavenly view through the round window onto the infinite, where there was no longer anything and beyond that still more nothingness, and if he were able to spot a pigeon or swallow flying in that blue circle, he took it as a good sign and as a sign from above to talk. The most terrible thing in the teaching profession is the noise and uproar, he said, but when you drink a bottle like this, you hardly hear anything anymore, or you hear it, but the uproar doesn't involve you somehow, the most terrible thing is the noise and uproar, the most terrible is the shouting.

But Faltys, that old cheater, was watching himself like a cat watches a mouse, and waited for the moment when his lost honour would start to annoy him. As long as they had played for 10-heller coins and matchsticks, it didn't bother him, but as soon as they started playing for honour, he started to watch himself and he was ready to bet with himself that suddenly something would burst in him, that suddenly something would break in him, and he started to search his conscience, he started to wake up at night and he discovered that he was actually splitting in two and that there existed one Faltys who cheated to his own benefit, and another Faltys who cheated to his own detriment, and he waited for those two to start fighting. He also discovered with astonishment that unsullied honour is somehow intangible, absent, yet self-evident, while lost honour is tangible and one is constantly aware of it and it constantly stands in the way. For hours and days Faltys felt nothing and nothing bothered him, he was just constantly on the look-out to see when this lost honour of his would start to haunt him.

Faltys started to really regret his lost honour and was really haunted by it on that very night when they nailed General Flemmer shut in his coffin and when, right at midnight, they carried him out of the house. The undertakers came and asked Houdek, Are you the bereaved? And Houdek said that he wasn't, and they asked Faltys if he was then, and Faltys answered that he wasn't either, that there were none and that they were only waiting for the funeral service so that they could bid General Flemmer farewell. And the chap from the undertakers said, almost mockingly, What kind of general is this, when he's so poor and has no family to mourn his death and the obituary notice will only be written in indelible pencil.

Faltys stood below at the front door, the door was lined with blue tiles with a willow pattern, like somewhere in a butcher's shop, and said General Flemmer had many opportunities to win battles and according to his own words he certainly won many battles and still more battles he lost only by a hair's breadth, he was a bigwig, as is well known, and the right-hand man of General Brusilov and the right-hand man of Marshall Foch and the right-hand man of the Duke of Aosta. Yet Faltys's life was poor in battles and in recent times poor in winnings, and in fact Faltys blamed General Flemmer for this, General Flemmer had robbed him. The fact that he had been losing his honour constantly and that he had therefore lost it altogether started to bother Faltys at the very moment when they carried General Flemmer out, and now after General Flemmer's death, the impossibility of any kind of satisfaction bothered him as well.

Since the general's death, Houdek had started to drink even more, and when the force of habit pushed him and Faltys up to their piece of heavenly attic, they suddenly didn't know what to do, so close to heaven and yet everything so futile, and Houdek opened a bottle and drank and smacked his lips and gazed at the round window and waited for chance to favour him, for a pigeon or a swallow or an eagle, a royal eagle, as he used to say, to fly across, and to this he added that he didn't think General Flemmer had been looking well lately, his face was too violet and he couldn't go up the stairs and he was rather excitable and so on, and Faltys didn't answer and was consumed by hatred for the dead general. He scowled at the big crate where the card-playing and drinking and debates and meals had taken place, and he looked at the letters VIA ASMARA and that hatred was regret for honour lost so many times, which he would never win back again, VIA ASMARA, and that hatred was hatred for a man who now meant so little, only dust and ashes, and who had nevertheless taken his honour with him, and so the hatred for the dead was also fear of his own death, as is usually the case.

And while the former teacher Houdek, sitting across from him, was poking around with a baffled fumbling, just poking around in the lazy and idle cards, Faltys said, Remember, or Christ's sake, remember, the last card that General Flemmer had, I know exactly what it was and it sends a chill up my spine, it was spades and spades are the cards of death, spades are death, said Faltys, and what if, added Faltys, only in spite, what if General Flemmer wasn't a general at all, and he pounded his fist three times on the crate, on which was written VIA ASMARA VIA ASMARA VIA ASMARA, he pounded as if it were the lid of a coffin. Houdek trembled and said, We can find out, he said it in a calm, even indifferent voice, but he thought to himself, Why should we find out, why for Christ's sake should we find out, I'd prefer to remember that I played cards with a general from three invincible and undefeated fronts, rather than finding out that he was some teacher from a primary school in a village, like I used to be, but I have the impression that his last card was hearts.

What if, said Faltys still more spitefully, the general wasn't a general at all? And what if his fronts were invented? What good is it to find out, said the startled Houdek, and the letters on the crate started to blur before his eyes, what good is it to find out, if the dead general was less than he seemed. I have the feeling, Faltys suddenly shouted, and because that shout required some sort of action, he grabbed the cards and started shuffling furiously, that all his talk of the French, Italian, and Galician mud and all that talk of Galician hunger and Italian caverns and French fires was just nonsense. Houdek couldn't stand shouting and intensely craved a swig of wine, at that very moment there was nothing at hand, nothing at all, and so he said only half-heartedly, But even if it were just nonsense. Even if it were just nonsense, repeated Houdek, still surprised by the incomprehensible aggressiveness of Faltys, it's such a pleasure to listen to nonsense while playing cards, and if I'm not wrong and if I recall correctly, each of us had our say and each of us uttered nonsense occasionally, and each of us came up with something which didn't entirely coincide with the truth, something rather to amuse or interest the others, but in a card game the most beautiful and wonderful things are precisely that nonsense, in my opinion. How do I know, confessed Houdek unwillingly and against his own will, if perhaps even that Well of Syene in the times of the ancient Egyptians, how do I know that it isn't just completely empty nonsense, either.

Houdek was loath to give up his Well of Syene. But one's duty justifies the means, he told himself. Faltys, however, was overflowing with dissatisfaction and resentment, he shuffled the cards and the cards made a wonderful fan in the air and fell perfectly arranged on the top of the crate, he picked them up and made a new fan, it looked like a rainbow of cards and one card after another landed regularly on the VIA ASMARA crate, the cards made another fan again and again, long, almost endless, and that fan caused a draught, and then Faltys picked up the cards again and as he did so his fingers worked with unbelievable speed, but in those days the speed was of absolutely no use.

What do you think, Faltys said to Houdek some days later, if I had been one year older, just one year older, and if I hadn't, as a result, missed serving in the war by a hair's breadth, I could have become a general, couldn't I? Houdek got absorbed in thought, he gazed at the round attic window, blue everywhere, he gazed at it for a long time, until a pigeon made its way across it akin to salvation and as usual brought him a thought and the courage to make a speech, and Houdek said charitably, Yes, you could have, you could have even become something more than an ordinary general, and with those decorations, you could have bedecked both collarbones, my friend, golly I remember you as a guy who wasn't threatened by anything, all muscle and all wit and above all the women, all those women, there were constantly some women giggling around you, right? and I also remember how that terrific chap, and he slapped Faltys on the shoulder, calmly threw half an ox over his shoulder as if it were nothing and didn't even, I tell you, didn't even sag under it, not only that, but didn't even wobble, you understand, I remember some sensational delivery man of the town slaughterhouse and I'll never forget him, that skill, that skill. Houdek spoke as if he wanted to convince Faltys of the qualities of some unknown person, he spoke and spoke until his doubts disappeared. Faltys hung on his words. That skill, that skill, he repeated as if in a dream. Yes, that skill, Houdek propped himself up, and following Faltys's example, pounded his fist on the table. I didn't have it so bad, Faltys said boastfully, and looked around as if it were a crowded arena, and I have the feeling that I could have easily earned those general's badges if it hadn't been for that one year I was born too late for the war. Not just badges, Houdek cried, longing for alcohol, stars! Yes, stars, said Faltys with renewed dejection. I don't doubt it, said Houdek fervently, you with your half-ox over your shoulder made a much greater impression on me and on everyone else than, and here Houdek pretended to search for words and sought to disperse the fear falling from above and finally just said, than that prig of a general, than that general of a general, than that whole Flemmer bloke! Houdek was hurt by his own words, like the scratching of an inflamed sore, he didn't like lies, but because in the presence of the dejected and dissatisfied Faltys he fully enjoyed the right to a charitable lie, and with the double right to a charitable lie for the living and dissatisfied Faltys, he went on slandering General Flemmer, Flemmer was an unbelievable prig and liar, yes, I tell you with full responsibility a liar, no lice, for God's sake, have you ever seen a general covered with lice, no mud, no dust on the general's boots, it's clear to me, yes, now it's completely clear to me, that the only wars that General Flemmer ever won, were those wars with us, and both of us know perfectly well what they were like.

He was a buffoon of a general, said Faltys, he was a nabob of a general and a prig and a liar, so you actually remember how I casually and nonchalantly hauled halves of oxen and several pigs at a time and rams and so on, do you really remember it? You were a real man then, said Houdek, and I can admit it to you now, I admired you tremendously, I envied you, I always envied you your wonderful figure, all muscles, and that skill of yours, God, that skill of yours, and those women always giggling all around, how could General Flemmer compete, he was a bag of bones and a wisp of a man and a poor wretch, yet you were enormously built like a breeding bull, upon my soul, like a breeding bull, and how those women always swarmed around you, and you handled them, how you could handle them, just like cards, you shuffled them, whirled them around, and your hat cocked nicely to one side and always a winner, what can I say.

Faltys dolefully watched Houdek's mouth and several times was at the very point of asking something, but then dropped it, he didn't want to interrupt this pleasant avalanche of words, where did it come from in Houdek, he hadn't been a teacher in vain, and Houdek spoke and spoke, Houdek recollected so many things of which Faltys hadn't the slightest idea and some of which he even doubted, but it was pleasant, quite pleasant, and Faltys listened and began to imagine himself as someone well known, but absent for a long time, absent but finally coming back to us, with a checked cap over one ear, with half an ox over his shoulders, and girls around him, where did so many women come from all at once, they giggle and he just whistles to himself, he looks at that mob of women, that gift for the taking, just out of the corner of his eye, and says to himself, which one, which one. And Faltys pursed his lips, maybe he was really whistling to himself, and Faltys's thoughts moved gradually from thoughts of death to life again, and as the days passed and as Faltys didn't stop listening to Houdek's talk and stories and chatter about the invincible delivery man Faltys, Faltys's thoughts moved on from the dead general and more towards life and Faltys went gratefully to get a bottle, a bottle and yet another bottle of red wine, because Houdek described the irresistible delivery man Faltys most picturesquely when he had drunk a half bottle or more, and slowly, as Faltys listened and as Houdek expounded, Faltys got a terrible urge to play cards.

Would you like to play cards, he said once early in the evening almost timidly, as Houdek's eyes followed an unexpected swallow flying across the blue balloon of the window, would you like to play cards, he said with his hands propped on the crate with the letters VIA ASMARA VIA ASMARA VIA ASMARA. Houdek nodded. With resignation. He had expected this, even though he wasn't overjoyed at the prospect of a card game. He had also expected something else. That is, he knew that Faltys didn't notice the letters written on the crate anymore, although they still cruelly and insistently reminded Houdek of some distant journey, *via* and *samara* and *mara* and *marasmus* and *massacre* and *amara* and *amaritude* and *Mars* and *mors*. Faltys started to shuffle the cards, once again in his able way, again the fan flew through the air and the cards landed and Faltys smiled, a little unsure smile that was still crooked, but he did smile, and again the fan flew wider and more daringly, of all three of them, only he could do it. And he dealt. Everything seemed all right. But Houdek knew Faltys, and he knew that Faltys knew that Houdek didn't want to play and that he longed just to drink, drink, drink. Let's bet a bottle of red wine, shouted Faltys all-knowingly as if lashing a whip, this sprightliness was almost impertinent, because Faltys knew into the bargain that Houdek never had any money. Houdek nodded. And Faltys didn't stop shouting and Houdek, because he couldn't stand shouting, took long swigs and drank the bottle dry, Faltys shouted, with beautiful clarity he articulated syllable by syllable and spait the last word in Houdek's face, something unprecedented, the bottle of wine will be paid for by the one who – wins! Houdek nodded resignedly. He knew Faltys well and he knew his tricks even better, and even now it didn't escape him that Faltys had hidden a card up his sleeve and one somewhere under his coat. Faltys had to cheat, otherwise he couldn't live, Faltys must, must, must cheat, because he was a born cheater.

What were they playing for now?

And was it still a game?

It seemed to Houdek that it was rather like violence, even though it turned out he gained from it. And so he surrendered fully to the will of the blue sky that showed itself in the little round window, and he still wasn't sure whether Faltys was thankful to him for that endless praise and would induce him to continue, or whether Faltys was, in a roundabout way, plotting his revenge for his humiliation at the hands of General Flemmer. Perhaps Faltys himself didn't know, even though he had a card up his sleeve or under his shirt. And so Houdek surrendered completely to the will of the cheater and told himself: one of us two will finally get spades, whether the stakes are high or low, he thought somewhat about the complexity of things and of the human soul and he noted a pigeon perching perilously on the round window-frame, and waited for it to take off again, and the pigeon took off, and then he waited for the end of the game and to see whether he would win or lose and whether in that case he would be able to play on and drink and play on and play on. He simply waited and waited and waited.

Translated by Charles Sabatos

SABRINA KARASOVÁ

Divine Trumpets

In this dream my life is at stake. 'What on earth, what can I do? How can I go on living?' I ask in despair.

Suddenly, the solution descends from the very heavens. A huge glass jar appears in the blue sky, full of men's arses preserved in lard like *foie gras*. They are floating down towards me. I can see them as juicy as apricot halves, each with a different shape, each a different tasty promise. Trumpets ring out, rejoicing is heard, a halo of light surrounds the jar. 'My God!' I cry in wonder: 'Is this all for me?'

Translated by Nancy Hawker

Biographical Notes

SVATAVA ANTOŠOVÁ was born in 1957. She is known as a Lesbian poet, and recently as the author of two novels, *Dáma a švihadlo* ('The Lady and the Whip', 2004) and *Nordickou blondýnu jsem nikdy nelízala* ('I Have Never Licked a Nordic Blonde', 2005). She lives in Teplice in northern Bohemia.

ALEXANDRA BERKOVÁ was born in 1949. A well-known television producer as well as a novelist, she is also a famous feminist who deals with issues of relationship breakdown. *Knížka s červeným obalem* ('Little Book With a Red Cover', 1986) was her publishing debut and made her name, but excerpts of her later work have also been published in English anthologies. She teaches in Prague.

TERA FABIÁNOVÁ was born in 1930 in Slovakia. She grew up in a rural settlement until she moved to Prague in 1946, where she still lives. She worked for more than twenty-five years as a crane operator. Self-taught in literature, she is a poet.

VIOLA FISCHEROVÁ was born in 1935 in Brno. In 1968 she emigrated to Switzerland. She has worked for the Czechoslovak radio, then Swiss radio and in the 1980s for Radio Free Europe. Her first published poetry collection, *Zádušní básně za Pavla Buksu* ('Requiem Poems for Pavel Buksa', 1993), was dedicated to her husband. She has published many collections since and also stories for children. She is a translator (from Polish and German), and since 1994 has lived in Prague.

SABRINA KARASOVÁ was born in 1970 in Most in northern Bohemia. She is the editor-in-chief of Czech *Cosmopolitan*. She has published five collections of short stories, most recently *Bílý pes* ('White Dog', 2000).

KVĚTA LEGÁTOVÁ was born in 1919. A teacher, she became suspicious to the communist regime and was relocated to remote villages in northeastern Moravia, an experience that provided material for her stories. The short stories in *Želary* (2001) were written in the 1960s and '70s, and were only discovered when she submitted one of them to a film script competition in the 1990s. The collection won her the State Prize for Literature in 2002. Her *Jozova Hanule* was turned into a film. She lives in Brno.

ERIKA OLAHOVÁ was born in 1957 in Zvolen in Slovakia. From the age of fifteen she worked in a factory and later as a cook. She has written short stories published in Romani journals. Her collection *Nechci se vrátit mezi mrtvé* ('I Do Not Want to Return Among the Dead', 2004) brings together stories based on supernatural and horror themes. She lives in Česká Třebová.

MAGDALÉNA PLATZOVÁ was born in 1972 in Prague. She is the editor-in-chief of *Literární Noviny* ('Literary News'). Her plays and short stories – *Sůl, ovce a kamení* ('Salt, Sheep and Stone', 2003) – were followed by her novel *Návrat přítelkyně* ('The Return of a Friend', 2004). Her short stories are translated into Croat and Slovenian.

LENKA REINEROVÁ was born in 1916 under the Austro-Hungarian Empire to a Czech father and German-speaking mother. She worked as a journalist for a left-wing Prague-based German newspaper in the 1930s and fled the country in 1938. She returned from exile in 1948, was persecuted by the regime until 1964, when she was rehabilitated for a short period until she was evicted from the Communist Party in 1969. She published short stories, memories of pre-war Jewish Prague (*Das Traumcafé einer Pragerin*, 'The Dreamcafé of a Prague Lady', 1996) and her memoirs, *Alle Farben der Sonne und der Nacht*

('All the Colours of the Sun and the Night', 2003). In 2002 she was awarded the title of Honorary Citizen by the Municipality of Prague for her contributions to Czech, German and Jewish culture in her home town.

Kateřina Rudčenková was born 1976, and has been a published poet since 1998. Her collection *Není nutné abys mě navštěvoval* ('It is Not Necessary for You to Visit Me', 2001) was translated to German and earned her the Hubert Burda prize for promising new talent. She also exhibits photography and writes short stories.

Kateřina Sidonová was born in 1964 in Prague. She first published a book dedicated to her father, Rabbi Karol Sidon, with a dissident press in 1989. She is a translator from English. She deals with life as a housewife in *Jsem Kateřina* ('I Am Kateřina', 2002). She has also published fairytales.

Věra Stiborová was born in 1926, and worked in publishing until 1968, when her political undesirability forced her to take up menial jobs, for instance in gardening. She published two titles before 1968 and then again after 1989: in the intervening period her books were published with dissident presses. In 2000 she published her autobiographical *Zapomeň, řeko, téci* ('River, Forget to Flow').

Alena Vostrá was born in 1938 in Prague. Following her drama studies, her plays were staged in 1968. Her debut, *Bůh z reklamy* ('The God from the Advertisement', 1964) was awarded the State Prize for Literature. After 1968 she was not allowed to publish books for adults, so she focussed on children's books and in the 1980s wrote detective stories. She died in 1992.

Anna Zonová was born in 1962 in Nižní Komárnik in Slovakia, into a Ruthenian family. She grew up in Moravian Sudetenland and she now lives in Moravský Beroun to the northeast of the Czech Republic, where she is the curator of an art gallery. Her novel *Za trest a za odměnu* ('In Retribution and In Reward', 2004) depicts the fate of two families throughout the 20th century in the Sudetenland.

TRANSLATORS

NICOLE BALMER was brought up in Britain, Switzerland and Hong Kong. She holds a degree in Chinese Studies from the University of London.

ALEXANDRA BÜCHLER is editor of *This Side of Reality: Modern Czech Writing* (1996) and *Allskin and Other Tales* (1998). She is also a translator and director of Literature Across Frontiers, which promotes literary exchange in Europe.

DAVID CHIRICO holds a PhD in Czech literature from the University of Cambridge, and has taught at the School of Slavonic and East European Studies (SSEES). He has worked with Romani rights organisations. He is a barrister at 1 Pump Court Chambers.

MARK CORNER is a Doctor of History and Theology. He translated Zdeněk Jirotka's *Saturnin*, published by Karolinum in 2003, Vladislav Vančura's *Rozmarné léto*, and more.

CRAIG CRAVENS is a lecturer in Slavic languages and literatures at the University of Texas, Austin. He has published translations of Vladimír Páral's *Lovers & Murderers* and several Jára Cimrman plays.

KATHLEEN HAYES holds a PhD in Czech literature from SSEES. She is editor and translator of *A World Apart and Other Stories: Czech Women Writers at the Fin de Siècle* (2001), and of *The Journalism of Milena Jesenská: A Critical Voice in Interwar Central Europe* (2003).

MADELAINE HRON is Associate Professor in English and Film Studies at Wilfred Laurier University in Canada. She has translated *Signs and Symptoms* by Róbert Gál.

CHARLES SABATOS is Doctor in Comparative Literature at the University of Michigan. He has published translations of Pavel Vilikovský's *Ever Green Is ...* (2002), and Lasica and Satinský's *Not Waiting for Godot* (2003).